MOUNTAINS
OF
STONE

Ned Eddins
2007

A HISTORICAL NOVEL

Ned_Eddins@msn.com
mountainsofstone.com
thefurtrapper.com

Published by
Council for Indian Education
2032 Woody Drive, Billings, MT. 59102

O.N. Eddins
neddins@silverstar.com
1-866-885-2400

Printed by
Peczuh Printing Company
Price, UT 84501

Printed in the United States of America

I.S.B.N. 0-89992-148-5

Cover: The Tetons
Photo By: A.S. Eddins

ACKNOWLEDGEMENTS

My Mother
Ada Sessions Eddins
Historian – Genealogist
Critic – Friend

My Brother
Albert S. Eddins
His help with the historical research was
invaluable.

My thirty-two grandparents – fourth to seventh generation,
that walked across the plains and over
South Pass between 1847 and 1854.

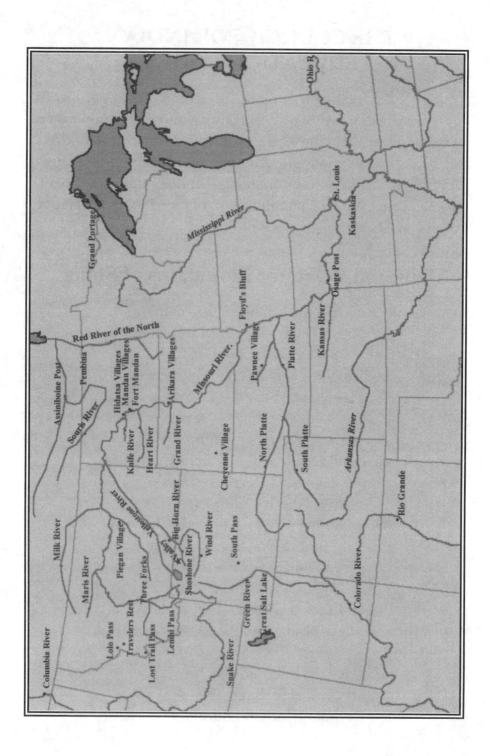

TABLE OF CONTENTS

To The Colonies..1

The Delaware..9

Walkers 28

St. Louis...42

Drouillard..57

Lewis and Clark..72

Loup River Pawnee 83

The Rescue 100

Black Hills Cheyenne 114

Hidatsa Trade Fair 130

North West Traders...145

Mountain Crow..154

Whispering Wind...168

The Valley...181

Arikara Warriors 194

Absaroka Winter 210

Shining Mountains 224

Colter Comes 234

Chouteau..248

The People..259

Biblography 271

TO THE COLONIES

Scotland, 1787

Sarah staggered to the wooden crib. She gripped the side, tearful eyes locked on her month-old son. The rhythmic up and down movement of the tiny chest provided slim solace for the anguish that ripped through her slender body. With a half sob, half moan, she gasped, "Henri is not dead." A grating squeak from the shuttered window caused her to whirl. Sarah cried out, "He cannot be."

Maure took hold of her shoulders. "Sarah! We must hurry. Men from the Jesuits will be here any minute."

In a daze, Sarah wrapped the blanket about her baby. She crossed to the stone-cased opening. Maure's outstretched hands took the tiny bundle as she crawled through the open window. Before her feet touched the ground, the front entrance gave way. Sounds of running men rolled along the stone-floored hallway.

Maure grabbed Sarah's hand. He pulled her into the foggy moor. Deep in the tangled heath, Maure stopped beside a rock-faced dugout. He handed Sarah the baby, then pushed open the door. Motioning to go inside, he said, "Wait here, I will fetch fuel for a fire."

Sarah moved to the darkest corner of the gale-battered

hut. She undid her bodice and let the baby nurse until Maure returned with an armful of peat. She fought back tears to ask, "Did those men kill my husband?"

"Yes, they have hounded us for three years." Maure's eyes hardened. "Henri and I were arrested in France for opposing King Louie and the Catholic Church's persecution of Huguenots. We were sentenced to the guillotine."

Sarah sobbed, "I do not understand any of this. Who are Huguenots? How did you get away?"

"Huguenots are French Protestants that follow the teachings of John Calvin." Pausing, he looked at Sarah. "One night, the cell door was left open." Maure's voice turned so low she barely heard the rest. "Only Henri's father could have arranged our escape."

Bewilderment filled Sarah's words. "Henri talked about France, but never his father. Will he help us?"

"I do not know," Maure replied. "Henri's father disowned him when we joined the Huguenots. Still, he is a fine caring man." Sarah gasped when he added, "His father is the Marquis de Soissons, one of the wealthiest men in France. My family has served the Soissons for generations. I was Henri's manservant as well as his friend."

Surprised and confused, Sarah could only say, "But, Clint is his grandson?"

"Even if the Marquis accepts you and Clint, revolution is brewing in France. Besides that danger, there is the Catholic Church. The Church will never give up its persecution of heretics."

Instinctively, Sarah cuddled the baby. "My uncle is head of the Stuart Clan. He will protect us."

Maure shook his head. "No, now that the Jesuits know we are here, it is not safe for me, or the boy." Maure touched the sleeping infant. He said, "The young of convicted Huguenots are taken and raised as Catholics."

Maure stepped off four paces along the back wall then

scraped away the dirt. Returning, he placed a black metal box containing papers, a signet ring, and two bags of gold coins on Sarah's lap. "Henri was afraid this might happen. A few days after the baby's baptism, we came here and buried this box. These papers verify the boy's lineage."

Sarah glanced through the documents. With the exception of her son's christening paper, all that she recognized were seals of the French Court.

Maure removed his jacket. Placing it around Sarah's shoulders, he said, "If you will be all right, I will go after food and warm clothes."

Sarah forced a smile of confidence. As Maure walked out, she snuggled the infant to her breast. When the baby was satisfied, she cried herself to sleep.

Maure returned with the light of a new day spreading across the heather. He placed a loaf of heavy black bread and a piece of goat's cheese on a rickety bench then woke Sarah. While they ate dry bread and cheese, Maure and Sarah decided the best place to hide would be in a crowded city. That night, they set out for Glasgow.

The streets of Glasgow teemed with activity. Horse-drawn coaches, rats, and people shared the hard beaten paths. The roads weaved through and around accumulated filth. Shallow breaths and hand-covered mouths cut the foul stench.

Sarah's admiration and respect for Maure grew. At first, she resented not using the coins. Deep down, she realized Maure was right – peasants with gold attract attention.

Maure strived to provide for Sarah and the baby, but each time they felt a measure of safety, he heard of men asking about a Frenchman with a Scottish woman that had a baby boy. With scanty belongings, he moved them deeper into the quagmire of dirty flats, hunger, and the ever-gnawing rats.

A year passed. Maure and Sarah could tolerate Glasgow no longer. With France embroiled in revolution, they decided the remaining gold coins would be used for passage to the

Colonies.

"Do you think I am crazy?" blurted out the sea captain. "No unmarried woman with a baby and a manservant books steerage passage." Displaying a lewd gesture, he sneered at Sarah. "Loose women cause nothin' but trouble."

Maure's eyes hardened, his hands knotted.

Sarah grabbed his arm. Her soft, grayish-green eyes pleaded with him. She whispered, "We will find a way."

Maure seethed with anger as Sarah led him down the street to the flat. Inside, he dropped on the wooden bench and stared at his rough, cracked hands.

Sarah sat beside him. She raised his callused hand to her cheek. "Maure, we must marry."

He stiffened at her words. Blood rushed to his head. His emotions reeled. He had kept his love hidden so long. In a voice barely audible, he moaned, "You are my master's wife."

Sarah's words were strong and forceful. "My husband, your master, is dead. Clint's only chance for a decent life is the Colonies."

Two days later, Maure relented. He and Sarah were married on the foredeck of a squalid three-mast schooner. With a bag of belongings over his shoulder, Maure led his new family below. The dark, filthy common area stank of unwashed bodies and slop jars. Forcing a path through the mingling people and their baggage, he found an empty grey-blanketed bunk bed. Not far away was a porthole. At least, there would be a little fresh air.

Out of Glasgow's protective harbor, the constant roll and pitch of the ship caused Sarah to suffer endless retching. The second night out, a fever racked her nausea-weakened body. By the next afternoon, the ague had diminished, but her breathing had a raspy sound. Afraid she had lung fever, Maure cajoled the First Mate into letting him move her onto the deck. Despite a canvas shelter, calm weather, and his constant nursing, Sarah's chills and fever persisted for ten days.

After her recovery, Sarah hated the occasional retching, but she dreaded the raging Atlantic storms worse. With Clint squeezed between them, she and Maure would huddle below deck. Screams of terrified passengers joined each lightning crack and thunderclap as the howling wind rolled wave after wave across the pitching schooner's deck. The screams and the constant creak of stressed timbers enforced the horror that the ship's leaky hull would give way and all would perish.

Forty-five days out of Glasgow, the battered schooner sailed into Boston harbor.

Maure carried Clint as he and Sarah trudged up the crowded street. They stopped at the first boarding house with a vacancy sign. The room contained a bed and wash basin. No better, no worse than the one in Glasgow. Sarah pleaded to use the few remaining gold pieces for a better place, but Maure refused – the coins were for land.

Maure left at daylight each day trying to eke out a meager existence for his family. After giving him several odd jobs, a hardware merchant offered him steady work and two rooms above the store. Upon learning Sarah could read and cipher, the owner offered her a job clerking behind the counter.

Sarah and Maure struggled until the worn coin pouch contained money for a team, a wagon, and a milk cow. When the merchant learned of their plans, he offered seed grain and tools on credit. Five days later, Maure, Sarah, and Clint left for the Ohio Country.

The grey team strained against the collars. The horses shod hooves dug out chunks of soft dirt as they pulled the tattered, canvas-covered wagon up the steep hill. On the crest, the spent horses paused to replenish air-starved lungs. A brindle cow tied to the tailgate dropped her head into tall succulent grass.

Maure and Sarah gazed across a verdant valley. Patchworks of summer flowers and scattered vivid-green trees covered the rolling ground. They both sighed as a breeze rolled wave after wave across tall, lush grasses.

Maure's weathered fingers covered his wife's bony hand. His throat tightened. Swallowing hard, he said, "We will mark the boundary trees with a tomahawk. Our land will be from the stream to that tree-covered ridge."

"Oh, Maure! It is so beautiful."

Maure drove the team off the steep slope. Sarah worked the brake lever to keep the doubletree from hitting the horses' hocks. Reaching level ground, the team broke into a trot. The horses smelled water.

With his horses' flared nostrils submerged in crystal-clear water, Maure glanced about. He smiled at Sarah and said, "Our first night on our own land will be here by the creek."

"Our land. Oh! Yes," cried Sarah as years of frustration and hardship slipped away. She crawled over the wagon seat to wake her son. The four-year-old boy slept on sacks of seed grain. With a joy she had not felt in years, she and Clint gathered wood.

Maure unhooked the sunken-hipped geldings. He removed the collars exposing fist-sized sores. After bathing the seeping sores with salt water, he covered them with axle grease. Satisfied he could do no more, Maure turned the weary horses loose in knee-high grass.

Through with his team, Maure hobbled the milk cow's hind legs. He stripped her flaccid teats. Another time or two, the cow would be dry.

Maure lit a small, smokeless fire. Confident the blaze would not go out, he went to the wagon. Removing the black iron pot and a sack containing a smattering of oats, he stared at the bare shelves of the grub box.

Maure returned to the fire as Sarah arrived with an armful of branches. He touched her drawn cheek. His voice softened. "Supper can wait. You are going to start coughing again. Please, rest here by the fire." Pointing across the stream, he said, "Tomorrow, I will build a lean-to between those oaks, then start splitting logs for a cabin. With a dry, warm cabin you will feel better."

Sarah smiled. "How could I not be fine now? You help Clint, I will fix something to eat."

She took the black pot from his hand and went to the stream. Sarah set the pot on the fire. At the first sign of bubbles in the water, she dumped in the grain. The handful of kernels barely covered the ten-inch bottom. After the hulls ruptured, Sarah divided the cooked oats into three wooden bowls. Setting their supper on the wagon's tailgate, she called for Maure and Clint.

Maure scrapped his half-finished bowl of cereal into Sarah's bowl. He stared at her gaunt face, then into her dark-rimmed eyes. Despite Sarah's happiness over having their own land, he felt she would die without rest and better food. Unconsciously, he reached over and straightened an errant lock of hair. Heavy hearted, he walked to the front of the wagon.

Maure returned a few minutes later with a flintlock in the crook of his arm. "I will look for a turkey or deer along the creek."

Clint jumped to his feet. "Can I come?"

Sarah glanced about. Her voice wavered. "It would be good for him to go. But, what about Indians?"

Maure bent and kissed her pale cheek. "It is a chance we must take. There is nothing left to eat except the seed grain. We will not go far." He glanced at Clint. "Fetch a crocus sack. There might be watercress, or asparagus along the creek bank."

Sarah watched her husband and son disappear into the willows. Once she was alone, the listlessness that plagued her movements returned. Sarah hated idleness. Now, she seemed always to be cold and tired. She hoped Maure was right about a cabin making her feel better.

Sarah took the dishes to the gravel bar and scrubbed them with streamed silt. Satisfied the bowls were clean, she placed them in the grub box before building up the fire. Perched on the one-legged milk stool, Sarah huddled over blazing branches to soak up the rising heat.

Dancing flames mesmerized Sarah. Her chest and throat tightened. A harsh coughing spell left a speck of blood on the corner of her mouth. Starting to shiver, Sarah looked down to see a thin ribbon of smoke coming off the blackened coals. Placing a handful of dry grass and a few small sticks on the coals, she fetched a shawl from the wagon. She returned to the one-legged milk stool in time to watch the sun settle below the horizon.

Sarah's attention returned to the fire. Blue yellow-tipped flames played back and forth across blackened branches. Her thoughts drifted...

A shadow passed in front of her. Gasping, she whirled. She did not see the Shawnee or his stone war club.

THE DELAWARE

The stillness of late afternoon settled over the meadow. A lanky man with a tow-headed boy at his side paused just inside the tree line. Across the clearing, a startled grouse flew off a gravel bar. Above them, a circling hawk set its wings and swooped toward the low-flying bird. Suddenly, the red-tailed hawk rolled sideways. Powerful wing strokes returned it to the safety of cottony clouds.

Struck by the hawk's action, Maure's eyes searched the willows on the other side of the clearing. His hand squeezed Clint's shoulder. Pointing at an old knurled oak, he whispered, "Wait under there."

Clint crawled beneath the low branches. His hand clutched a broken-bladed pocketknife. Minutes passed. To a four-year-old, it seemed hours. With the last rays of the sun filtering through the trees, Clint's legs came up. His chin rested on bony knees. Uncontrollable sobbing racked his frail body. His father was not coming back.

As Clint started to crawl from under the tree, a grisly Indian stepped around a nearby clump of willows. A string of light brown hair dangled from his hand.

Clint pushed himself back under the tree. He pressed

against the tree trunk. Rough bark cut into his back, still he pressed harder.

The Indian smirked. He shook Maure's scalp.

Clint's eyes hardened. Between two low branches, he scrambled to his feet. A jerk of his arm raised the broken-bladed knife.

At sight of the boy's courage, the Indian hesitated. His piercing eyes softened. A wide grin crossed his face. He dropped the scalp and emitting soft soothing sounds held out his hand. Slowly, he inched forward.

Leaves of the timeworn oak began to rustle.

The Indian froze. His head tilted, his mouth opened. A low, eerie wailing rolled back and forth through the tree branches. The mournful sound grew louder.

Clint shrank against the tree. The knife dropped to his side. Staring at the rigid Indian, he heard a gasp just before the warrior's head exploded in a spray of blood.

A red film blurred Clint's vision. As he rubbed his eyes, powerful hands pulled him from under the tree and swung him in the air. Settling on a bare back, Clint's arms wrapped around the man's thick neck. The broken-bladed knife fell from his hand.

Picking up the knife, the warrior trotted off into the forest. The Indian stopped, his head tilted. Satisfied with what he heard, he set the boy down.

"Lame Bear, me friend."

Clint stared at the tall, heavy-muscled Indian. A single white feather attached to his coal-black hair dangled over the left shoulder. On the right side of his face, a jagged scar ran from hairline to jaw line. A wide leather flap circled his narrow waist. Clint's inquisitive eyes settled on the blood-covered stone hatchet. His eyes went from the hatchet to the bow and beaded quiver.

The left side of Lame Bear's mouth raised in a crooked smile. He pointed at the stream.

Clint dropped on his stomach and scooped a handful of water. As his hands came up to his mouth, they flew apart. The water had turned red. He stared at his hands then touched his blood-covered face. After scrubbing his hands and face, Clint watched a thin ribbon of the dead Indian's blood trail into the rapid current.

Finished, he walked over to Lame Bear. The big Indian held out several plums. Grabbing one, Clint chewed off the meat. Spitting out the pit, he reached for another.

Lame Bear growled. Picking up the stone, his darting eyes searched for other telltale signs. Lifting Clint on his back, Lame Bear took hold of a thick limb and swung out into the middle of the rock-bottomed creek. He waded twenty-yards downstream. Nudging a small round stone with his foot, he turned upstream.

Curious, Clint glanced over his shoulder. The only sign of Lame Bear being in the water was a slight sand-filled depression left by the stone.

Around the first bend, Lame Bear paused. His hand squeezed Clint's arm.

Sounds of splashing water come from below them. There was a loud grunt. The Shawnee had found the rolled stone. When the excited voices faded away, Lame Bear continued toward a rockslide. Where rocks had rolled into the water, he stepped onto a flat rock, and crossed the talus slope into dark, dense timber.

Lame Bear stopped near a tree with smaller ones around it. Lowering Clint, he motioned to crawl under the trees. When Clint grabbed his hand, Lame Bear smiled his crooked smile. He placed the broken-bladed knife into Clint's hand and gently pushed him into the dark space.

Cold, tired, and hungry, Clint fell into a troubled sleep – images of Maure's scalp, the Indian's head, the blood, would not go away. His eyes popped open. He whimpered, "Mamma, Mamma." Rubbing the cobwebs of sleep from his eyes, Clint saw his new friend in the flickering light of a small fire.

Lame Bear held out a forked stick with a fish on it. Clint grabbed the half-cooked fish. A growling stomach could wait no longer. Finished with it and another one, he noticed a tin box beside the fire. When Lame Bear nodded, Clint pried open the lid. The ash-covered box contained a ring, a sheaf of papers, and several gold coins; none of which meant a thing to a four-year-old.

Lame Bear used gestures and a few English words to make Clint understand Shawnee had killed his mother and burned the wagon. Clint started to cry. Lame Bear placed a reassuring hand on the boy's shoulder. The hand stayed until Clint cried himself to sleep.

A faint grey line had formed beneath eastern stars when Lame Bear and Clint left the protective shelter. Clint carried the black box under his arm.

The four days it took to reach Lame Bear's village were almost too much for Clint. The tired sore-footed boy lagged behind. At first sight of growling dogs and screaming people, he hurried beside the big Indian.

Lame Bear ignored the commotion. Reaching the village center, he stopped. A hush settled over the crowd.

Lame Bear talked several minutes. He pointed at Clint. From Lame Bear's gestures and the staring people, Clint realized he was telling about him and the Shawnee. The People admire courage. This boy had faced a Shawnee warrior with a broken-bladed knife.

A bright, round hunters moon appeared before Lame Bear broke away from the gathering. He took Clint to a bark hut. Inside, a man and woman sat by a circular fire pit.

The warrior rose and stood beside Lame Bear. After a few words from Lame Bear, he smiled. He motioned Clint was welcome. Lame Bear gestured the man was his brother, Running Deer. Clint could not understand Lame Bear's signs for the woman's name.

Pulling Clint outside, Lame Bear pointed at the night sky. He continued shaking his head until Clint finally pointed at a bright star on the western horizon. Lame Bear smiled and led him back into the wigwam.

Bright Star crossed the room. Her face beamed with kindness. Smiling, she touched his hand. Her soft, warm touch filled his eyes with tears. Bright Star gently wiped the tears away. She led him to a bed of tanned robes covered by a Hudson's Bay trade blanket. Secure in the warm bed, Clint dropped into a dreamless sleep.

Clint woke to stare at herbs, ears of corn, and strips of meat hanging from the willow ceiling. Realizing where he was, he snuggled deeper in the soft tree-bough bed. He was almost back to sleep when a noise brought him to his elbows.

Bright Star bent over a black kettle above the fire pit. Clint watched her fill a bowl with stew. Smiling, she placed the bowl by his bed then went outside.

Clint reached for his clothes. His pants and shirt were gone. Across the foot of the bed, were a pair of moccasins, a cloth like Lame Bear's, and a beaded shirt. A bear claw on a leather thong laid across the shirt – Bright Star had spent the night making and beading the shirt. The claw had come from the bear that scarred Lame Bear's cheek.

Clint's eager fingers grabbed the thong. He put it around his neck before putting on his new clothes. He had barely started on the rich stew when Running Deer and Bright Star entered. One look at Clint and they began to laugh.

Bright Star walked across the lodge. She placed her cheek next to Clint's cheek. Removing the loincloth, she put it on right.

Rattled, Clint dropped the wooden bowl. His eyes searched the lodge for his friend. Running to the entrance flap, he started out, then stopped. He turned to see Running Deer pick up the bowl and refill it. Running Deer held it out towards him. When Clint took the bowl, Running Deer gestured Lame

Bear was gone, and that he and Bright Star were his new parents.

Clint accepted his new life as a duck takes to water. At first, he tried to fetch water and gather wood, but Bright Star would not let him. He was to be a warrior. Warriors did not do women's work.

Clint knew, that if he asked, Running Deer and Bright Star would take him to a white settlement, but who wanted to go there? For him, there was nothing better than being an Indian boy. He and his many friends hunted birds, rabbits, squirrels, and other small animals. When not hunting or shooting at targets, there were games. If they tired of the contests, they could always make the girls chase them by raiding the meat racks or gardens.

As soon as Clint understood enough Delaware, he asked, "Why does Lame Bear stay away from the village?"

Running Deer smiled, he motioned to sit. "Many snows before you came to the People, a Shawnee war party discovered Lame Bear's wife of two days picking berries. She fought her attackers, and even managed to kill one with her skinning knife before the other warriors killed and scalped her. When she did not return, Lame Bear went to look for her. He found her mutilated body in a bramble bush." Running Deer paused. "My brother's cry of anguish could be heard throughout the village. He sat with her cradled in his arms, and sang her death song until the Grandfather's first rays appeared on the horizon. Lame Bear stood and faced the Giver of Life. Slowly, he raised the defiled body high overhead. With sobs of anguish, Lame Bear offered a prayer of eternal vengeance against the Shawnee."

"Has he hunted the Shawnee every since then?"

"Yes," Running Deer replied, "his hatred has been so fierce and unrelenting that many Shawnee believe Lame Bear is of the Spirit World – a Wind-of-Death."

Clint stared at Running Deer. "When Lame Bear saved me

from the Shawnee warrior, I heard a strange wailing sound."

Running Deer shook his head. "I have heard this is true, but I do not know. My brother never talks about the Shawnee."

Days turned into weeks, weeks into months, months into years, Clint's white life blurred then disappeared entirely from his thoughts.

Ten harvest seasons had passed since Clint's arrival at the village. He spoke and thought in Delaware, and thanks to his mother, understood the common language of the Iroquois. Bright Star had been taken from the Tuscarora – sixth member of the Iroquois League – while still a child.

Among his friends, he shot a bow the fastest and with the most accuracy. Despite his ability with the bow, he liked running the best. Clint could beat anyone in the village, except Running Deer, for a half-mile and most of the warriors over longer distances.

The only thing Clint missed was Lame Bear. No one had seen or heard of him for several moons. Stories of his death at the hands of the Shawnee circulated among the village warriors.

Shortly after the Harvest Moon, the villagers and dogs created such a commotion that it woke Clint. He rushed outside to hear the name Lame Bear being passed back and forth across the village.

Clint's happiness over Lame Bear's return soon faded. He saw little of Lame Bear or Running Deer for the next three days. Feasting and councils kept both his fathers away.

The third sunset after Lame Bear's return, Clint entered the wigwam to find his fathers seated at the cooking fire. Lame Bear motioned to sit.

When Clint dropped down between them, Lame Bear placed a slender, leather-wrapped object in his son's lap. "The time has come for your manhood name. It has been decided you shall be known to the People as – Broken Knife."

Excited by a new name and a present, Broken Knife opened

the soft leather cover. He saw a taper-bladed throwing knife.

Lame Bear smiled. "My son needs a better knife for the Shawnee than a broken-bladed one. Tomorrow, we will see how well he throws it."

The morning dawned bright and clear. Before the sun appeared, Broken Knife was out in the village. It was hard to maintain his casual indifference when several older warriors, calling him by name, stopped to talk and look at his knife. One did not show pride in such things; however, it did not hurt to be friendly.

That afternoon, Broken Knife followed Lame Bear to a secluded glade. His father showed him how to balance and throw the knife. Hard as Broken Knife tried, the blade would not stick in the tree.

"What does my son think about when he runs?" his father asked.

Not understanding the question, Broken Knife shrugged his shoulders.

Lame Bear smiled. He pointed at a nearby tree. "When the Blue Jay chirps, beat me to the blackened stump." After his son nodded, Lame Bear innocently added, "While we wait, think about how hard you must run."

Broken Knife concentrated on beating Lame Bear. His father was nearly as fast as Running Deer. The longer they waited, the more Broken Knife felt his muscles tense.

At the bird's chirp, the runners were off. Lame Bear won easy. Smiling at his son's dejected look, he said, "We will try again. This time, listen to the rustling leaves, the singing birds, the flowing water. Breath deep the forest smells; feel them spread through your body."

Broken Knife won the next race. He was more confused than after the first one.

Lame Bear held out the knife. "Now, take a deep breath. Slowly release the air. Feel your muscles relax."

Unaware just when the knife left his hand, Broken Knife

saw the handle vibrating in the tree.

His father grinned. "Try a few more times then we will go back." Lame Bear hesitated. "Never forget – stay calm and relaxed. Of all that I teach you, those two things are the most important. Many times the Shawnee's fear, or excitement, made the arrows miss. An enemy's fear, or his over confidence, is your best ally."

That night seated around the fire, Lame Bear announced he would leave early the next morning. Bright Star glanced at her son. She grinned at his solemn look. "It is too bad that no one wishes to accompany Lame Bear."

Broken Knife started to speak. Seeing the look on his mother's face, he realized that he was going with his father. Overwhelmed, he stared into the fire.

The next morning, when Running Deer and Lame Bear left the lodge, Bright Star held out four robin-egg-size green stones. "These are for my son." Her eyes misted. "A great Chief of my people left these stones to his son. After I was married, we visited my father. He gave me the Medicine Stones. If you are troubled look deep into a stone's center, and our spirits will be as one."

Tears flowed down her cheeks as she said, "I have prayed for Manitou to watch over my son."

Broken Knife's voice cracked when he replied, "My heart is also heavy."

Running Deer entered the lodge. He laid down a beaded quiver and a new long bow. Turning, he walked out without a word. Confused by his father's action, Broken Knife stared at the entrance flap.

Bright Star sobbed, "Your father is sad. He told me during the sleep, he would see his son no more."

Broken Knife held his mother. His cheek next to hers, their tears flowed together.

Once they were clear of the village, Lame Bear broke into a steady ground-eating trot. Proud to be going with his father,

Broken Knife felt unrestrained. He wanted to jump, run ahead, and yell as if a little boy. After three days of the same pace, he struggled to keep his father in sight.

With twilight of the third day settling about them, Lame Bear crossed the Scioto River and started up a narrow canyon. He had gone a half-mile or so when he stopped near a small stream. The twisting water flowed from the base of a cliff high above them.

Lame Bear studied his son. "The camp is near. Tell me where?"

Broken Knife searched the base of the sheer walled cliff and the rocks, nothing. He looked across the canyon at thick underbrush and heavy timber. Confidently he pointed at a dense stand of trees. "Over there."

His father's eyes remained expressionless. "Step where I do."

Where the stream crossed the trail, Lame Bear hopped onto a rock, stepped to another, then hesitated. Satisfied Broken Knife had not left a mark on the path, Lame Bear continued over the rocks. Climbing to the base of the cliff, Lame Bear stopped where water bubbled up from under the rock slab.

To his surprise, Broken Knife saw the sheer wall was not flat as it had appeared from the trail. Near where the water flowed out of the rocks was an offset crevice. Broken Knife glanced across the canyon. When he looked back, his father was gone. Stepping into the crevice, he saw it was the entrance to a cave.

His father held out a tallow candle. "Good, my son found me. Can he find the pool of water at the back of the cave?"

Red-faced, Broken Knife took the candle and bark pitcher. As he filled the container, he saw a dim light beyond the pool. Returning with the water, he looked around. There were containers of salted meat, pemmican, corn, and dried fruits. Besides the food, he saw heavy robes, cooking utensils, two

18

rusty muzzleloaders, two bows, and a parfleche containing metal tipped arrows. Stacked firewood, bed platforms, and backrests lined the opposite wall. Through with his inspection of the cave, Broken Knife started for the entrance.

Lame Bear glanced up. He growled, "Never leave that way." Seeing the hurt look on his son's face, Lame Bear's voice softened. "Many snows ago, Shawnee warriors chased me into this canyon. Searching for a place to hide among the rocks, I saw the crack and discovered the cave's entrance." Hesitating, he continued, "The Shawnee have trailed me here many times, but the warriors have never searched along the cliff." He eyed his son. "Why have they never looked on the rocks?"

Broken Knife thought a minute before he said, "Because there was no place to hide."

Lame Bear smiled. "You must always hide where your enemies do not look with a close eye. Once, while Shawnee searched the brush along a creek, I laid spread out on a bare knoll. Two braves glanced at me. Their eyes did not see me because they thought no one would hide there. Before going to sleep, consider this. Why are deer hard to see standing in brush?"

The next morning Broken Knife grinned at his father. "A hunter's eye detects movement, so the deer remains still."

"Yes, when my son hides, he must do the same." Pleased, he continued, "This morning your lessons begin. We are in Shawnee territory and must be careful. Do exactly as I say."

The dim light beyond the water pool filtered through a pile of downed trees near the canyon rim. While Lame Bear studied the open country, Broken Knife realized the importance of not using the cliff entrance. Anyone on the trail would see you first; whereas lying under the piled trees, you could scan the whole area without danger of being discovered.

Leaving the deadfall, Lame Bear started a training routine that did not vary. Mornings, they studied the ways of the forest. Loud chatter, or lack of it, from squirrels, marmots, and chipmunks, as well as bird calls, indicated nearby danger. If a large trout's fins did not quiver, or it would not rise for a grub, something had waded the stream. Had the morning sun dried the moisture off the grass? Or had the moisture been knocked off? If brushed off, had an animal or an Indian done it? From its tracks had the deer been standing, walking, or running?

Afternoons, Broken Knife practiced with the bow and knife. At some point while he was preoccupied, Lame Bear would disappear. For a ways, his father's tracks were easy to follow, but eventually, he would find a distinct moccasin print on soft ground, after that nothing. Giving up and going back to the cave, he would find Lame Bear patiently waiting.

Lame Bear made Broken Knife tell him everything he had seen and heard. When Broken Knife finished, he and his father went over each detail.

Days and weeks blended into months. Ten excitement-filled months passed without any change in the routine. By this time, Broken Knife saw signs while trotting that he once crawled to find.

With a late spring snow storm raging outside, Lame Bear and Broken Knife hovered around the fire. Lame Bear said, "In mid-morning, if there is a fresh deer track near a stream is the deer going to eat, or lie down? If the track is a big buck, will it hide in brush, or high up under ledges?" He hesitated. "Understand what you track then search where its instinct takes it."

Broken Knife started to ask a question. Lame Bear stopped him. "This you must decide by yourself. Your senses must become one with what you track. Remember what you have learned about each animal, then I will answer your questions."

Five days later, Broken Knife woke to find Lame Bear gone. He grabbed his bow, a handful of parched corn, and headed for the cave exit. Lying under the deadfall, he considered what his father said about knowing the habits of what you tracked. Shawnee, his father hunted the Shawnee.

Several miles from the cave, Broken Knife found a partial track. He had guessed right. Lame Bear had gone to the nearest

Shawnee village.

Broken Knife paused on the edge of an open meadow. He watched a hawk climb higher and higher. The bird did not search for food. It had been scared.

The hawk still circled when Lame Bear appeared on the other side of the clearing. Seconds later, five Shawnee broke out of the trees into the open area. Broken Knife moved to a large tree. As his father ran by, he said, "There are only five Shawnee. Why do you run away?"

Lame Bear stumbled. He sprawled out on the ground.

Confident of taking his scalp, the Shawnee screamed, "Wind-of-Death! Wind-of-Death!"

When the Shawnee were thirty paces away, Lame Bear jumped to his feet. Broken Knife stepped out from behind the tree.

The warriors slid to a stop. As they did, three began singing death songs.

Lame Bear shot the two on the left, Broken Knife the two on the right. The one in the middle turned back. Broken Knife waited. When his father did not shoot, he raised his bow.

Lame Bear knocked it down. He shouted in Shawnee, "Let the dog go. His people should know the bravery of Wind-of-Death's son, Broken Knife."

Broken Knife had no regrets about killing Shawnee. Scalping them was something else. Aware of his son's discomfort, Lame Bear said, "I do not scalp dung heaps. Many Shawnee believe I am a Wind Spirit." Grinning, he continued, "Everyone knows a spirit does not need scalps. Besides, it is a bad thing used by red-coated soldiers."

Back at the cave, Lame Bear stared into the lambent flames. Finally, he said, "My son makes me proud. Any Delaware can kill a Shawnee, only Broken Knife can follow Lame Bear." After putting more wood on the fire, he looked at his son. "In the beginning, I wanted you to carry on my vengeance. Now, I think my life should not be yours. When I am gone do not pursue the Shawnee." Taken back by his father's words, Broken Knife said nothing.

Lame Bear studied his solemn-faced son. "Someday you will choose between the Indian and white worlds. Running Deer and I have taught you our ways. We cannot guide you in the ways of the white man. I know little of the white man except one thing, never trust his paper words."

Two days later Lame Bear was gone. Sure that his father hunted the Shawnee, Broken Knife started after him. He searched until the sun approached the horizon without finding any sign. In heavy timber and about to quit, Broken Knife heard sounds of turkey buzzards. His every sense cried danger.

Broken Knife dropped to his hands and knees. He crawled through tall grass and around downed trees toward the squawking birds. Reaching the tree line of a small clearing, he froze. His muscles refused to obey. He could only stare. Two vultures fought over Lame Bear's blood-torn shirt. Other vultures ripped his lifeless flesh.

Gut-wrenching sobs racked Broken Knife's body. Then, overwhelming rage replaced the sorrow and anguish. He would continue Lame Bear's vendetta. No Shawnee would escape his wrath. Lying there plotting against his enemy, a cold sweat drained him of all emotion. Too weak to move, a warm, overpowering calmness spread over him. He felt Lame Bear's presence – their spirits joined as one.

Broken Knife studied every bush, every tree. He saw nothing out of place until a buzzard shied near a deadfall. He notched an arrow and waited. It was not long before a Shawnee moved. He buried the arrow in the Indian's side. The dying warrior's jerking legs scared the scavengers away; this made Broken Knife feel a little better. It had been hard to watch buzzards tear at his father's flesh.

Balancing the long bow on his back, he slithered through the grass to retrieve the arrow. Before he could pull it from the dead Shawnee, he sensed movement. He crawled into the deadfall and waited. Seconds later, a large Shawnee stepped into view. The warrior died with his eyes fixed on the wooden-handled knife. It pinned the beaded medicine bag to his chest.

Broken Knife remained under the brush pile. When the buzzards returned, he put an arrow through the largest vulture's head. The bird's futile efforts to fly scared the others away. Using the smallest warrior's blanket, he gathered Lame Bear's scattered remains. He placed the tied bundle beneath a deep undercut in a dry wash.

Broken Knife built a small fire by his father's blanket-wrapped remains. After dropping braided sweet grass on the low flames, he breathed deep of the Grandmother's Perfume then sang his father's death song. Tears run down his cheeks as he chipped away at the bank. Dirt, rocks, and grass-laden sod covered his father.

Not satisfied with killing the warriors, Broken Knife scattered their medicine bag contents to the wind. Finished with that, he dragged each body to a tree near where Lame Bear had died. He used a leather rope to pull the smallest Shawnee high into the tree. After securing the rope, he bound the big Indian's ankles near the slipknot. He yanked the loose end. The small Indian dropped. The weight of the falling body helped raise the other warrior. He retied the knot. The hair of both Indians barely touched the ground.

Broken Knife paused for a last look. A gentle breeze moved the ankle-tied warriors back and forth. He could not help but think – what better tribute – Shawnee guarding the place where Lame Bear's spirit had joined his.

As he left the clearing, Broken Knife saw a number of Shawnee tracks headed toward his village. Afraid for his parents, he cut cross-country for their village. Two days later, black smoke and persistent wailing confirmed his worse fears.

Entering the burned-out village, Broken Knife grabbed hold of a boyhood friend. "Deer Hump, where are my parents?"

"Dead, all dead. My mother, my grandmother, Running Deer, Bright Star, all dead." Mumbling to himself, the boy disappeared among the burned lodges.

Broken Knife staggered to the ruins of his mother's wigwam. Numb with grief, he sat on a black charred log. He stared at his little finger. Blood oozed from around the white knuckle joint of his left little finger. The tip of the finger and the blood-covered knife lay at his feet. Nothing mattered anymore.

With the light of dawn spreading across the blackened village, Broken Knife placed moss over the bloody stub. He used his teeth to bind it with a leather strip.

Broken Knife walked over to where two men huddled over a fire. One of them was his uncle. Antler told him that white men dressed as Indians had attacked the village. The raiders had sneaked up on the village and fired without warning. His wife and daughter were killed in the first volley. Antler touched Broken Knife's shoulder. He said, "Your father killed one white man before a bullet tore the top of his head off. When Bright Star ran to her husband's body, a heavyset man hit her with the butt of his gun."

"I am sorry about your loss, Uncle. Where were the other warriors?" Broken Knife asked.

"They were hunting." Antler paused. "The same two whites killed Running Deer and Bright Star."

Broken Knife sensed Antler was leaving something out. "What else happened?" he asked.

Antler looked away. "The two white men threw water on Bright Star and raped her," the old warrior replied with downcast eyes. "That is all."

"No! Tell me."

Antler's voice broke several times as he said, "The small man cut her breasts off. The big one slit her belly open to see if she carried a child. Bright Star did not die for sometime."

Broken Knife threw up, and then he cried as if he was a baby.

24

That afternoon, a warrior showed Broken Knife a round disk he had found by the dead white man. He pointed at one word. "This is on a building five days journey from here. Maybe, men live there."

That night, Broken Knife cut his hair and started for the settlement. Four nights later he reached the outskirts of the town. He spent the night in a barn where he found an old pair of pants and a shirt hanging on a peg. Rummaging around the barn, he found a wide brim hat made from straw.

Uncomfortable in the baggy pants and hat, Broken Knife hugged the buildings as he walked up and down the settlement's only street. Several times, he paused by groups of talking men. He could not understand their words. The approach of darkness brought forth sounds of raucous men inside the town's tavern.

Broken Knife went inside. He made his way to an uncrowded corner of the noisy saloon. From the dim-lit corner, he watched gaunt, red-faced frontiersmen reel back and forth across the dirt-packed floor. A black-bearded man stood behind a rough hewn plank bar dealing out tankards of black rum.

After several minutes, his attention centered on two men. The loud pair was arguing with a man wearing a broadcloth suit. The man shook his head. He snarled something. When he did, the smallest braggart yanked out a breast-skin tobacco pouch. His partner held up a scalp with a deer-antler ornament attached to the hair.

Broken Knife gasped. He had carved the hairpiece. Consumed by rage, he started forward. He had not gone far when he felt Lame Bear's presence. His father's words – calm and relaxed – echoed in his ears. He stood several seconds then went outside and leaned against the porch railing. He waited.

Broken Knife had not been there long when the saloonkeeper pushed the drunken pair out into the street. Arm in arm, they staggered down the black deserted roadway. He

25

could have slit their throats easy, but while waiting on the porch, he had decided woman killers deserved more. When they entered the same cabin, he waited a few minutes, then followed them inside.

Both men lay passed out on the bed. Searching in the dim glow from the fireplace, Broken Knife found a short piece of rope. He used it to tie their hands and legs to the bed frame. By the time he finished, the pair was cold sober and shouting threats.

Not understanding the words, Broken Knife smiled as he pulled out each man's shirttail. He soaked the ends with coal oil, then carefully arranged the oily material over each man's crotch.

Using two sticks of firewood, Broken Knife carried embers from the fireplace. He placed the glowing coals between the pleading cowards spread-eagled legs. Black smoke rose off the oil-soaked material. The woman killers broke into screams of sheer terror. The big man passed out. Broken Knife revived him with cold water and a willow switch. He wanted the butchers of an innocent woman to enjoy this last warmth between their legs.

Broken Knife wrapped Bright Star's hair and the tobacco pouch in a blanket. As he finished tying the blanket into a tight bundle, the first yellow-tipped flame broke out of the black smoke. The only sounds from the killers of his mother were pitiful whimpers. He walked out leaving the sagging door open.

Broken Knife climbed onto a knoll near the cabin. On the top stood an old, knurled oak much like the one where Lame Bear had found him. He buried the bundle under the tree. Removing one of the green stones from his medicine bag, he pushed the stone into the soft dirt. Broken Knife moved into the Grandmother's light and sang a prayer for his mother. Having done all he could for Bright Star, Broken Knife watched the burning cabin light up the night sky.

Nothing at the Delaware village interested Broken Knife except the black metal box. He retrieved it from a lightning-scarred tree. With the box under his arm, he headed for Lame Bear's cave.

At the cave, Broken Knife built a fire and roasted a chunk of deer meat. He ate the meat and a handful of parched corn before putting a pack together. The pack contained a robe, shirt, leggins, extra moccasins, pemmican, dried fruit, and the box contents. Pausing at the cave entrance, he took a last look at the metal box setting on Lame Bear's favorite willow back-rest.

WALKERS

Broken Knife climbed an ancient trail that wound through trees and over rock ledges. At the tree line, he made his way along the barren ridge to a weather-scarred tree. Exposed roots anchored the lifeless tree on the rocky summit. Over countless years, eagles perched on its branches had turned the few remaining limbs stark white.

The vision seeker built a low fire. As the flames died down, he dropped a handful of sweet grass on the gray-rimmed embers. He straddled the fire. The rising smoke bathed his body. With deep breaths, he pulled the fragrant smoke into his lungs. Purified in body and spirit, he faced the ghost tree.

A soft, low song began his spiritual quest.

The fourth night of his fast, sheet lightning flashed across a black ominous sky. The storm intensified. Cracks of lightning and rolling booms of thunder filled the heavens. Lost in his vision search, Broken Knife sat unaware of the storm's fury.

A jagged streak split the aged tree. The simultaneous crack and boom aroused the vision seeker from his semi-conscious state. He stared at the smoking tree.

Lame Bear stood in the acrid blue-gray light. Wobbly legs gave way as Broken Knife struggled to stand. By the time he reached his feet, his father had vanished.

Broken Knife stared into the darkness. Reaching out toward the smoldering tree, he moaned, "Thank you, Father," before staggering down the steep, winding trail into a tree-lined canyon.

Broken Knife built a wikiup to keep out the rain. Deer, turkeys, a creek full of fish were nearby. Grieving for his parents, his only solace was the bow and knife. Relentless practice dimmed his worst images: Lame Bear and the vultures, Bright Star and the white men.

Three weeks of practice and song prayers softened Broken Knife's grief. Tired of his seclusion, he checked the surrounding country. He had covered several miles when he crossed the trail of three Delaware.

His curiosity aroused, Broken Knife followed their tracks to the white man's wagon road in the next valley. He stopped on the edge of a stand of oaks. Just ahead, three Indians stood behind trees. They watched a white man tighten the hub nut on a wagon wheel. Behind the man, a skinny, narrow-faced woman stood by two mules.

The Indians waited to make sure the two whites were alone then stepped into view. The woman gasped. Her hand flew to her mouth.

The largest warrior held up his hand palm out. Another one rubbed his belly.

Broken Knife moved behind the warriors. He snarled, "Do Delaware beg as if filthy Shawnee?"

The big Indian whirled. His hand dropped to his knife. He stared at Broken Knife. In a voice full of contempt, he said, "Who are you to speak bad of us?"

The reply was equally contemptuous. "Broken Knife, son of Lame Bear."

After a quick glance between them, the three Delaware trotted off into the trees.

Surprised by the Indians abrupt departure, the man blurted out, "What did you say?"

Broken Knife did not understand the words. Struggling to form words of greeting, something his father had said on occasions just popped out. "Gawd-All-Firelocks."

The man doubled over laughing. With a loin-clothed savage before her, the woman remained stiff and pale. She relaxed slightly as Broken Knife stammered, "Me white, me Clint."

Red-faced, the man straightened. In a warm friendly voice, he introduced himself and his wife. Broken Knife caught one word, Bill. The man turned to his wife. "He is probably hungry. I will finish the wheel. You fix something." Bill motioned Broken Knife to stay then headed for the wagon.

Broken Knife watched Bill's yellow hair bounce off the wool shirt that stretched tight across his broad shoulders. Instinctively, he felt this white man could be depended on. The dark eyed woman, he was not so sure.

While Bill tightened the nut and greased the wheel hub, Broken Knife walked about the camp. There were two wagons, a milk cow, four mules, and a stockin' legged horse. The lead wagon carried furniture. A water barrel was on one side and a grub box on the other. Tools and equipment filled the second wagon. As he looked in the wagons, Broken Knife tried to recall the English word for things he recognized.

His inquisitiveness satisfied, Broken Knife returned to the fire. As he walked up, the woman pointed at the stream. He washed his hands and face. About to go back, he broke into a snicker. His white mother had made him do the same thing.

The food tasted different, so he ate little. Somehow, he did not think that this woman would take it kindly if he threw up.

Bill finished eating. He set his plate and cup on the log. Looking at Broken Knife, he motioned he needed a driver for the second wagon. Broken Knife knew nothing about driving mules, but he had been thinking about going West. Nodding at Bill, he pointed toward his camp then jogged off.

Broken Knife returned two hours later. He wore a

buckskin shirt, loincloth, and leggings. His bow was in one hand and a beaded pouch in the other.

Mrs. Walker went to the wagon. She returned with a pair of wool pants. Pointing at the loincloth, Mrs. Walker held out the pants. When he felt the heavy, stiff material, he dropped them and shook his head.

With a grin, Bill said, "Fetch him the flannel ones."

Broken Knife changed behind the wagon. The pants were too big around the waist. Rummaging in the wagon, he found enough twine to hold them on. As he finished, a grin crossed his face. It was a good thing he had cut his hair or she might have scalped him.

Bill had the cow and sorrel horse tied to the lead wagon, so Broken Knife climbed on the seat of the other wagon. He picked up the lines and tried to move behind Bill's wagon. The mules refused to budge.

Bill grinned and clucked to his team. When they started to move, the mules Broken Knife was driving fell in behind and down the road they went.

Late that afternoon, Bill pulled off the rutty road into a clearing where water and grass were plentiful. Broken Knife watched Bill unharness his team. When he tried to unhook his mules, they threw a fit.

Bill came over. With a chuckle, he unhooked and hobbled the ornery pair. The four mules went straight to a small patch of bare ground, dropped to their knees, and rolled on their backs. Each one twisted from side to side before getting up and shaking off the dirt.

Broken Knife watched the mules grab mouthfuls of succulent grass. They seemed contented, but Lame Bear had taught him caution. He did not want unexpected visitors. Retrieving his bow from the wagon, he circled the meadow then went into the trees.

Mrs. Walker had a makeshift table set when Broken Knife returned. The food tasted better, still he ate little. When they finished eating, Bill doused the fire. He motioned for Broken Knife to follow.

Bill had the four mules tied to trees before Broken Knife caught and tied the horse. They left the cow loose. She would not stray. Besides that, Indians did not care for cow meat.

Broken Knife spread his night robe near the sharp-eared mules. The pawing of their flint-like hooves would wake him if anything prowled about the camp. At the first hint of grey light, he crawled from under his robe. With bow in hand, he made a large circle to check for pesky Indians. Convinced there was no danger, he headed back.

Bill was setting the coffeepot down when Broken Knife stopped beside him. Startled, Bill dropped the steaming cup of coffee in his other hand.

Seeing what happened, Mrs. Walker brought two more cups. She offered one to Broken Knife. After a slight pause, he shook his head and walked to the stream.

Bill stared at Broken Knife's back. "Nobody should be able to move through dried leaves and twigs so quiet."

"I am glad that I saw him coming," she said as her face took on a more serious look. "He wanted the coffee, but thought he had to wash first. At least, he has some civilized up bringing. I hope that we are doing the right thing."

"Now, Mother quit worrying. I am sure we are."

Breakfast over, Bill hooked up the mules. Broken Knife and Mrs. Walker put the few things they used back in the wagon. Broken Knife's team followed the lead wagon leaving him nothing to do except stare at the rear of Bill's wagon. He passed the time trying to recall the English word for what he saw. It did not take long until the words began coming back.

After the first week, Broken Knife could tell Mrs. Walker's curiosity was killing her. That night when she finished the dishes, he told about the Shawnee killing his white parents and parts of his Indian life. When Bill asked about the Indians who raised him, Broken Knife replied white men had killed them. A dull knife would have cut the stillness.

"Other day, it sounded like you said two names to those Indians. Who are they?" Bill asked.

Broken Knife hesitated. "One was my father. The other my Indian name." Bill did not say anymore, but he had a strange look on his face.

Mrs. Walker rose and without a word went to the wagon. She returned carrying a pan of water, two small jars, and a piece of cloth. She mixed a white powder into the water then reached for his hand. With warmth in her eyes, she removed the dirty leather bandage and submerged his hand in the tepid water. Yellow thick pus oozed from under the scab just before it came loose. At sight of the bone tip, her hand tightened on Broken Knife's wrist. Tears filled her eyes. She knew why he had cut the finger off. Mrs. Walker bandaged the stub then kissed his cheek before going to her wagon. Sounds of a broken-hearted woman drifted across the night air.

Bill rested his hand on Broken Knife's shoulder, before he went to console his wife.

At his first opportunity the next day, Bill took Broken Knife aside. "Why did those Indians take off when you mentioned your name?" he asked.

Broken Knife hesitated then told him about the Shawnee and the two white men.

Dumbfounded, Bill blurted out, "Holy Mother of God! No wonder they left in a hurry."

Broken Knife said, "I would as soon Mrs. Walker did not hear any of this. She would not understand."

Bill nodded in agreement. "And you be careful who you tell. If the law learns about it, they will hang you for sure."

Several days later, a wagon train bound for an old French fort below St. Louis caught up with them. The fort, called Kaskaskia, was where Bill planned to start a blacksmith shop, so they joined the train.

Not wanting to attract attention, Broken Knife put away

his buckskin shirt. He wore one of Bill's linsey-woolsey shirts. With the collar buttoned, it hid his medicine bag and bear-claw necklace. He tried, but could not stand the stiff shoes. He continued wearing his moccasins.

Broken Knife stayed away from the other travelers, and none of them came near him. He suspected Bill had told them that "the boy's tetched." He still checked the countryside night and morning. Afraid somebody might notice his bow and ask questions, he left it in the wagon. In its place, he carried his knife.

The mules stayed skittish, but Broken Knife made friends with the horse. He was brushing the sorrel gelding when Bill asked if he had ever ridden. When he shook his head no, Bill bridled and saddled the gelding. Holding out the reins, he said, "Cotton is gentle. Just pull a rein in the direction you want to go."

Broken Knife rode every evening. Occasionally, he stopped in the trees, or on a knoll, and watched the settlers. Several times, he crawled into the camp and listened to the men talking around the night fires.

Broken Knife could not help but compare the wagon people with Indians of his village. Of all the differences that he noted, three things stood out. No one swam in the streams where they camped. Parents continually hollered at their kids. One man picked up things that did not belong to him. In a Delaware village, everyone swam each morning, no one hollered at children, and no one stole from members of the village. The strange part was these same people often referred to Indians as dirty, thieving savages.

If the wagon train stopped early, there would usually be footraces. Since he did not want trouble, Broken Knife stayed away from the races. Bill told him the best runner was Jack James. He added the only good thing about the loud-mouthed bully was the stallion he rode.

The wagon train reached Kaskaskia just before the first

winter storm. The McClendons, relatives of Bill, had a house and barn ready for them. The barn would make a good blacksmith shop.

After the wagons were unloaded, Broken Knife gathered his things and prepared to leave. The Walkers insisted he stay. When Broken Knife finally agreed to wait until spring, Bill broke into a grin.

"Good," he said. "We will start on the shop tomorrow. By spring you will be a first rate blacksmith."

With a pleased look, Mrs. Walker added, "And I will teach you to read and write." She took his hand and led him to the back bedroom. "This will be your room, and please call me Louise."

That night after supper, she said, "You have never mentioned your white parents. How old were you when they were killed?"

"I am not sure, maybe four or five," Broken Knife replied. Getting up, he said, "There is something in my room that I would like you to see." He returned with the beaded leather pouch. He handed it to her. "These are all I have of them."

Mrs. Walker removed the papers, ring, and coins. It was several minutes before she looked up. "You were christened Henri Clint Soissons. Your parents were Henri and Sarah Stuart Soissons. Except this fifty dollar note to a merchant in Boston, I cannot read the other documents."

Puzzled, Broken Knife said, "My father's name was Maure."

Bill asked, "Could that have been a nickname?"

Broken Knife shook his head. "I do not know. What does christened mean?"

"It means you were given a name and baptized into a Christian Church." Broken Knife did not understand what she meant. Before he could ask a question, Mrs. Walker said, "Nothing here indicates you have relatives in America. This coat of arms on the ring is not familiar to me, but my father would recognize it. He teaches American and European history at a university near Washington. He is also an advisor to President Jefferson. Would you like me to send him the papers and ring?"

"It does not matter," Broken Knife replied with a shrug of his shoulders. "Come spring, I am going West, maybe clear to the heighth of land. Lame Bear told me that someday I would choose between the Indian and white man. After watching the people on the wagon train, it is not a hard choice." He hesitated. "Sometimes at night, I listened to the wagon train men. All they talked about was more – more land, more money. Everything with the white man is more, whereas, Indians want little except to live as they choose. With Indians, there is a sense of freedom few white men will ever understand. I want to be free, not bound by a struggle to have more."

With sadness in her voice, Mrs. Walker said, "Not all white people are the same."

Smiling, Broken Knife touched her cheek. "I am sure they are not, but I miss the life of an Indian village. There everyone is family. I had Aunts, Uncles. Here, I am a stranger in a strange land. Let me keep the merchant's note. Someday I will send him the money."

Broken Knife enjoyed the blacksmith work. At first, he hated the reading and writing lessons and would have quit, but Mrs. Walker would not hear of it. The one thing he did like was her talking about the country's history. Through her father, Dr. John Fitzpatrick, she knew many important government officials including Thomas Jefferson. She often talked late into the night about the West and its relationship to France, Spain, and England.

On several occasions, she talked about one of her father's former students. He was the President's personal secretary. His name was Meriwether Lewis. She told Broken Knife that Captain Lewis was preparing for an overland expedition to the Pacific.

Blacksmith work in Kaskaskia consisted mainly of

shoeing horses and replacing wagon wheel rims. It was not long before Broken Knife could fit a hot rim with a ten-pound hammer in either hand. Busy fitting a rim, he did not see, or hear, Jack James and another man come into the shop.

The stranger grabbed Broken Knife's shoulder. He growled, "I'm talkin' to you boy."

From across the shop, Bill yelled, "Leave him alone."

The big man stepped toward the smithy. "An' who's gonna make me?"

Broken Knife did not see the blow, but he heard a loud thud. The man staggered and went down. Bill's harsh voice vibrated throughout the barn. "James, drag this bum out, and do not come back."

Bill chuckled at his helper's face. "They come hunting trouble. There is no use gabbing about it."

"I have never seen anyone do that. Would you teach me?" Broken Knife asked.

Bill nodded as a broad grin crossed his face. "In my younger days, I fought some for money. Tomorrow, we can rope off a back corner, but do not tell Mrs. Walker."

Over the next couple of months, Bill taught Broken Knife to block punches, duck and weave, balance on the balls of his feet, to jab, and throw combinations.

With a storm raging outside, Broken Knife asked if they could box. It had been over a week since he and Bill last sparred.

Broken Knife's youth, quickness, and stamina were too much for Bill. After several hard rounds, he held up his hands. His face beamed with pleasure. "You are wearing me out." He hesitated then added, "It is hard to believe how you have filled out this winter. That shirt use to be big across the shoulders. Now you fill it out fine. I would bet you are close to six foot and weight one-ninety or so. You have the size and ability to be a professional fighter."

Broken Knife had no idea how tall he was, or what he

weighed, still the compliment pleased him. After cleaning up, he walked into the house with a lighter step. His newfound pride soon vanished.

Mrs. Walker scowled, "What happened to your eye?"

"Aaaaah, ah horse hit me with its head."

Glaring at Bill, Mrs. Walker said, "You promised me no more fighting."

Bill looked sheepish. "We were not fighting just playing around."

Holding out a primer, she said, "If you have all this time to play around, you can spend more time doing your lessons."

A few days later, Bill and Broken Knife were talking about knives. When Broken Knife mentioned his throwing knife, Bill asked to see it. He studied it for sometime then said, "Would you like me to improve the balance on this?"

"That would be good," Broken Knife replied. "I cannot throw it very well if I hold the handle."

Bill removed the wooden handle. Over the next two days, he reshaped the shaft. Finally, he cut grooves in the metal and inlaid silver strips. When Bill was done, Broken Knife attached the knife sheath to the thongs of his bear-claw necklace. He added two more long thongs to the tip of the sheath.

Bill held out the knife. He said, "You should be able to throw it holding either end now."

Broken Knife balanced the knife. "That is better. Thanks for fixing it," he said as he slipped the necklace and sheath over his head. When he tied the lower thongs, the sheathed knife fit snug between his shoulder blades.

Bill nodded. "No one would ever guess you are carrying a knife there."

"It does feel good. Could we put up a target? I need to practice with it and my bow." His eyes twinkled as he added, "There were several guns in our village, but none of them worked. I have never fired a gun. Could you teach me that too?"

"Raising you is about to tucker me out," Bill replied with a grin. "Trade guns have always got something wrong with them. I have been thinking about doing gun repairs. If we do, you will get tired of looking at them."

Robins fighting over small territories of worms signaled the coming of spring. The sounds and smell of a new season made Broken Knife restless. A couple of nights later, he announced his decision to leave.

Mrs. Walker's eyes filled with tears. Walking into the bedroom, she returned carrying a gun wrapped in linen. "We want you to take this. Mr. Gallatin gave it to us. We have no need for such a fine weapon. You might."

Broken Knife uncovered the flintlock. He stared at the meticulous engraving and workmanship. He laid the rifle on the table. "I cannot accept this."

Mrs. Walker's stern voice put a stop to his protest. "Yes, you can. We owe you our lives. You sent those Indians away, and I know why you were gone night and morning. Even here, you sleep outside most nights."

Smiling, Broken Knife said, "It is hard for me to sleep without stars above me." He kissed her cheek. "Thank you. I will always be beholden."

Bill put an arm around his wife's shoulder. His own voice sounded heavy. "Just remember, you always have a home here with us."

The next day, Bill and Broken Knife went to the general store. Jack James's father was the proprietor. Mr. James was admiring Broken Knife's rifle when his big-bellied son sauntered through the door. Mr. James scowled, "Where you been? You should 'ave been here hours ago."

Jack reached for a piece of hardtack. "Me an' some ah the boys were harassin' some filthy Injuns, an' I lost track ah the time."

Broken Knife smiled. His eyes were hard. "Jack, your dad likes my flintlock. If you are not afraid, race me to the tree by the blacksmith shop and back. The rifle against your stallion."

Jack smirked. "Pa, you're goin' ta 'ave a new gun." He glared at Broken Knife. "Then, we'll see who's afraid."

Broken Knife sneered back. "Can you run as well as you brag, fat boy?"

When Jack lunged toward Broken Knife, Mr. James grabbed him. "He's just gettin' your goat. Settle down, or you're beat 'fore the race starts."

As they approached the tree, Broken Knife led by ten yards. He circled the tree, and when he passed Jack, he thumbed his nose at him. Broken Knife stopped at the finish line. He looked over his shoulder. Jack was walking back with his head down. Even from that distance, Broken Knife could see the anger and frustration building up in the dejected runner.

Broken Knife removed the saddle and set it on the hitch rail. A pistol hung from the horn. He asked, "Could I bring the bridle back this afternoon?" When the storekeeper nodded, Broken Knife untied the reins. He turned to see Jack standing in front of him.

Jack's clenched fists looked like granite blocks.

Broken Knife's eyes twinkled. "The spirits of my Indian mother and fathers thank you for the horse, and I thank you, fatty."

Jack lunged for the pistol. "Ya filthy, stinkin' Injun. I'll kill ya."

Broken Knife's hand went behind his neck. His fingers were on the handle of the knife.

Bill jumped between them. He grabbed Jack's hand. "You have already lost once," he said, "but you are alive. Your next loss will change that."

Jack hesitated. He did not understand what the blacksmith meant. Mr. James stepped forward and took the pistol. "He beat you fair and square. Leave him alone."

Broken Knife chuckled as he and Bill walked away. "He

will wait until he and his friends catch me alone, but I got news for him. Come morning, all that will be left of me in this town is a track, and I doubt if he is smart enough to find it." Touching Bill's arm, he continued, "I have no need for a horse. Mrs. Walker likes this one. I would like to give it to her."

Bill smiled his appreciation. "At one time, her father raised thoroughbreds. She mentioned once that this one was as fine as any she had seen."

Broken Knife tied the stallion to the hitch rail. He went after Mrs. Walker. When she saw the horse and he said it was hers, she squealed, hugged him, hugged the horse, and hugged him again.

ST. LOUIS

A buckskin clad man stepped into the drizzling, predawn rain. Unconcerned by the rain, or heavy mist rolling in from the distant river, he tilted his head. His mouth opened, his nostrils dilated. Convinced splattering drops of rain were the only unusual sounds, he returned to the shallow cave.

Broken Knife went to his possibles sack and removed a compact clump of punk. He arranged the fire-starting moss in a depression created by a pile of sticks. He scraped flint across fire steel to produce a wisp of smoke. Bending over, he gently blew on the punk. A yellow flame broke out of the smoke.

Adding small sticks to the fire, he placed a kettle of cold water on the blazing branches. A handful of Arbuckle floated on the water. While waiting for the coffee to boil, he leaned against the rock wall and chewed a dried strip of deer meat.

Finished with his morning coffee, Broken Knife dumped the coffeepot grounds on the smoldering ashes. He covered the ashes with dirt then set the pile of sticks back over the fire pit. Leaning his rifle and powder horn against the cave wall, Broken Knife put his possibles sack and other weapons in a deep crack at the back of the cave. Sticks and dry leaves concealed his cache. Using a leaf-covered branch, he swept the dirt floor.

With powder horn and rifle in hand, Broken Knife stepped from under the rock overhang. He listened to the chatter of squirrels and birds. Reassured that it was safe, he started toward the wagon road. His light, certain step left undisturbed the glistening moisture on underbrush and grass. At the hard-beaten roadway, Broken Knife's long, flowing strides carried him toward the Mississippi ferry.

A heavyset bald man collected the nickel fee without so much as a nod. Moving to the bow, Broken Knife stared across the river at St. Louis.

The surly boatman started yelling and cursing.

Broken Knife turned to see a young woman trying to drive a buckboard onto the bobbing ferry. When the balky team reared, the girl's face paled.

Broken Knife moved behind the odious man. "Quit cussing and help the lady."

The boatman whirled. His eyes locked on Broken Knife's cold, grayish-green eyes – death permeated the air. The man's neck swelled with words he could not utter as a cold-clammy sweat spread across his shoulders and down his back. The boatman's face drained of color. His knotted fists opened. He used a dirty shirtsleeve to wipe his brow. Cowed, the boatman trudged to the buckboard.

A grey-haired man stepped from behind a wagon. He said, "You sure lit a fire under ol' Jake."

Broken Knife returned the man's grin with a slight bow of his head. He said, "If you will lead the horses, we will get behind them." The old-timer yanked the horse's heads about. With the boatman and Broken Knife pushing, the team stepped on the ferry.

When Broken Knife moved away from the horse that he had pushed, the buckboard driver touched his shoulder. A low, warm voice whispered, "Thank you."

Broken Knife looked into black flecked, lupine-blue eyes. Hanging from under a wide brimmed hat, burnished-blonde curls framed the driver's stunning face.

The beautiful girl smiled. Her even white teeth and blue eyes sparkled.

Flustered, a red-faced Broken Knife stammered, "Your servant ma'am." He hurried toward the two mules that powered the ferry.

On the St. Louis side, the boatman dropped the rail. He scowled as the girl drove onto the dock. The sinister look on the man's face made Broken Knife uneasy. When the girl turned and waved, he smiled back, and promptly forgot the boatman's icy stare.

The ferry owner followed Broken Knife off the boat. He stared at Broken Knife's back, then the rifle. A cruel smile flickered across his wind-blown face. He hurried past Broken Knife toward the town.

Broken Knife stopped on the outskirts of St. Louis. He stared down the main street. Carriages and large freight wagons filled the muddy road. Boisterous men jammed boardwalks and hard-packed dirt paths. The men shouted, clapped each other's backs, and fired guns in the air.

Rather than force his way through the exuberant crowd, Broken Knife stayed on the rutted road. He weaved his way between wagons toward the town's center. Mercantiles, saloons, and office buildings lined the right side. On the riverside, big storage buildings faced the main street.

Ragged Indians approached Broken Knife with outstretched hands. When he grunted, the hangdog expressions left their faces. They scurried away. In front of a two-story building, painted women wiggled hips and beckoned. He ignored the gestures.

Broken Knife stopped to watch dock workers. A large keelboat was being loaded with crated supplies and equipment. Bales of pelts and buffalo hides were hoisted aboard another one. Other boats were unloaded into warehouses and wagons. Watching the bustling activity, he understood why trappers referred to St. Louis as "Gateway to the Wilderness."

The Town Square was full of people. All eyes were on the ceremony at the base of the flagpole. Unable to go any farther, Broken Knife looked at the swarthy man beside him. He touched the man's arm. "Excuse me, sir. My name is Clint. What is going on?" he asked.

"I'm Manuel Lisa. Today's the ninth of March 1804. It's a day to remember. Official word arrived yesterday that the United States has bought the Louisiana Territory from Napoleon." Pausing, he added, "Even local Spanish authorities hadn't received official notice that the territory had been sold. In fact, everybody I know thought Spain owned it. Now they find out, France had owned it for three years 'fore they sold it to the Americans last April."

"I heard President Jefferson wanted to buy New Orleans. Napoleon must have sold it all. Are those men raising the Stars and Stripes?" Broken Knife asked.

Lisa shook his head. "Naw, they're hoisting the French Flag for twenty-four hours. It's a salute to the French founders of St. Louis." He watched the Spanish flag come down. "I'm Spanish, but this is the best thing that could have happened to the fur trade."

"I do not understand. In what way is it good?" Broken Knife asked.

"Spanish officials in New Orleans have restricted trading above the Platte to Clamorgan's Company," Lisa replied. "Word is the country beyond the Platte River is the best fur and hide country in North America." Lighting his pipe, he continued, "You can bet it won't take Kentucky- and Tennessee-Irish trappers long to get upriver. See the man next to that one with the flag?"

"Wearing the army hat?" Broken Knife asked.

"Yea, that's Meriwether Lewis. He and a William Clark are taking an expedition to the Pacific Ocean. Those men will open up the whole territory." Lisa stuck out his hand.

"I'm raisin' money now for a trading post on the upper Missouri. Be gone three, four years. If you're interested, come see me."

"Thanks, I will do that."

Broken Knife sauntered about observing the sights. Two streets paralleled the main thoroughfare. Several roads ran crosswise. The crossroads ended at a bluff containing an old fort and several mansions. Green grass, flower gardens, trees, and high ornamental-iron fences surrounded the large houses on the high bluff.

Below the sheer-faced bluff, log cabins lined the narrow streets. The logs of the cabins stood side by side in the French fashion. From a distance, the town had appeared clean. Here on the side roads, hard beaten paths wound around decayed animal carcasses and piles of debris.

Broken Knife returned to the docks. After dangling his muddy feet in the water, he leaned against a shaded crate. He pushed his feet out to let the sun dry his moccasins. The rhythmic lapping of the water had almost put him to sleep. He sensed movement. Turning, he watched a gray-haired man stroll onto the quay. Broken Knife nodded.

The stranger sit beside him. "Are you enjoying the sun young man?" he asked.

"Yes, sir, it had me daydreaming." Broken Knife glanced about. "Until today, I would not have believed any river could be this large."

"Aye, she's a big one. I'm Josh McBain, retired Captain of the Orleans Queen."

"My name is Clint. I was thinking about the first white men to float the Mississippi. Do you know who they were?" he asked.

"The earliest I've heard about is two Frenchmen, Jolliet and a Jesuit Priest named Marquette." McBain subtracted numbers on the dock boards. "That was 1673. When the explorers saw the size of the Missouri and Arkansas rivers,

Jolliet realized they were not on the River of the West. He decided the river must flow into the Gulf of Mexico. Afraid the Spanish would throw them in jail, the party turned back. Jolliet wanted to inform Quebec of their discovery." McBain hesitated. "Fifteen- or sixteen-years later, La Salle followed the river to the gulf."

"River of the West?" Broken Knife asked with a puzzled expression.

"There's no such river," McBain replied. "For generations, explorers have hunted a waterway that connects the Atlantic and Pacific oceans. This mythical river has been called everything from the Northwest Passage to the Strait of Anian." Glancing at the sun, he continued, "When La Salle reached the gulf, he claimed the drainage of the Mississippi River for his King. Those words by La Salle gave France the land between the Appalachian and Rocky Mountains."

Broken Knife said, "I had heard about La Salle, but not the other two. It does not seem right for Kings to claim land that way, especially when people already live there."

The Captain nodded in agreement. "A Catholic Priest told me, that during the Crusades, the Mother Church declared Holy Wars to be just. Christian governments use this church decree to justify claims on foreign lands. The officials claim to be bringing heathens to the Mother Church." McBain grinned then added, "These same governments reason if any infidels resist, it's all right to kill a few. After all, enlightened white men are saving savage souls."

Sobering thoughts silenced them. Both men listened to the lapping water. McBain broke the silence. He asked, "Had you heard about France owning the Louisiana Territory? Until today, I figured Spain owned it."

Broken Knife replied, "Through a secret treaty, Spain returned the Louisiana territory to France four years ago. When President Jefferson found out, he had emissaries approach Tallyrand, the French minister, about buying New

Orleans. During the negotiation, Napoleon must have offered the whole territory."

"Why did Napoleon want to keep it quiet?" McBain asked out of curiosity.

"France has financial problems." Pausing, he added, "Napoleon sent his army to Haiti, and what had seemed an easy conquest turned into disaster. Yellow fever and bloody fighting depleted Napoleon's military prowess, and his treasury. Until France recovers from this Sugar Island debacle, it cannot defend New Orleans. Bonaparte probably felt selling the territory to the Americans beat the English taking it."

Impressed, McBain asked, "Maybe you can answer something else that's always bothered me. Why was New Orleans under Spanish control anyway?"

Broken Knife changed positions. "It goes back to the French and Indian War. From 1754 to 1763, France and England fought over shipping, free trade, Indians, and the Canadian and Louisiana borders. In 1763, the Peace of Paris Treaty forced France to relinquish its North American claims. Through this treaty, England took possession of Canada and the land from the Appalachian Mountains to the Mississippi River. The treaty did not include Spanish Florida."

"But New Orleans is considered east of the river. It should have gone to the British," McBain said. "That's what I don't understand."

Broken Knife said, "Before signing the Treaty, the French King ceded Spain everything west of the Mississippi River and the mouth of the river, including New Orleans. Some think the King did this to pit the British against the Americans." Pausing, Broken Knife looked at McBain. He added, "Despite winning a seven-year war, the British did not control the best water route to the Ohio Country. Spain controlled entrance to the Mississippi."

"Those old Kings were sure enough tricky. Where did you learn all this?" McBain asked with a smile.

"I stayed in Kaskaskia last winter. On cold evenings, we huddled around the stove while Mrs. Walker talked about history and governments. Her father is a college professor, and an advisor to President Jefferson." Pausing, he said, "A few minutes ago you said Rocky Mountains. I thought they were called the Stony Mountains."

McBain smiled. "You'll hear 'em called four different names: Chippewaynean, Stony, Shining, and Rocky. Who knows which name will stick?"

Dock workers moved toward the two men. The workers were talking about a sixteen hundred mile boat trip and soldiers wintering at a Mandan village. The gist of the conversation was that seven soldiers would return the keelboat in the spring. The other twenty-seven, a slave, and an interpreter would go on to the headwaters of the Missouri. There, the Captains hoped to get horses from the Snake Indians (Shoshone) and cross the mountains to the Columbia River.

"Sounds simple enough," McBain said as the workers moved off, "but Lewis and Clark are wasting time. It would be faster to cut across Panama, or sail the Horn."

"President Jefferson's got more in mind," Broken Knife replied. "He is interested in Indian commerce, fixing the Louisiana's western boundary, and bolstering the United States' claim to the Oregon country."

McBain stared across the water. "I wondered if there wasn't more to it. I've never sailed the Pacific. Where is this Oregon country?"

Broken Knife traced out a map. "Spanish California forms the southern border. Louisiana's western mountains form the east border. The Pacific is on the west. The dispute is over the northern boundary with Canada. In 1792, an American named Robert Gray crossed treacherous breakers and sailed into an immense estuary. He named the river after his ship, the Columbia. Gray's discovery plus an overland expedition will help settle the northern boundary."

His interest aroused, McBain asked, "Where do the British think it ought to be?"

"At the Columbia River," Broken Knife replied. "A North West Company partner named Alexander Mackenzie left Fort Chippewaynean on Lake Athabasca. Accompanied by Alexander Mackay, six French Canadians, two Indians, and a dog, he went up the Peace River to the Parsnip River. Following the Parsnip to the Continental Divide, the men made an eight hundred and forty step portage to a lake. Mackenzie believed the lake was the headwaters of the Columbia. A couple of hundred miles later, cataracts and falls made the waterway impassable."

Broken Knife stopped to change position. "Friendly Carrier Indians told Mackenzie the river could not be traveled by canoe. The Carriers also said the Indians downriver were hostile. When two Carrier Indians offered to serve as guides, the expedition headed cross-country toward the ocean. Reaching the Bella Colla River, the expedition followed it to the Pacific.

"Mackenzie waited a couple of days for clear weather to determine the longitude and latitude. While waiting, Mackenzie carved his name on a rock. He wrote – Alexander Mackenzie, from Canada, by Land, the twenty-second of July, One Thousand Seven Hundred and Ninety-three."

"Will the British claim to the Columbia stick?" McBain asked.

"It is doubtful," Broken Knife replied. "Mackenzie was on the Tacoutche-Tesse River. His mark is hundreds of miles north of the Columbia River's mouth. Besides that, Mackenzie's journey was a year after Gray's discovery of the Columbia." Hesitating, Broken Knife said, "Another North West trapper, Simon Frazier managed to float the Tacoutche-Tesse three years later. It is now called the Frazier River."

McBain checked the sun. "I better go, or I'll miss dinner. I've enjoyed our talk, maybe we can do it again."

"I hope so," Broken Knife replied.

Heading back toward the ferry, Broken Knife saw ten- or twelve-dirty men blocking the boardwalk. The loud voices and the way some used the building for support showed they had celebrated all day. Broken Knife noticed a big redheaded man watching him.

The man slurred, "Gimme' thet gun."

Broken Knife ignored the man. Before he could step out in the road, a short, dirty man grabbed the rifle. He handed it to his boss.

Broken Knife's voice sounded a sharp warning. "Give the gun back."

Red ignored him. He stared at the gun. Finally, he said, "Ya stole this, an' iffen tha owner cun fin' me, he cun ask fer it." He finished in a thick-tongued sneer, "But, he'd be ah wastin' 'is time."

The ragtag and bobtail roared.

Broken Knife reached for the gun. The big man knocked him down. He growled, "This har Coon's goin' ah slit yer throat."

Broken Knife collected himself. He dove headfirst into Red's soft belly, then jumped to his feet.

Bent double, the bully gasped new air into his lungs. Red forced himself erect. The wild-eyed man had dropped the rifle. His hand held a pistol.

Broken Knife's hands moved behind his head. "Cock that hammer and you will be worm or fish feed." He smiled. "It depends on, whether this scum digs a grave, or throws you off the dock."

Red's followers howled at anyone dumb enough to make threats with his hands clasped behind his neck.

The rawboned man failed to see the humor in anything. He was busy feeding his air-starved lungs.

The short gun-grabber cried, "Shoot 'im, Red. I needs me sum mogasins."

Red's thumb tightened on the hammer. "Ya son-of-a-bitch. I'll kill ya."

Broken Knife's arm dropped.

Red's eyes bulged. Confused, he turned toward his men. The silver knife handle in his throat reflected the afternoon sun.

Rooted in place, five men stared. The rest ran down the street.

Red's claw-like fingers dropped the pistol. He grabbed the blood-covered handle. His hand slipped off. He tried again. Once more. His strength gone, Red toppled backwards. Blood from his slack mouth ran between boards on the boardwalk.

Broken Knife stepped across Red's heaving chest. He picked up the rifle by its barrel. As he raised up, he swung the stock between the gun-grabber's legs.

The lackey's face drained of color. Whimpering, Shorty doubled over. Broken Knife drove the gun butt into his jaw. The sharp, brittle crack of the jawbone stopped the pitiful moaning.

Wrapping Red's long hair around the knife handle, he pulled the knife out. The space left by the blade filled with dark, thick blood. Broken Knife rolled the quivering body over. He wiped his hands and knife off on Red's flannel shirt.

Oblivious to the dead man, Broken Knife smiled at the four men still standing there. His eyes were warm and friendly. "Tell Shorty, it is not polite to grab, or covet another man's moccasins."

A tall, dark-complected man crossed the street. A Kentucky rifle rested on his arm. The man's light, easy step gave an impression of ability and confidence. He looked at Red's followers. Raising the rifle, he said, "I would take those two and git 'fore this young man gets riled."

The riffraff picked up Shorty and Red's body. They disappeared down the first side street.

The stranger held out his hand. "George Drouillard."

"Thank you, sir. My name is Clint."

"Do not thank me. You killed the cock-of-the-walk, and

not one of them knows how the knife got in Red's throat. Those boys were buffaloed." Drouillard looked sheepish. "In fact, I did not see it myself. Providin' you do not object, I would admire lookin' at your gun."

Broken Knife grinned. He handed over the flintlock.

While Drouillard examined the rifle, Broken Knife studied him. They were the same height, but Drouillard's hair was darker and longer. He wore a buckskin shirt, brown wool pants, and moccasins. A wide beaded belt held his pants up. Broken Knife liked the man's appearance despite the fact Shawnee beadwork decorated his belt and moccasins.

Drouillard checked the polished stock, the fine, deep engraving, and the overall quality. Bringing the gun to his shoulder, he sighted down the barrel. He sighed and handed it back. "This is the finest rifle I have ever seen."

"Thanks."

"A friend of mine from Quebec is the Police Chief. We better go see him." Broken Knife seemed surprised, so Drouillard added, "With all the French-Canadians here, a Canadian can control them better."

Broken Knife told Drouillard that Mrs. Walker had given him the gun and a certificate of ownership. He added a Mr. Gallatin had given the rifle to her. Drouillard looked surprised, but he did not say anything.

Drouillard introduced Broken Knife to the Police Chief then explained what happened. Yves studied the certificate. He asked a few questions. Satisfied, he smiled at Broken Knife. "Monsieur, the man you killed is no loss. Men like Red McCloud needed to be hung, or run out of St. Louis long ago. His followers are a gutless bunch, but like dogs, they are dangerous in packs. Be careful of them."

Drouillard glanced at dark, storm clouds forming in the northwest. "It is goin' to be rainin' before long. Where you stayin'?" he asked.

"Across the river."

"Me too. Let's go together. Even if they are a gutless bunch, it won't stop them from back-shootin' you."

"Thanks, I am fine."

Drouillard ignored Broken Knife's reply. He steered him down the street. Drouillard said, "I am Lewis and Clark's interpreter and hunter. Our camp is on the East Side of the Mississippi across from the mouth of the Missouri." Pausing, he said, "The Captains wanted to winter near St. Charles, but the local Spanish Commandant said no. He would need official permission to let American soldiers camp on the Missouri. When Captain Lewis told him that Americans had owned the country for close to a year, the Commandant shrugged his shoulders. He still needed permission from New Orleans."

Broken Knife smiled. "Just goes to show you how slow governments are."

The hunter pointed at a white house on the bluff. "That belongs to Auguste Chouteau. He laid out the first trading post here for his stepfather, Pierre Linguest Laclede. Chouteau was thirteen at the time. Now, he is the richest man in town."

"That reminds me of a question I wanted to ask Lisa."

Surprised, Drouillard asked, "You know Manuel Lisa?"

"Not really," Broken Knife replied. "I asked him about the celebration today is all."

"I do not know him either, but word has it he is the best field trader on the river. What is your question?"

"Does the Platte River divide the lower and upper Missouri country? How far is it?"

"It is the dividin' line all right," Drouillard replied. "If you follow the Big Muddy (Missouri), the Platte's six hundred and fifty miles upriver. Few white men have gone beyond the Platte." He chuckled. "Even Dan'l Boone is at La Charette, and it is only sixty miles up the Missouri."

As questions were asked and answered, both men watched the streets, buildings, and people. On the outskirts of town, a stocky, deep-chested man stepped into the street.

54

Behind him, several men and one woman stood on the saloon's porch. The man's flat nose, scarred eyebrows, and thick ears implied a riverfront brawler. The pug-nosed tough glared at Broken Knife. "McCloud wuz my frien'. Iffen he'd been sober, you'd be on the slab 'stead ah him."

Broken Knife handed Drouillard his rifle. "I am sorry, sir. Were you addressing me? If so, are you drunk?"

Surprised by the polite response, the fighter's oversized fists relaxed. "Naw, whatsa ta ya?" he asked.

Broken Knife leaped forward. His fist sank into the braggart's soft mid-section. Hot, fetid air exploded from the man's mouth. A bone-jarring right snapped the man's head back. Another right, followed by a hard left to the solar plexus buckled his knees. Red's friend sprawled face first in a mud puddle.

The silent crowd gaped at their champion. Finally, a big-busted woman thrust her hip out. She yelled, "Yo, George. Bring yer frien' an' com' on oer."

Red-faced, Broken Knife reached for his gun. He said, "St. Louis is sure a friendly place. Everywhere you go, someone wants to admire your gun, stop and talk, or invite you over. It bothers me when people are this nice."

"I have noticed that, Hoss." Drouillard's eyes twinkled as he added, "When we part, try smilin' or wavin'."

Broken Knife grinned and walked away.

Drouillard peered at the man lying in the street. He hurried to catch up. "Why did you ask if he was drunk?"

Glancing over his shoulder, Broken Knife replied, "I did not want him to use the same excuse he did for Red. We better step on it, or we will miss the ferry."

The boatman forced a smile as he took the nickels from Drouillard and Broken Knife. Watching the pair make their way forward, his smile turned into a black, menacing scowl.

Broken Knife sat on a hard plank. His thoughts were on Drouillard and the Pacific, but not for long. The rocking motion of the boat put him to sleep.

Broken Knife's piercing eyes opened flat and cold. The gun raised off his lap. Seeing Drouillard's outstretched hand, he flashed an embarrassed smile. "Sorry, I should have warned you. I am a light sleeper."

Despite his ashen-colored face, Drouillard's voice sounded calm. "We are about to dock, I was goin' to wake you."

Drouillard moved to the rail. He gripped it for a minute then lit his pipe. After several puffs, he returned. Standing by Broken Knife, he said, "I'm nosy, which must be the French in me. I hope you do not mind questions. Who taught you to use your fists?"

Broken Knife yawned. Starting for the gangplank, he said, "Last winter, I worked in a blacksmith shop. Most days were spent swinging a hammer, but on slow days, the owner gave me some pointers."

The boatman smiled and thanked them as Drouillard and Broken Knife walked off. Puzzled, Drouillard said, "Tanner seemed surprised to see us. Now he is polite which is not like him. You know why?"

"Tanner?"

"Jake Tanner, he is the boatman."

"Oh, I did not know his last name," Broken Knife replied. "Jake and I had a little chat this morning about helping ladies. Maybe, he is changing his ways." Before Drouillard could ask anything else, Broken Knife held out his hand. "Good day to you, Mr. Drouillard. It has been my distinct pleasure and honor to have made your acquaintance."

Drouillard responded with a firm grip. "Now, wasn't that easier than killin' or hittin' someone?"

A mischievous smile crossed Broken Knife's face. "Seemed like wasted words to me."

Drouillard grinned as he shook his head. "That road goes to our camp. Come visit, and we will go shoot a deer."

Nodding, Broken Knife trotted off.

DROUILLARD

Stars were fading in morning light when Broken Knife gathered his goods and left the shallow cave. The possibles sack hung off his right shoulder. Over his left shoulder were the long bow, quiver, and powder horn. The rifle rested in the bend of his arm. A small kettle, ten-inch butcher knife, and a shot pouch swung from his beaded belt. He carried the cumbersome burden with ease.

Broken Knife stopped on a haze covered bluff. He watched the round, golden-red ball dissolve the remnants of a heavy fog. The vanishing mist revealed the mouth of the Missouri River.

The sharp contrast in the diagonal line formed by the muddy-brown Missouri and the slate-grey Mississippi explained why settlers referred to the Missouri as "too thick to drink and too thin to plow." Shop loafers had mentioned that trappers had dubbed the Missouri the Big Muddy. Indians called it Smoky Water. To Broken Knife, neither name did the violent river justice.

The turbulence and sheer power of the debris-ridden river held him as if a magnet. The raging Missouri was drawing him toward the mountains where streams, creeks, and rivulet formed the angry river. Broken Knife had no doubt these far off waters were to nourish his life's blood.

The bluff road ended among the fourteen log cabins of the Lewis and Clark Wood River Camp (Camp River DuBois). At the first campfire, Broken Knife asked for Drouillard. A pudgy man pointed toward the last cabin. Squatted around cooking fires, several men watched Broken Knife pass, but no one spoke.

Drouillard sat cleaning his rifle on the sunny side of his cabin. At sight of the heavy-laden Broken Knife, he grinned. Holding out his hand, he said, "I did not expect you this soon, Hoss. You have not threatened a bully, or rescued a distressed damsel, and gotten in trouble again?"

A straight-faced Broken Knife replied, "Naw, but there is hope. The day is still young." He asked, "How about going to the Pacific with you, or at least as far as the mountains?"

Drouillard paused. "Your goin' is fine by me." Grinning he added, "You might find it kinda dull without St. Louis bad men around to pick on." Drouillard stared at Broken Knife's variety of weapons. "Settlers have killed off the game close around. I could use help huntin' now, and goin' upriver. How is your huntin'?"

"I am pretty good with a bow and at tracking, so-so with a gun."

Drouillard eyed the bow. He asked, "Have you lived with Indians?"

"The Delaware. When Shawnee killed my white parents, a Delaware named Lame Bear saved me."

Drouillard dropped the gun. His face turned pasty white. "Wind-of-Death!" exploded from his half-opened mouth.

Drouillard picked up the gun. His grip on the barrel turned his fingernails white, then red. "I hunted last fall with Shawnee that were there when Lame Bear went under. The tribe's two best warriors stayed behind to ambush Lame Bear's son, Broken Knife."

Drouillard's black eyes locked on Broken Knife's gray

58

ones. "This boy killed both warriors, then hung them upside down under a tree." His voice dropped to a whisper. "That was you?"

Broken Knife nodded.

Looking as if a club had hit him in the stomach, Drouillard leaned the gun against the cabin. He asked, "How old are you?"

"I am not sure, sixteen or seventeen."

"That could be a problem. Everyone goin' to the Pacific is in the army except myself, Captain Clark's manservant York, and Captain Lewis' dog Scannon (Seaman). The youngest private is Shannon, and he is seventeen which is the minimum age for joining the army." Pausing, he said, "Captain Clark just went into his cabin. Let's go talk to him."

Drouillard hesitated outside the Captain's cabin. He said, "Let me talk to him first." Within a few minutes, he stuck his head out and motioned at Broken Knife.

The tall, redheaded Clark had a friendly grin, straightforward eyes, and a strong handshake. He pointed at a chair. "I am glad you stopped by. Drouillard mentioned you and your rifle last night. George tells me you want to go with us?" When Broken Knife nodded, Clark said, "The expedition is set for the Pacific, but we could use help to the Mandans. You are welcome to go that far."

Broken Knife grinned from ear to ear. "Thank you, sir."

"Good, now can I take a look at your gun?"

Clark examined the firearm from all angles. He handed it back. "You mentioned to Drouillard that a Mr. Gallatin had owned it. Do you know who he is?"

"Yes, sir," Broken Knife replied. "He is President Jefferson's secretary of the treasury. Napoleon gave him the rifle during negotiations for the Louisiana Territory."

Clark said, "Secretary Gallatin contributed a great deal to our route selection. Besides his vast knowledge of Canadian trapper journals and charts, he commissioned the best cartographer in Boston for a new map."

Clark walked over to his desk. He pointed at the map. "Regrettably, the mouth of the Missouri, the Mandan village, and the Columbia estuary, are the only places located with accurate longitudes and latitudes. Still, it is a big help." He glanced at his watch. He held out his hand. "I am sorry. I have a meeting. Captain Lewis will want to meet you. We can talk some more when he is here. Drouillard can find you a place to stay."

Drouillard piped up. "He can stay with me. There is an extra bunk in my cabin."

Broken Knife placed his possibles sack and weapons by the empty cot. He went back outside to see Drouillard sitting on a six-foot log.

Drouillard leaned over on his right hand. "Hoss, that silver-handled knife has me curious. Yesterday, you put it in your belt, but it is not there now. Mind tellin' me where you pack it?"

Rubbing his neck, Broken Knife glanced around to make sure no one watched. His hand dropped. The knife quivered between Drouillard's fourth and fifth finger. "Between my shoulder blades," he replied with a smile.

Drouillard's hand did not move, his expression did not change. "I am glad your knife throwin' is a bunch better than pretty good." With a hard look at Broken Knife, he said, "McCloud did not stand a chance. The funny part is, he did not even know it."

"Maybe not, but he had a choice. His mistake was cocking the pistol. The two best fighters I have known were Lame Bear and Bill Walker. In different ways, they said the same thing – 'hit 'em first, and hit 'em hard.'"

Piqued with interest, Drouillard asked, "You mean while Red and the other guy bragged about what they were goin' to do, you hit them?"

"That is right." With a grin, Broken Knife added, "As you

60

observed, it stops drawn out conversations and long good-byes."

Drouillard removed the knife. His tears of laughter obscured the blade. He handed it back. "Grab your gun. Let's see if we can rustle the cooks a deer."

Broken Knife nodded his head. Breaking into a smile, he said, "If you expect me to get one, I better take my bow too."

The hunters long, smooth strides carried them over rolling hills covered with grass, blooming flowers, and scattered hardwood trees. On a small stream that emptied into the Wood River, Drouillard spotted a doe and young buck. He shot the doe.

Broken Knife missed the forked-horn. Holding out his rifle, he said, "Watch this thing. I will fetch the buck."

Broken Knife circled to get ahead of the deer. When he crossed a well traveled game trail without seeing fresh tracks, he turned down the beaten path. He had not gone far before he saw the twitching ears of the forked horn. His arrow severed the neck vein and artery below the horn. Leaving the deer where it fell, he went back to where he had seen turkey signs. Not far off the trail was a gobbler and hen feeding on a bull-berry bush. He shot the hen in the head and the tom as it flew off.

Broken Knife returned to the deer. After cleaning it, he dug a hole and buried a piece of liver as an offering to the deer's spirit for providing food. With the deer across his shoulders and a turkey in each hand, Broken Knife returned to where he had left Drouillard.

His friend sat puffing his pipe. Behind him, the doe hung with a stick between her hind legs. Downwind, blow flies swarmed on the discarded entrails. Drouillard knocked the ashes out of his pipe. His voice hid his admiration. "Kind ah careless body-shootin' the tom, Hoss?"

With mock concern, Broken Knife replied, "Lame Bear could do it, but for me, a flying turkey's head is tough to hit."

Drouillard raised off the log. "Let's cool these out before we head back." After hanging the deer and turkeys, he said, "You must be more than good with a bow too."

"The bow is fine." Looking at Drouillard, he said, "I would appreciate any suggestions about the gun though."

Drouillard said, "Never shoot if the deer is lookin' at you like the fork-horn was. The flash of the gun and the powder smoke will spook it every time. The deer will be gone before the rifle ball ever gets there." He picked up Broken Knife's bow. Removing two arrows from his quiver, he said, "Let's see how good you are. Behind you is a three-inch sapling. Try and put one of these in it."

Broken Knife whirled. Two arrows and the silver-handled knife were in the tree trunk.

Drouillard saw it. He did not believe it. Stepping off forty paces, he removed the knife and arrows. His palm covered the three holes.

Broken Knife peered over Drouillard's shoulder. "That bottom hole is a tad off center. Think I better practice more?" he asked.

Drouillard stared at Broken Knife. "Holy Mother of God! I cannot believe it, and you wanna practice more?" He shook his head in bewilderment. "Most of my life has been spent around Indians. I would have never believed anyone could shoot that far with such speed and accuracy. No wonder the Shawnee fear your medicine."

Broken Knife started to say something then stopped.

Drouillard smiled. "Afraid I will not understand about medicine?" His hands dropped to his side. "There is something I need to tell you." Pausing, he said, "Maybe, I better sing my death song first. My mother is Shawnee."

Broken Knife's eyes sparkled. "Your response to Lame Bear's name, and the beadwork on your moccasins said you had lived with the Shawnee." He held out his hand. "I want a friend, not an enemy."

Drouillard

Drouillard gripped Broken Knife's hand.

Broken Knife sit on a nearby log. "I better start at the beginning, or you will be asking questions forever."

Drouillard listened with rapt attention. When Broken Knife mentioned Lame Bear had taught him to be aware of air current changes, even while asleep, Drouillard interrupted, "Yesterday, crossing the river you felt my hand move?"

"Yes. Of all the things he taught me, that was the hardest to master."

Amazed, Drouillard urged him to continue. When Broken Knife reached the part about finding Lame Bear's body, Drouillard felt an aura of spiritual power emanate from his friend. Overcome by deep emotions, he asked, "Your spiritual guidance comes from Lame Bear?"

"Whenever there is danger, my father's spirit guides me." Hesitating, Broken Knife said, "Our spirits were joined where Lame Bear was killed, and he appeared to me where eagles perch on the ghost tree."

"I have prayed many times at the ghost tree," replied a solemn faced Drouillard.

The two men sat lost in deep thought until Broken Knife broke the stillness. He said, "I scattered the Shawnee warriors' medicine bags knowing their spirits could not enter the Spirit World without the medicine symbols." His voice softened. "I should not have done that."

Drouillard nodded his understanding. "Lame Bear was my peoples worst enemy. My own mother cut off her finger because of him. Still, I am sorry for the way he died. Lame Bear's vendetta made the Shawnee a stronger people. Our warriors' skills were better because of his hatred. The warriors should have honored his spirit." Hesitating, he added, "Young Shawnee braves found the swayin' bodies, and were afraid to cut them down. It might anger the Wind Spirit. Now, many of my people believe you are a spirit."

Broken Knife did not know what to say. He went to the

deer and started taking them down.

On the way back to camp, Drouillard said, "Despite countless hours of campfire tales about Lame Bear, I do not even know what started his hatred. What did?" he asked.

"Lame Bear never talked about it, but Running Deer told me a Shawnee war party killed his bride."

Drouillard shook his head back and forth. "I have never known an Indian to seek revenge so long. He acted like a white man. Many of them will not be satisfied until all Indians are dead."

"You are right about that. Lame Bear was obsessed with killing the Shawnee, but unlike whites, he hunted only warriors." Pausing, he said, "Bright Star believed the Wind Spirit had placed a cloud behind his eyes. Now it is my turn to ask a question?"

"What?"

"You have lived in the Indian and white worlds, but seem to prefer the white. Why?"

"Not really," Drouillard replied. "Being a half-breed I am not really accepted by either." He hesitated. "A common thread that binds all peoples is prejudice."

"Until the Walkers, my life, my thoughts, were Indian. Now, I am dangling somewhere between the two worlds."

A solemn faced Drouillard said, "That is exactly how I felt at the missionary school in Montreal."

The hunters left the deer and turkeys at the cook shack. On the way to the cabin, they paused to watch Joseph and Reuben Fields, John Potts, John Colter, and George Shannon playing cards.

When Drouillard introduced Broken Knife, Colter remarked, "We've 'eard about 'im. Wiser cum back 'is afternoon, an' says St. Louie's goin' ta be ah talkin' about this kid till the cows cum home." He smiled. "Tha' guy ya hit's still groggy."

"Yea," added Potts, "an' Big Bertha sends greetins, an' ta cum oer iffen ya can." At this, the group and a red-faced

64

Broken Knife roared.

Drouillard spoke up. "Clint's goin' to the Mandans with us. Any of you goin' to St. Louis pass the word. If there is talk against him, I want to know about it."

Several others welcomed Broken Knife and offered their help. The heavyset Newman summed up the men's feelings. "We's all Indian fighters an' backwoods men, an' ah reckon, iffen push cums ta shove, we'uns cun handle any ah St. Louie's riffraff."

The men kept glancing at his gun, so Broken Knife handed it to Colter. After each one had sighted down the barrel, the whole bunch agreed when Reuben Fields said, "I'd ah gutted tha bastard iffen he tried fer mine, an' it's nothin' like this hyar' un."

Declining to play cards, Broken Knife and Drouillard went on to their cabin. As they entered it, Drouillard asked, "Anything else you are good at?"

"Naw, except maybe running," Broken Knife replied.

Excited, Drouillard asked, "How fast are you?"

"Two years ago at the fall harvest ceremonies, I outran everyone except Running Deer." Broken Knife smiled. "He was the Delaware's best."

"Somebody is always gettin' up a footrace around here. Colter's the fastest, an' if you could beat him," a sly grin crossed his face, "we would clean up."

Broken Knife shook his head at his scheming friend before going after an armful of wood. When Broken Knife returned and stoked the fire, Drouillard said, "You mentioned trouble with five warriors. Were those the Shawnee you killed?"

"How in the world...."

"Two of them belonged to my mother's clan." His voice dropped. "One was her younger brother."

"I am sorry about your uncle," Broken Knife said before explaining what happened.

Drouillard sighed. "It is hard to believe. I am indebted to Lame Bear. His knocking down your bow spared my half-brother."

Broken Knife did not know what to say except, "I am glad too."

"You did not scalp them. Why?" Drouillard asked.

"Those were the first warriors I had killed, and I was not keen on the idea. When Lame Bear saw my discomfort, he said the Shawnee believed him a spirit; therefore, he had no need for scalps. That night, I received the best praise my father ever gave me. His words were, 'Any Delaware can kill a Shawnee. Only Broken Knife can follow Lame Bear.'"

"After the Shawnee spent all those years trying to find him, I would say that is real praise," Drouillard said with a smile. "If my people heard an eerie, low-moanin' wind, a Shawnee warrior would be found dead. Did he make that noise?"

"I am not sure," Broken Knife replied. "Lame Bear mentioned spirits only that one time." Pausing, he said, "When he rescued me from the Shawnee, I heard a strange rustling of the leaves just before the Shawnee warrior's head exploded in a spray of blood."

Drouillard said, "My white half says Lame Bear made the noise. My Indian half says spirits did it."

After adding wood to the fire, Drouillard said, "You have never talked about your white parents. Do you remember them?"

Broken Knife shook his head. "Mostly dim memories of a bouncing wagon. When I use to try to picture my mother, all I could see was her gaunt face. The one thing I do remember is being hungry."

Drouillard stared into the fire a long time, before saying, "You know, despite all the tall tales, I would not recognize Lame Bear if he walked in right now."

Broken Knife blew out the candle. "One thing for sure,

you would never forget him. He was taller than I am and weighed at least twenty pounds more. Lame Bear moved with the quickness and grace of, or he could be as patient as, a stalking cat."

Drouillard yawned. "He must have been something to elude the Shawnee for twenty years."

The next day it began raining. It did not stop for five days. Lack of game forced the hunters to range farther inland. They often took packhorses and camped out. After two days of hard hunting, Broken Knife and Drouillard were sitting around the night fire. Drouillard asked, "Did you cut your finger off for your Indian mother?"

The breeze shifted. Broken Knife moved out of the smoke. "Bright Star never hurt anyone." His voice dropped to a whisper. "She did not deserve to die the way she did."

Drouillard waited a few minutes then asked, "What did happen to her and Running Deer?"

Broken Knife wiggled around until the log he leaned against fit his back. "After Lame Bear was killed, the Shawnee tracks headed for our village. When I reached the village, an Uncle told me white men dressed as Indians had killed Bright Star and Running Deer."

Drouillard stirred the coals. "White men often dress as Indians in the hope the raids will be blamed on other Indians."

Broken Knife casually mentioned it did not help two white men. When he did not say anymore, Drouillard blurted out, "What happened? Do not stop now."

It still hurt to think about Bright Star. Broken Knife had to collect himself before he could go on. When he finished, he paused. "The shirts caught fire too soon. The woman-killers needed to suffer more."

Drouillard eyes expressed his sympathy. "Some whites take great pride in killin' an Indian. A few years ago, it was nothin' to see Indian heads and hands impaled on stakes around white settlements. Infuriated Indians retaliated by raidin' isolated farms. This cycle went on and on." Yawning, he added, "Feels like it is gettin' time for bed."

Come morning, the hunters separated. Broken Knife worked a brushy draw. At its head, he crossed the trail of five Indians. The tracks headed in Drouillard direction. With a five to one advantage, there could be trouble.

Broken Knife stopped on the edge of a hickory grove. Ahead of him, a fat warrior leaned against a tree trunk. The other four warriors surrounded Drouillard. One had his gun, another his knife.

Broken Knife's arrow pinned the leader's jacket to the tree. When the other Indians whirled about, Drouillard grabbed back his gun. Broken Knife notched another arrow. He gestured that he had shot at a bird and missed.

The Indians jabbered and motioned they only wanted to look at the white man's gun and knife. Finished with their explanation, they took off. The leader went a little ways. He turned and snarled, "White man lern shoot, get um hurt."

Two arrow shafts between the Indian's pigeon-toed feet ended any need for further conversation. The pudgy warrior hurried after his friends. He moved as if he had curled up toes, but it did not slow him down any.

"Those were Iowa warriors," Drouillard said with a chuckle as he watched the fat warrior's belly bounce. "I let them look at my knife, then the big one grabbed..."

Broken Knife interrupted. "If those heathens had taken your gun, you might have wanted mine." His mischievous eyes twinkled. "Without my rifle, I am defenseless. I could not protect myself from these devilish demons."

Drouillard shook his head. He started after the horses. On the way back to the Wood River camp, Drouillard killed a black bear. Broken Knife shot two deer. The deer's hindquarters, long back muscles, and the tenderloins were loaded on two horses. They packed the bear fat and hide on the third horse.

Headed toward camp Broken Knife asked, "Do you

suppose Indians and whites can ever live in peace?"

"No! The white man will never be satisfied until he has our huntin' grounds. That means killin'." Pausing, Drouillard added, "What gets me is when they kill in the name of religion. I heard a preacher thank his Father-In-Heaven for deliverin' heathen savages unto his children." Drouillard scowled. "The Huron women, children, an' old people delivered by the white-man's God had lived in peace for years. Makes you wonder who the savages are."

"Running Deer felt the same way. Once when we were fishing, he talked about the Lenni Lenape. The Lenape consisted of many different tribes with a territory above and below the Hudson River. Since the arrival of white men, their diseases and warfare have reduced the Lenni Lenape from eighty to a hundred thousand to a few thousand. Now, only the Delaware and Munsee tribes remain." Pausing, Broken Knife said, "Pressure from the whites and Iroquois have forced them west of the Appalachian Mountains."

Drouillard nodded. "The same thing happened to the Shawnee. It just took the white man longer to get there."

"Running Deer told me the British and Americans had signed over a hundred treaties with the Delaware. Most of the treaties guaranteed white soldiers would protect the Delaware's remaining land. Once white men moved onto the new ground, they always took more. If any Delaware resisted, local politicians and land-grabbers pressured the government into sending soldiers. Not to protect – as the treaty had promised – but to force the Delaware into signing a new treaty."

Drouillard lit his pipe. He said, "My father was a French-Canadian. He made me attend a Catholic Mission School in Montreal. One missionary wrote on the blackboard: French embrace the red man; British despise the red man; Americans kill the red man."

Broken Knife looked grim. "Mrs. Walker believes

President Jefferson is going to establish an Indian Nation in the desert of the Louisiana Territory. He wants the eastern tribes moved across the Mississippi away from settlers. When I asked about this forced relocation, Mrs. Walker's eyes filled with tears. She replied, 'Throughout man's history, one people take another people's land.'"

Drouillard shook his head, then said, "It does not seem right."

"No, it is just the way things are," replied Broken Knife. "Is your father still alive?"

"He traps for the XY Company in Canada," Drouillard replied.

Broken Knife looked at Drouillard. "I have never heard of them."

"The XY was started by several wealthy merchants in Montreal to compete against the North West Company. Three years ago at the North West's annual Grand Portage rendezvous, Simon McTavish had a fit when he learned Mackenzie was comin' back from England to head up the XY Company."

Broken Knife said, "I thought Mackenzie was a North West man."

"He was. After he got back from the Pacific, he wanted the Hudson's Bay and North West to join forces. Mackenzie argued that if the companies merged, they could control all the country above Spanish California. McTavish would not hear of it. After pulling the Quebec and Montreal independent traders together to form the North West Company in 1787, McTavish was not about to give up control.

"Mackenzie and McTavish had a big fight over merging the two companies. Not long after that meeting, Mackenzie went to England to talk with leaders of the Hudson's Bay Company. As far as I have heard, all he has accomplished is to be knighted. He is Sir Alexander Mackenzie now." Pausing, Drouillard said, "While in England, he wrote a book about his

70

travels. Mackenzie's book was behind Jefferson gettin' an expedition off to the pacific coast."

Broken Knife nodded. "Mrs. Walker said President Jefferson had the expedition planned long before buying the Louisiana Territory."

"The President and Capt'n Lewis had talked about it for several years," Drouillard said as they rode into the Wood River Camp.

LEWIS AND CLARK

Camped on the Wood River since early December, the soldiers were tired of drilling and guard duty. With the warm days of early spring, the favorite diversion was foot racing, but no one would run against Colter.

Broken Knife had no idea how fast Colter was until they were hunting. After watching him run down a wing-shot turkey, Broken Knife knew the man could move.

A few days later, everybody was sitting around the cook shack. As it inevitably did, the talk turned to running. After the men had discussed each detail of Colter's last race, Drouillard chimed in, "If you boys haven't got cold feet, you can watch Broken Knife beat your speedster."

Men all around the room shouted, "What do ya wan' ta bet?"

Potts looked as if the shifty half-breed was up to something. He growled, "What ya pullin' now?"

Drouillard, the picture of innocence, drawled, "Couple ah days back, he jumped an ol' sow an' her cub. He seemed ta come over where I was tolerable fast." Yawning with boredom, he added, "Sides, what else ya got ta do. Just ta make it interestin', I'd be willin' ta risk a little at, say, five ta one."

Potts and his friend Drouillard bickered back and forth.

72

They finally agreed on odds of three to one.

Lack of script and coins complicated the betting. Most of the men were broke until they returned and collected their five dollar a month pay (sergeants eight dollars and Drouillard twenty-five dollars). There were bets for doodads, tobacco plugs, whiskey allotments, knives, and one gun. Arguments over the value of each item dragged on and on. Finally, Broken Knife went to bed. After he left, the matchmakers decided if they waited a few days townspeople might bring cash money.

Broken Knife learned at breakfast that Potts and Drouillard had agreed to three races: a quarter of a mile, a mile, and two hundred yards. The races were to be held in five days. Potts mentioned a thirty-minute break between races. Broken Knife let out a sigh of relief. "Good, I cannot run far, but with a little rest, I will be fine."

Winking at his shifty friend, Broken Knife walked outside. After he left, Potts and Drouillard argued over raising the odds. The pair finally agreed on the winner of two out of the three races.

Broken Knife finished five yards behind in the quarter-mile race. During the rest period, he whispered to his sour-faced friend that the bets were safe. Smiling from ear to ear, Drouillard headed toward the town gamblers. He still had a couple of twenty-dollar gold pieces. Maybe, he could get better odds.

Broken Knife won the mile race. More people favored Drouillard's runner, but the Colter backers had nothing left to bet. When Broken Knife won the last race, Drouillard jumped up and down. He grabbed his runner in a bear hug.

An exuberant, Drouillard said, "Hoss, we are splittin' the winnins' down the middle. Providin' everybody gets back and we collect on the notes, we have cleaned up. Right now your share of the town's gambler bets is thirty-five dollars."

Before Broken Knife could answer, Colter came over. "I'm too old fer 'ese shenanigans. If ya 'adn't ah 'eld back, we'd only 'ad ta run twice." Smiling, Colter clapped the victor's back then went to join his dejected supporters.

Broken Knife finished breakfast as Drouillard came through the door. Drouillard said, "The Captains want to see you."

"Do you know why?" Broken Knife asked.

Drouillard shrugged his shoulders. "Let's find out."

This was Broken Knife's first close look at Lewis. The Captain had short brown hair, steady eyes, and a prominent nose. He had a quick nervous way of talking and laughing. It did not take Broken Knife long to peg Lewis as a visionary. In contrast, Clark had struck him as a doer.

Lewis motioned to a nearby chair. He looked at Broken Knife. "Auguste Chouteau wants to meet you. If you can be of any service to him, Captain Clark and I will be grateful. Chouteau's aid has been invaluable. Now, I need his help again. Voyageurs are refusing to help if they have to winter at the Mandan village."

"I will do anything I can, sir," Broken Knife said.

Lewis broke into a broad smile. "Good. It is imperative that we reach the Pacific. Without his help, our expedition could be in serious jeopardy."

"Yes sir, I am aware of its importance." Grinning at the doubtful looks on the faces of the two Captains, he continued, "President Jefferson has charged the 'Voyage of Discovery' with: numbers and locations of Indian tribes; collecting plant, animal, and rock specimens; geology of the country; longitude and latitude of rivers and mountain passes; detailed maps and journals.

"Equally important: you are to investigate Indian commerce, Louisiana Territory's boundaries, augment a claim to the Oregon country, and decide the feasibility of an overland route for the China and West Indies trade."

The Captains were flabbergasted.

In a high pitched voice, Lewis cried out, "Only a few advisors were privy to the President's guidelines. How can you possibly know this?"

Broken Knife smiled. "As President Jefferson's personal secretary and a student of Dr. Fitzpatrick, you were a frequent visitor to his home. The woman I stayed with last winter is his daughter."

Lewis stared. "Louise!"

When Clark and Drouillard looked blank, Broken Knife said, "Her father is an advisor to the President."

"Louise is a brilliant, gracious lady. Her rejecting eligible suitors to marry a blacksmith and move West kept Washington tea circles humming weeks on end." Lewis walked over and glanced out the door. "Looks like a storm is brewin'. Maybe, we can beat it." Smiling at Broken Knife, he said, "We can talk on the way."

Four apprehensive men watched black thunderheads roll out of the northwest. In places, heavy mist lines extended from grumbling clouds to the ground. As they approached the ferry, the violent storm struck in full fury. The bone-biting wind was bad enough without a deluge of rain. The wet, miserable travelers paid Jake Tanner the fare then looked for shelter on the open deck. Huddled between wagons, Broken Knife saw the boatman's ragged helper coming toward him.

"We'uns ain't goin' 'till 'em waves ain't sa 'igh." He held out rope and canvas. "'Ese ar' fer scarin' thet ornery ol' bastard 'alf 'ta death."

Cold hands quickly rigged a cover between freight wagons. The makeshift shelter kept out wind and rain, not the penetrating cold. Captain Lewis wiped water from his red face. Pushing frozen fingers under his arms, he asked, "How did you meet Louise?"

Broken Knife hunched in closer. He told about the three Delawares, and how scared Mrs. Walker had been. When he mentioned the Indians abrupt departure, Lewis interrupted, "I don't understand. They just left?"

"Nothin' happens with Indians that does not spread like

a wind-fed grass fire," Drouillard said with a smile. "Those warriors pictured Shawnee swayin' in the breeze and remembered important matters elsewhere."

Broken Knife grinned at the confused leaders. "That is another story. Drouillard can tell you another time."

"Yes, please continue," chipped in Lewis.

After Broken Knife finished, Lewis grinned. "As you found out, Louise is extremely knowledgeable and persistent. How does she like the backwoods life?"

"Fine, Bill has relatives in Kaskaskia. A couple of his cousins' wives are her age. When I left, she wanted to start a school in the fall."

When the boat jerked, Clark peered out. "We are getting under way. The wind has died down, and it is clearing off. How about moving out in the sun? I am freezing."

Lewis touched Broken Knife's elbow as they walked off the ferry. "I will visit Louise when we return. She will be pleased with how much you have helped us."

Chouteau's Negro servant, Tobias, opened the ornate door. He asked them to follow him. Several bronze statues and marble busts lined the foyer and wide hallway. Oil paintings covered the walls. The servant opened double doors at the end of the corridor. He stepped aside and motioned to enter.

The large room contained shelves of books, a hardwood desk, and leather chairs. A distinguished man turned away from the stone fireplace. "Welcome, gentlemen. Please, be seated." Waving at the chairs, he smiled at Lewis. "Captain, my man Deschamps and nine voyageurs will accompany you. Weather permitting, seven wish to return before the river freezes." Chouteau sit down before adding, "The other two, Pierre Cruzatte and Françoise Labiche, would like to join your army and accompany you to the Pacific. They are experienced traders and river pilots. I can highly recommend them both."

Lewis's eyes expressed his relief. "Is it possible to meet these men?"

"Certainly, they are at the Front Street warehouse."

"If you will excuse us then, we will leave." Lewis smiled at Broken Knife. "When you are through, meet us at the Missouri Mercantile Store."

While Chouteau saw the Captains and Drouillard to the door, Broken Knife took a book off the mantle and thumbed through it. Engrossed by a drawing of men jousting, he did not hear his host return.

Chouteau looked over Broken Knife's shoulder. He said, "I spend many an evening with my books. That one is about King Arthur." He pointed at a chair by the hearth. "Please, here by the fire. Do you care for coffee or tea?"

"Thanks, coffee sounds good."

Chouteau twirled a round silver bell. Shortly, Tobias entered with coffee and cakes. After taking a sip of coffee, Chouteau said, "Thank you for helping Jeannie." When Broken Knife looked confused, he hastily added, "The girl on the ferry. Her name is Jean Schwist, but everyone calls her Jeannie. She is my niece."

With a chuckle, Broken Knife said, "I did not do much, except mention to the boatman he should stop cussing and help the lady."

Chouteau's eyes gleamed. "From the description my niece gave of Tanner's face, you must have a forceful way with words." Pausing, he said, "The saloon talk about you has reached my ears. Before I ask your help, let me tell you what has happened. Nine years ago, Jeannie's older brother came from Virginia to help me. I sent him to the Osage Post, and two years later, he married an Osage woman. They had a daughter and a son. The children are seven and four."

Broken Knife interrupted, "I am not familiar with that tribe."

"The Osage live along the Missouri this side of the Platte." He continued, "A few months ago, my nephew struck a drunken Pawnee named Lone Dog. That night, the Indian returned and killed my nephew and his wife. He took the boy and girl captive. I have tried to ransom the children, but so far, Lone Dog has refused every offer."

Chouteau sipped his coffee. "Jeannie has had a hard time accepting her brother's death. Like a foolish old man, I agreed to let her visit the Osage Post. Two days ago, I received word an Osage hunting party had found her burned wagon. The charred body of the driver was there." His voice wavered. "My niece was gone."

"You believe Lone Dog is behind it?" Broken Knife asked.

"It must be him," Chouteau replied. "I will be blunt. This miserable Indian has caused my family enough sorrow. I want him dead and Jeannie and the children back." When his request did not raise an eyebrow from Broken Knife, Chouteau hastily added, "A saddle horse, two packhorses, and anything else you require will be provided. The animals and equipment are yours regardless of the outcome. When you return with Jeannie and the kids, there will be a five hundred dollar bonus."

Before any more could be said, Tobias knocked. He entered with the Police Chief. After an exchange of the amenities, Yves said, "I have received information Red McCloud, Jake Tanner, and a Pawnee called Lone Dog were in cahoots. Tanner told McCloud about Broken Knife's gun, and he sent word to Lone Dog of Miss Schwist's arrival. There is no proof, but Tanner probably notified the Pawnee when she left for the Osage Post." Yves hesitated. "That is all I have found out so far. If you will excuse me, I had better go. There has been another waterfront stabbing."

Broken Knife waited until Yves left, then said, "At least, we can be fairly sure Lone Dog has her. Does anyone else know about your plans?"

"Only my cousin Pierre will be told. He is coming from the Osage Post. Pierre should be here by morning to take you to Lone Dog's village."

"Good, if Lone Dog finds out we are coming, he will kill

her and the children."

Chouteau's face brightened. For the first time since Jeannie's disappearance, he had hope. "You accept then?"

"Yes. I will get my possibles and be back by noon tomorrow. If Pierre is here, we can leave then."

Broken Knife met Drouillard at the mercantile store. The Captains had gone with Deschamps to inspect the pirogues. Broken Knife and Drouillard started back. On the way, he related what Yves had said.

Drouillard growled, "I never did like Tanner. He is too sullen. We can soon find out if he is involved."

Broken Knife shook his head. "Leave Tanner to me. You just make sure no one interferes."

The only other passenger on the ferry was a wagon driver. The teamster appeared to be the kind that minded his own business.

Halfway across the choppy river, Broken Knife saw Tanner settle in a canvasback chair. When the boatman's head started to bob, Broken Knife took a short rope. He tied one end to an iron anvil. The other end, he dropped over Jake's head.

Jake grabbed at the rope. Turning, he hollered, "What in hell's goin' on?" His wind-burnt face paled when he saw Broken Knife on the other end of the rope.

Placing the eighty-pound anvil on the wooden side rail, Broken Knife let Jake watch it teeter. He said, "This is a memory jogger." Broken Knife removed one hand. "Your first lie, it goes overboard. Did you send the Pawnee word about Miss Schwist?"

Jake screamed, "What er ya talkin' 'bout. Ya can't do this. I'll 'ave tha law on ya'."

The anvil tilted toward the roiling water five feet below.

Jake's grip tightened on the rope. "Yes....Yes!"

"I would let this go, but that is too quick. When townspeople hear what you have been doing, your life will not be worth a plug nickel." Broken Knife let the anvil fall on the deck and walked away.

Drouillard shouted, a gun fired.

Broken Knife jumped. He turned with his knife poised.

Tanner lay in a rapidly spreading pool of blood. His hand clutched a pistol.

Drouillard, the boatman's helper, and the wagon driver stared at the fist-sized hole in Jake's chest. The teamster held a smoking gun. Broken Knife touched the stranger's arm. "Thanks, mister."

The burly man growled, "I eered wat ya asks 'im. River scum likes 'im kilt my woman an' 'ittle girl."

The hate-filled man spit. Tobacco juice ran off Jake's chalky face. Removing the rope, he rolled the body overboard with his foot. "I needs ah anvil."

That night, Broken Knife outlined to Drouillard what Chouteau wanted. "If I fail and the girl is still alive, will you and Colter go after her when you get back?"

"We will do it, but you will have her home way before we get back here."

"I hope you are right. It would please Mrs. Walker if you took my gun to the Pacific." Broken Knife broke into a mischievous smile. "Besides, it is too good a rifle for someone that shoots as bad as I do."

"I do not know what to say except thanks. I will take good care of it." Holding out his hand, he said, "You be careful going up the Missouri. Many Shawnee trap for the North West Company. I have notified my mother's village that Wind-of-Death's son wants peace with the Shawnee. Until the word spreads, the son of Lame Bear is big medicine for any Shawnee."

Broken Knife stopped at Captain Clark's cabin to say good-bye. As they shook hands, Clark said, "Tanner got what he deserved. I am just glad no one connected with the expedition shot him." He placed his hand on Broken Knife's shoulder. "Captain Lewis wanted me to give you his best. If you are not back before the expedition leaves, you are welcome

Lewis and Clark

to winter with us at the Mandans."

Tobias escorted Broken Knife into the library. Chouteau and another man sat in the leather chairs. Chouteau said, "This is my cousin Pierre Laclede."

The small man grinned. "From the stories, I expected you twice as big and blowing fire out of each nostril."

Broken Knife liked the man's looks. Pierre's sun-parched face appeared tough as twang leather. Coupled with a firm handshake and straightforward eyes, he gave the impression he would know which way the stick floated.

Grinning back, Broken Knife said, "People tend to exaggerate." He glanced at Chouteau. "Tanner did send Lone Dog word."

"Yes, Pierre heard about him at the tavern."

The wiry guide looked at Broken Knife. "Lone Dog and his buddy, Hurt Leg, have not been seen lately. I would bet they have Jeannie at the Loup River village."

"How far is that?"

"With horses, two weeks or better." Pierre eyed his new companion. "But, there is a faster way."

Broken Knife realized that Pierre meant on foot. He smiled. "I will try to keep up. Mr. Chouteau, could someone meet us below the village with packhorses? We will need things for Jeannie and the kids."

The trader interjected, "Rene LeClerc knows that country good as anybody around here."

"He is at the dock," Chouteau replied. "We can arrange it now."

While Pierre searched for his friend, Broken Knife looked around the warehouse. "Can I leave some of my things here?" he asked. "All I need is my bow."

Chouteau stared at the bow and quiver. "Are you sure about no gun?"

"I am sure. If it makes you feel better, send a couple with LeClerc on the packhorses. There is one other thing. If I fail,

Drouillard promises he and Colter will go after Jeannie when they return."

With confidence, Chouteau replied, "You will not fail."

Pierre walked up to the two men and said, "One time, Rene and I killed a silver bear and her yearling cubs about a half-day from the Loup village. He will meet us there in two weeks. Holding out a light pack, he said, "Here is a three-point trade blanket, extra moccasins, dried corn, and pemmican. Auguste, if we cross the Muddy at St. Charles and beeline it for the Platte, it will save several days."

Chouteau nodded. "When you reach the Pawnee village ask Gervias for any help you need." At Broken Knife's blank look, he added, "Joe Gervias is a trader at the Loup River village. He can be trusted."

LOUP RIVER PAWNEE

Out of St. Louis, the trader set a blistering pace. The guide's flowing strides reminded Broken Knife of Lame Bear and the day they left the Delaware village. Across the river from St. Charles, Pierre broke into a walk. When Broken Knife came along side, Pierre said, "We could stay here or," a smile lifted the corners of his mouth, "if you are not too tired, we will make a few more miles before dark."

Broken Knife forced a weak grin. He headed for the river.

Pierre chuckled. He went into a nearby tavern to hire a man to row them across the Missouri. Seated in the small boat, the trader faced Broken Knife. "Myself, I would have preferred a soft bed."

Broken Knife stared at Pierre. Every breath felt as if he had swallowed a horseshoe rasp. "I will just bet."

"There is a good Indian trail on the other side of the Missouri clear to the Platte. Let's hit it for awhile, then sleep until the moon is up then hit it again." Pierre grinned and closed his eyes.

The next several days were the same: they ran, they ate, they slept, they ran. The only breaks were occasional stops behind a bush, or sips of creek water. On the ninth day, the runners reached the mouth of the Platte.

Pierre glanced at Broken Knife. "I have a canoe cached upriver, we will cross over in the morning. I will fetch it, while you rustle some meat. I am sick of corn and pemmican."

Broken Knife nodded. He headed into the trees.

Pierre returned to find a small fire and six headshot squirrels, but no Broken Knife. Skinning the squirrels, Pierre placed them on a hastily made spit.

Broken Knife arrived a few minutes later. He had a small deer across his shoulders. "Those smell good. When do we eat?"

At sight of the yearling, the cook licked his lips. "Cut out the backstrap and tenderloin. The meat can cook while we eat these taste teasers."

Pierre wiped greasy hands on his leather pants. He asked, "What is your plan?"

"Right now, I do not have one. How much farther is it?" Broken Knife asked.

"From here, a day and a half."

Broken Knife hesitated then said, "That gives us five days before we meet Rene LeClerc. We can talk to Gervias and go from there."

Pierre said, "Most Pawnees do not like Lone Dog or Hurt Leg. They are an arrogant, mean pair. I doubt if anyone will interfere if we keep the fight between them and us."

Broken Knife shook his head back and forth. "We cannot risk you being hurt. If anything happens, you must get Jeannie and the kids home."

Pierre hated the idea even if Broken Knife was right. "All right, but that does not mean I like it."

"You do not talk like most frontiersmen," said Broken Knife as he tossed a stick on the fire.

"I attended college in London, but my drinking and fighting were an embarrassment, so Father decided I should visit our cousins in America. Once here, I liked the Indian life and stayed."

Pierre got up and went to the packs. He tossed a blanket at Broken Knife. "By tomorrow night, we will be on the other side of the Pawnee village. If we approach the village from the northwest, maybe Lone Dog will think we have been visiting other tribes."

The runners paddled through the Missouri's morning mist to the opposite bank. After hiding the boat, Broken Knife followed the long-striding Pierre the rest of the day. It was long after dark before they collapsed under a shallow rock overhang, too tired to eat.

Come morning, Broken Knife rolled out at first light. Stepping out of the night camp, he stared across a broad plain. The vastness of the flat open country held him spellbound.

Pierre shook off his blanket. He stood beside him. "Your first look is a real treat. There is nothing like the prairie." Turning, he paused. "How does a big breakfast sound?"

"Fine, what?" Broken Knife asked.

Pointing south, the guide licked his lips. "This morning, I fancy liver and hump-ribs." He motioned at his gun. "Take that an' shoot a young cow, they are best."

Far off, Broken Knife made out black bumps – buffalo. He shook his head. "I might miss. I would hate spoiling this big breakfast."

"Buffalo have poor eye sight, but a keen sense of smell." With confidence, Pierre held out the gun. "Approach the herd from downwind, and you can poke it in one's ribs."

Broken Knife and Pierre crawled within twenty yards of a fat cow. Pierre moved beside him. "A heart shot is about all that drops a buffalo in its tracks. Aim above and slightly behind the elbow."

Pushing the gun barrel through the tall grass, Broken Knife lined up the rear and front sights. He pulled the trigger.

The short-horned heifer humped its back, spewed mucus through flared nostrils, and walked off.

Disgusted, Broken Knife reloaded. He aimed higher. This time, the heifer dropped to her knees. She let out a mournful bellow before toppling over. A curious bull ambled over and sniffed then wandered off with its head down eating.

As the herd grazed away, Pierre cut the belly wall and removed a chunk of liver. Cutting it in half, he handed Broken Knife a piece. Consuming the delicacy, he said, "Boy, this tastes good." A loud belch underscored his appreciation.

"It is all right," Pierre replied, "but there is something better. Build a fire."

"Now, just what with?" Broken Knife asked as he glanced about. "There is not a tree or bush in sight."

Pierre pointed at scattered disks of sun-dried manure. He said, "Buffalo chips make a hot fire."

Broken Knife built a fire while Pierre peeled back the wooly hide. He cut out two chunks of fat-marbled, hump meat. Pierre tossed the meat and the buffalo's tongue on the hot coals. Popping fat and the odor of seared meat made Broken Knife's belly growl.

"I take it those are hump-ribs?" he asked.

"There is nothing like them," Pierre replied. "Why, I have seen hungry trappers eat eight, ten pounds, sleep awhile then take on more."

Finished eating, Broken Knife dug a small hole with his knife. He removed the buffalo's heart and buried it in the grass-lined hole.

Surprised at his action, Pierre asked, "Why did you do that?"

"To honor the buffalo's spirit. The cow provided food, and we should express our gratitude. If food is scarce, a prayer will do, but always offer something for what the animal provides you."

Stomach cramps from the rich meat forced a slower pace. By the time they spotted the village, the sun sat high overhead. Pierre fired his rifle. He tossed his blanket in the air, and let it spread out on the ground. Turning, he said, "Announce your arrival and even if you are the tribes worst enemy, you will be given presents and allowed to leave. Did the Delaware do this?"

"They signaled, but not with a blanket." Broken Knife appeared puzzled. "Those lodges are sure spread out."

"Pawnee build them among the corn fields," Pierre replied. "Gervias and other traders have told the warriors it is safer to have the houses closer together. The warriors just shrug, and say it is the way of the Ones who walked before."

Pierre repacked his blanket. They had not gone far when a rider galloped toward them. Pulling up, the horseman nodded at Pierre. He handed his gun to Broken Knife. "I'm Gervias. Leave your bow here. We'll fetch it tonight."

Broken Knife took the rifle. Before he could say anything, the rider turned and started back.

As they approached the town, the barking dogs and playing children made Broken Knife homesick. Nothing has the sounds of an Indian village.

Gervias stopped outside a dirt lodge. He motioned for Broken Knife and Pierre to go inside. Kicking his horse into a lope, he disappeared among the lodges.

The weary travelers entered the dirt lodge. As they dropped their packs, a woman entered with two wooden bowls of meat. Both men had finished eating by the time Gervias returned.

The Pawnee trader smiled at Broken Knife. "I just returned from an Iowa camp. All those warriors would talk about was a white man shooting arrows between Fat Belly's toes. Was that you?"

Pierre broke in, "What is all this?"

After Broken Knife explained what happened, Gervias said, "When I saw you packing a bow through my spyglass, it hit me how to get the girl."

"Jeannie's here?" Pierre and Broken Knife blurted out in

unison.

"Yes. So far, Lone Dog has ignored her. She and the kids are in Tall Elk's lodge. His wife is Lone Dog's sister." Gervias paused. "Comanche are on their way with stolen Spanish horses. Awhile back, Lone Dog beat these same warriors in a game of arrows. They'll be anxious to try again. If Lone Dog wins, the arrogant bastard will bet anything. Providin' he hasn't heard about a bow-shootin' white man, you might win her back."

Broken Knife asked, "What are the rules?"

"Whoever shoots the most arrows before an arrow hits the ground wins." Gervias added, "Seven or eight usually wins the contest."

With a smile on his face, Broken Knife said, "Sounds like a good game. What about seeing Jeannie?"

Gervias thought a minute. "Tall Elk is the village Chief. He usually smokes with any white visitors. I just told the girl you're here and that she's to ignore you." He hesitated. "If you're careful, it should be safe enough."

Pierre stretched and yawned. "Joe, dragging this kid around tuckered me out. You two smoke with Tall Elk while I catch up on some shut-eye."

Broken Knife enjoyed walking through the spread-out village. It felt good to do something besides watch Pierre's back. He stopped by one house and studied the dirt-covered structure. "I have never seen lodges built this way."

Joe kicked at a yapping dog. "The Pawnee build a solid house. After the corn's planted, they follow the buffalo herds 'til harvest time. While they're out hunting, they use wikiups or skin tepees."

As Gervias walked away, Broken Knife said, "What a beautiful little girl! She does not look Pawnee. Who is she?"

Joe glanced over his shoulder. Without missing a step, he muttered, "A Crow."

Confused by the trader's reaction, Broken Knife watched

her enter a lodge. He caught up with Gervias outside Tall Elk's lodge. After Gervias introduced Broken Knife, the aging Chief invited them to smoke. He was lighting his ceremonial pipe when Jeannie came through the entrance.

Jeannie's blue eyes locked on Broken Knife. There was not a flicker of recognition. The Chief's wife hit Jeannie across the legs with a willow switch and shooed her outside.

It was nearly dark when the two men returned to Gervias' lodge. Broken Knife waited until it was good and dark to retrieve his bow. His last thoughts that night were about the Crow girl and Jeannie, mostly Jeannie. She was a good actress or had forgotten him.

Broken Knife shot out of bed. He held his knife. "What was that?"

Gervias laughed. "The Comanche are here. Those damn bucks drive the horses through the village to announce their arrival." He pointed at the meat pot. "Eat, then we'll take ah look at the horses."

The trio left the village and followed the river to an open valley a half-mile away. Bunches of horses were scattered in every direction. Surprised at the number of horses, Broken Knife blurted out. "I cannot believe it. How many are there, Joe?"

"The Pawnee had seven, eight hundred. The Comanche brought another hundred or so."

Broken Knife walked closer. There were browns, bays, grullas, grays, chestnuts, and a few pintos. The short-backed horses were about fourteen hands and weighed on average seven hundred pounds. Their short necks ended in common heads. The horses had well-developed shoulders and rear ends with fine-boned legs ending in small, brittle hooves.

Broken Knife went back to Gervias and Pierre. He asked, "Are they as tough as they look, Joe?"

"Most of 'em could run all day. If necessary, they can live on cottonwood bark."

Two Comanche rode up and started talking to Gervias. The warriors sat on hair, or grass, stuffed buffalo-hide pads. A leather strap around the horse's girth held the pad in place. Braided rope served for a bridle.

Broken Knife took in every detail of the bridle. The leather rope had a small loop braided into one end. Three feet from the eye-end, the rope wrapped around the horse's lower jaw. The loose end continued over the horse's neck and through the eye-end forming a loop. This loop served as a rein. The rider coiled the excess rope and placed it under his belt.

As the two warriors rode off, Broken Knife looked at Joe. "I have never seen bridles made that way. How long are those braided ropes?"

"About thirty feet. Indians call 'em war bridles. If a rider is thrown, he grabs the bridle rope and hangs on. That way he doesn't end up losing his horse." He smiled before adding, "Lose your horse on a buffalo chase, or on a war party. You'll more than likely get yourself killed."

He nodded toward the two Comanche. "They're headed back now. The arrow game will start 'fore long. It should be a good one. Those two told me that a warrior called Many Horses come with them. He's regarded as the tribes best shooter."

Several warriors had shot, and the top score was seven. A powerfully built Pawnee sauntered forward. Pierre nudged Broken Knife. "That is Lone Dog."

The haughty Pawnee looked over the crowd without seeing anyone or anything. He raised his horn bow and shot eight arrows. Lone Dog strutted off like a rutting deer.

Gervias snarled, "He's an arrogant bastard. I hope you take him down a peg or two."

Broken Knife smiled. "Today is the day."

The last warrior finished shooting. Many Horses and Lone Dog had each shot eight. In the shoot-off, the Comanche shot eight, the Pawnee nine.

Broken Knife touched Gervias's arm. "Make Lone Dog mad enough to bet the girl."

As the wild cheering subsided, Gervias shouted, "A white man says Lone Dog shoots like a woman."

Lone Dog scanned the hushed crowd. He saw Gervias and sneered, "No white man beat me."

The trader pointed at Broken Knife. "He bets two guns and a gallon of whiskey against the yellow-haired woman."

Lone Dog hesitated. He looked around.

Gervias scoffed, "The white man said if Lone Dog was afraid, he could have the whiskey for courage."

A handful of Comanche that understood Pawnee roared.

The Pawnee screamed something back. Broken Knife had no doubt Lone Dog had accepted. While his friends went after the guns and whiskey, Broken Knife stretched out under a bush and closed his eyes.

Words of astonishment rolled through the gathering. The white man slept.

When the traders returned, Broken Knife leered at Lone Dog. "Joe, tell the woman-shooter he can keep the nine, or shoot over."

Gervias's eyes popped out. "You're crazy! He can't do it again. No one can shoot ten."

"Go ahead, tell him." Broken Knife smiled. "It is harder to lose if you believe you have already won. There is still the boy and girl."

When Gervias said he could take the nine or shoot again, Lone Dog puffed up like a toad. The Pawnee motioned the white man to shoot.

Broken Knife stepped forward. He pushed ten arrow points into the soft ground. The crowd gasped at the tenth metal-tipped arrow, and then roared, until the first one hit the ground. Not a warrior there doubted that the white man could have shot two or three more.

Lone Dog was livid. Tall Elk and several others moved

between him and Broken Knife. The enraged Pawnee pointed at Broken Knife's bow. He yelled, "The bow."

Broken Knife held up his bow. "Tell them Lone Dog is right. This is a medicine symbol. I will show the People its medicine."

Looking around, Broken Knife saw some boys kicking a grass-stuffed buffalo bladder. He motioned at Pierre to come with him. After considerable coaxing, one boy handed Pierre the ball. When Pierre threw the ball in the air, Broken Knife buried three arrows into the bladder. A fourth arrow pinned it to the ground.

Awe spread through the onlookers. No Pawnee could have hit it once.

Broken Knife and Pierre had started back when Jeannie threw herself at Broken Knife. He shoved her aside. He shouted at Gervias. "The white woman is happy to be rid of such a weak shooting warrior."

Gervias translated and a snicker rolled through the Pawnee warriors. The Comanche did not snicker. They roared.

"Joe," Broken Knife grinned, "you are doing fine. Ask if he can run any better than he shoots. The girl against the two kids."

When Gervias offered the new bet, Lone Dog snarled. He pointed toward a large boulder. The rock was a good quarter of a mile away.

Broken Knife shrugged his shoulders.

The runners were side by side on the way to the rock. As they circled it, Lone Dog faded. Broken Knife poured it on. Crossing the finish line well ahead of the Pawnee, Broken Knife's hand rested on his neck.

Lone Dog stopped short. His icy, pinpointed eyes left no doubt that someday, he would kill the white man.

When Hurt Leg led Lone Dog away, Broken Knife glanced at Gervias. The trader said, "Jeannie and the kids are safe. Tall Elk had four warriors take them to my place. They'll stay with them 'til we get there."

Excited Comanche crowded about Broken Knife. Many Horses insisted Broken Knife and his friends smoke. As the pipe passed from warrior to warrior, each one rose and commented on what he had witnessed. Most believed that in a previous life, this white man had been Comanche. The smoking ended as the sun settled below the horizon.

Broken Knife and the two traders entered the lodge. Jeannie rose off a backrest. Broken Knife bowed slightly. "I am sorry about pushing you, ma'am. I hoped the insult would make Lone Dog risk the kids."

Jeannie crossed the room. She stood on tiptoes. Her moist lips touched Broken Knife's ear. She whispered, "I understand the push, but if you ever call me ma'am again, I will take a horsewhip to you." She pulled back and gently kissed him.

Her words shocked Broken Knife more than the kiss. He had expected her to cry and carry on about heathen savages. Instead, she had scolded him for calling her ma'am.

Jeannie smiled at the look on his face. She led him across the room to her niece and nephew. In a low voice, she said, "Mary understands, but I cannot tell about John. If he learns we are leaving, he may sneak away. He has many friends here and does not want to go home."

Broken Knife grinned at the kids. He whispered to Jeannie. "Have Mary watch him. We are meeting one of your uncle's men in three days."

Gervias went to a wooden trunk. He returned with a comb, a mirror, and a small sack. "Jeannie, take these. Years ago, I packed in a round tub. If you'd like a hot bath, we'll walk down by the river."

"Oh! Could I?"

Outside, Pierre nudged Joe. "Tell Broken Knife what you told Lone Dog."

Gervias repeated what he had said. Broken Knife laughed. "No wonder he acted fit to be tied."

"Once you leave here, Lone Dog will be hot on your trail. Since your bow demonstration, the only one he can depend on is Hurt Leg." Gervias hesitated. "You've made a bad enemy, but plenty of friends among the Pawnee and the Comanche. Ask, and those Comanche warriors will pack you through Chouteau's front door."

Broken Knife shook his head. "I wanted Lone Dog to start something after the race. If he does not follow us, I am coming back after him. I am not waiting for him to sneak up on me some dark night."

Broken Knife turned toward Pierre. "What if we leave day after tomorrow? We could spend the night somewhere on the way. That would give Lone Dog a chance to hit us before we meet Rene."

"Sounds good to me," replied Pierre. "The quicker this is settled the better."

The three men sat by the river and watched the slow current. Each one lost in thought. Finally, Gervias said, "Who would believe ten arrows? Moreover, you do it easy. Where did you learn to shoot?"

Broken Knife talked a little about his Delaware life, then said, "After we get Jeannie home, I am headed for the Mandans and the Stony Mountains. Do either of you know about the Indian tribes there?"

"Campfire tales have the Crow and Blackfeet the most powerful," Gervias replied. "I know little about the Crow, except they and the Pawnee steal each others horses. All I have heard about the Blackfeet is they're fighters. How about you, Pierre?"

"Nothing about the tribes, or the country." Pierre yawned. "I am tuckered out. Suppose Jeannie has finished?"

Gervias rose. "Plenty of blankets in the storeroom. You and I can sleep there."

Everybody was asleep at the lodge. Broken Knife moved quietly to his sleeping area.

The lodge was dark when Broken Knife woke. He lit the fire and started after more firewood. Jeannie stirred. Raising on her elbows, she said, "Please, wait."

Broken Knife returned to the fire. Jeannie moved beside him. "I am sorry about last night. I tried to stay awake, but being safe and clean was too much."

Jeannie stared at the flames. Her voice trembled. "Lone Dog and Hurt Leg are vicious killers. They will not let us go."

Broken Knife's eyes softened. His fingers caressed her cheek. "There is nothing to worry about. You and the kids will soon be in St. Louis."

Warmed by the lightness of his touch, Jeannie's head settled to his shoulder. Firelight reflected in her moist eyes. "It is you." Her voice wavered. "I am worried about you. I had seen you that one time, but I just knew the blushing young man would save me. Now, I am sorry you came."

Jeannie's hand pressed Broken Knife's hand to her cheek. Her tearful eyes searched his. Broken Knife felt a strange warmth churn and radiate deep inside. Before he could respond to the invitation in her wistful eyes, they heard Joe and Pierre.

Both traders brightened at sight of the gingham-dressed girl. Pierre grinned. "Jeannie, you are mighty pretty this morning."

"I am glad someone noticed." She grimaced at Broken Knife then smiled at the trader. "Thank you, Mr. Gervias. I hardly expected a tub, or a dress."

"I'm glad it fit. I bought the dress for my Indian wife. She died in the 'ninety-two smallpox outbreak and never had a chance to wear it."

Broken Knife wrinkled his nose at Jeannie's scowl. "I am sorry about your wife, Joe. Could you find out if Lone Dog has left the village yet?"

The trader nodded. "How many horses will you need? I'll have a boy picket 'em by the lodge tonight."

"Three to ride should be enough, thanks."

As Gervias walked out, Broken Knife turned to Pierre. "Yesterday, I saw the prettiest, longhaired Crow girl. When I asked Gervias about her, he acted funny and last night, he did not mention her. Can you find out who she is?"

Jeannie's face drained of color. Her eyes filled with tears. She walked to the bed and laid down facing the dirt wall. With no one to talk to, Broken Knife went to his sleeping area and promptly fell asleep.

Gervias coming through the entrance woke Broken Knife. Seated by the fire, the trader said, "I must have talked to half the village. Lone Dog, Hurt Leg, and a seventeen-year-old brave are three miles downriver."

"Good. When Pierre gets back, I will explain what I have in mind."

Gervias got up. "I need a few things from the storeroom. It'll only take a minute."

Broken Knife looked at Jeannie. "I know you are not asleep." He asked, "Did I do something? Please, come and sit by me."

Jeannie moved to the fire. She raised her doleful eyes. "Who is the Crow girl?"

Broken Knife broke into a mischievous smile. "She is every bit as pretty, as you are beautiful. She must be at least nine-years-old."

The traders entered before the red-faced girl could reply. When Pierre nodded slightly, Broken Knife said, "Gervias said a young brave, Hurt Leg, and Lone Dog are waiting downriver. Lone Dog will send the brave back to watch what direction we take. While he is going back to tell Lone Dog, I can slip away and find them first."

The men nodded in agreement. Jeannie shook her head. She sobbed, "Not alone. You did not see what Lone Dog and Hurt Leg did to that poor wagon driver."

Broken Knife brushed a hanging tear off her cheek.

96

"Pierre must stay with you. If Joe or the Comanche come, Lone Dog will back off. I am not bragging, but if I meet them face to face, there is little danger." His voice lowered. "Believe me, it is safer to end it now."

Jeannie went back to the bed. By the time Joe and Pierre left, she had fallen asleep.

Left alone, Broken Knife stared at the fire. Low flames changed from blue to orange to yellow as they danced back and forth consuming their playground. His eyes were getting heavy. He was about to go to bed when Jeannie snuggled beside him.

"Please, do not say anything," she whispered, "just hold me."

The coals were black. The lodge cold. Jeannie and his arm were asleep. Her slender body snuggled against his had aroused sensations he had never experienced. He hated to move, but it would not be long until dawn. Reaching under her long legs, he lifted her as if a child. The sleeping girl stirred. When he hesitated, she settled back into a trouble-free sleep. He kissed her softly then lowered her to the bed.

Broken Knife walked out on the moonlit prairie to ask for the Grandmother's help. As he sang his prayer, bright rays shimmered off a white prairie lily. The flower's resplendent beauty made the others appear drab. Finishing his prayer, he cut the long stem. Broken Knife placed a small multi-colored stone on an adjacent bloom, an offering for the gift of beauty. Returning to the lodge, he laid the flower beside Jeannie's golden hair.

The sun was high overhead when the small party bid Gervias good-bye. At the first stream, Broken Knife stopped halfway across. Sliding off his horse, he placed Mary in the saddle.

Jeannie, with John behind her, urged her horse beside Broken Knife. Her fear-ridden eyes belied her resolve to be unafraid. She bent down and whispered, "Thank you for the flower." Her soft lips touched his. She pulled back. A weak smile flitted across her face. "If you are not back by dark, I will never speak to you again."

Pierre waved then led Jeannie and the kids on across the creek. Watching until they were out of sight, Broken Knife waded downstream to a small knoll. Crawling on top of it, he lay curled around rocks and low brush. He had been there several hours when three Pawnee rode toward the creek.

Lone Dog slid off his horse. He searched the ground along the edge of the water. Satisfied, the horses had gone straight across. He remounted and followed Pierre's trail.

Broken Knife was about to follow them when two other riders came along, Joe and Many Horses.

With the sun on the horizon, Lone Dog's party turned into a dry wash. After building a fire, they squatted around it chewing jerky.

Broken Knife walked into the camp. He grunted.

The young brave froze. Lone Dog and Hurt Leg lunged for weapons. An arrow pierced Hurt Leg's heart. The knife split Lone Dog's breastbone.

Lone Dog dropped the lance. He sank to his knees. Struggling to rise, his defiant eyes clouded. He fell across the flames.

Broken Knife rolled Lone Dog's body out of the fire. He removed his knife, then glanced at the brave. He had not moved from the fire. Broken Knife wiped off the soot-covered handle and bloody blade. Looking over his shoulder, he yelled, "Come on in, Joe."

An embarrassed trader and a jabbering Comanche came forward. Gervias stared at the bodies then Broken Knife. He shook his head. "You are one hell-raisin'-rip-snorter. Many Horses is so damned excited I can't understand a word he's saying."

Broken Knife motioned toward the young Pawnee. "Joe, tell him he can keep the horses if he takes those two back." He held out his hand. "I have to get going."

Broken Knife was halfway out of the gully when Gervias called out. "If you don't like the mountains, you're welcome here, or with Many Horses and the Comanche."

THE RESCUE

The Lewis and Clark Expedition left St. Louis on the fourteenth of May. Two weeks later, Broken Knife arrived with Jeannie and the kids.

It had been a month since his return and his feelings for Jeannie had grown with each new day, but with this love, came an obligation to live as a white man. Broken Knife had convinced himself Jeannie was all that mattered until he spent a day helping Pierre load supplies for the Osage Post. The talk and activity with his old companion brought back a hunger for the Indian life that he could no longer suppress.

That night, after Tobias served the dessert, Broken Knife said, "Pierre is leaving tomorrow. I am thinking of going with him."

Jeannie looked at him for a moment. Laying her napkin down, she helped Tobias clear the table.

Chouteau turned to Broken Knife. "Let's take our coffee in the study." Seated in front of the darkened fireplace, Chouteau said, "I hoped you would live here and help me."

Broken Knife shook his head. "I appreciate all you have done, but I cannot live in a town or even a trading post." Pausing, he said, "Then, there is Jeannie. By staying here, I will make both our lives miserable."

Chouteau nodded his understanding. "Pierre mentioned this afternoon you might leave, and I suspected your answer. Your supplies and trade goods are ready at the warehouse. Do you want me to invest your five hundred dollars?"

Broken Knife held out a piece of yellowed paper. "This is a note to a merchant for goods he gave my white parents. Would you see that he or his family is paid? Do what you want with the rest of the money. If I do not return, give it to Jeannie."

Chouteau paused at the door. He glanced over his shoulder. "You will be back. Wait here, I will find Jeannie."

As Jeannie stepped through the door, Broken Knife said, "I am sorry for not telling you first, but I did not know what to say."

The sadness in her face pulled him to her. Holding her close, he whispered, "My spirit is torn. Half cries for you, half for my Indian life." Lifting her chin, he gazed into her eyes. "It would kill me to see hate replace the love in your eyes. For me to live as a white man will destroy us both."

Jeannie placed her hands on his shoulders. A joyless smile crossed her face. "Let's walk in the garden."

On a path that overlooked the town, Jeannie and Broken Knife paused to watch a small bright dot shoot across a brilliant night sky. When the shooting star died out, Jeannie cradled his hands. She held them against her cheek. "Coming back from the Pawnee village, I saw you climb onto a big boulder and raise your arms to the rising sun. As I listened to your song prayer, I knew you could never live as a white man. It was selfish of me to let our love grow." Her breath caught. "I could not help it."

Broken Knife removed a green stone from the medicine bag under his shirt. "Bright Star gave me four of these. They belonged to her peoples' ancient ones. When you are troubled, look deep into this stone and our spirits will be joined."

The emerald reflected the Grandmother's rays. Jeannie cried out, "Oh, it is beautiful."

Jeannie's arms circled his neck. "I watched your eyes when Pierre said, 'After the Pawnee corn is planted, the Crow girl will be sacrificed to the Morning Star.' You are not going to the Osage Post. You are taking that little girl back to her people. And, I love you for it."

Broken Knife led two packhorses and Pierre a string of eight mules out of St. Louis. The travelers stopped the first night below St. Charles. Broken Knife unsaddled and hobbled the horses before rummaging through the four panniers. Surprised at the amount of trade goods, he glanced at Pierre. "I cannot believe you packed this much on two horses."

Pierre dropped a handful of Arbuckle in the coffeepot. "Auguste said to pack tools, traps, Indian presents, and anything else you might need. I loaded them heavy. Where you are headed, those trade doodads are worth more than gold." He hesitated. "The old man went out this morning, and bought the spyglass, compass, and Kentucky rifle."

"It is good of him to send this much," Broken Knife said as he studied an iron trap. "I know nothing about these things. Could you show me how to set a couple?"

Pierre nodded. "We will hit a good stream in a few days."

"There is another problem," Broken Knife said with a grin. "You had the horses loaded when I got there this morning. All I have packed is game. Do you suppose that in the morning you can give me a hand tying on the panniers?"

Pierre shook his head in disgust. "You better find a nice wife. Then you won't have to worry about these details." He paused. "Sounds as if the coffee's boiling, let's have a cup?"

Seated by the fire Pierre said, "When you hook the bags on the packsaddle make sure they weigh close to the same amount. If one is slightly heavier, place it on the off side. Keep anything you put on top low and flat."

"Drouillard used a diamond hitch to tie on the packs. What do you use?" Broken Knife asked.

"I like a box hitch better," Pierre replied. "If you are alone, it is easier to tie. I will show you how to throw it in the morning." His eyes twinkled. "If a packsaddle starts to turn, stop and re-tie the whole thing. A packsaddle under a horse's belly is real exciting."

Broken Knife chuckled at the thought. "That is one I will take your word for."

The next day, he had trouble with his packs, but he would not let Pierre help. He had to learn. By the time they reached the beaver stream, his packs were riding as well as Pierre's.

Pierre stopped beside a willow-lined creek. He nodded at Broken Knife to tie the horses. "We will camp here tonight. There are several beaver ponds above here where we can set the traps."

At the first pond, the broad tail of a beaver slapped the water as it dove to safety. The danger signal broke the stillness of the evening air. Both men paused to watch a series of ripples spread across sharp images reflected in the water.

Broken Knife breathed deep the pristine beauty of the pond with cottony clouds drifting in blue sky above it. He expelled his life's breath slowly, then turned to watch Pierre.

The trader cut a thick willow. He sharpened the big end before cutting the stick into two lengths. With the biggest piece in his hand and the smaller one tucked in his hind pocket, he waded into the pond.

Pierre set an iron trap under ten-inches of water. He used his foot to stir mud over the iron jaws. Wading further out, he drove the willow stake through the ring on the three-foot chain of the trap. Returning to the trap, he dipped the end of the green willow from his pocket into a brown bottle, then forced the other end into the bank. The smelly, green-leafed end hung above the iron jawed trap. Soaked to the waist, Pierre waded out of the water.

Pierre drained the water out of his moccasins. He looked at Broken Knife. "The beaver smells the castor and goes to investigate. When the beaver stands on its hind feet to eat the willow, its feet are caught in the trap."

Broken Knife wrinkled his nose. "Is that stinking stuff called castor?"

Pierre chuckled. "That or castorum. It comes from two glands at the base of the beaver's tail."

"You mean like a skunk?"

"Yes, and do not waste it. A small bottle of castor sells for ten- to twelve-bucks in St. Louis." He paused. "Trappers mix castor with cloves, nutmeg, cinnamon, alcohol. The Lord only knows what else. Each trapper guards his recipe and swears it is the best."

Pierre looked back at the silt-covered trap. "Make sure the chain is tight and well anchored. If the beaver can reach the bank, all you will find in your trap is a chewed-off paw. Once the beaver panics, it dives into deep water and drowns."

Sour-faced, Broken Knife said, "Those things seem awfully cruel to me."

"Cannot argue with that. They are cruel, but effective. North West traders have used iron traps the last few years, but they are just beginning to filter into this country. With these traps on the upper Missouri, one trapper will take more beaver pelts in one season than a whole passel of Indians." Pierre hesitated. "Now, Indians catch beaver on shore, or else they tear their houses apart, and then shoot, lance, or club them to death."

Broken Knife finished setting the last trap. Pierre nodded with satisfaction. "Tomorrow morning, we will have beaver. Right now, I am wet and starved."

On the way back to camp, Broken Knife shot two willow grouse. While he cleaned them, Pierre built a fire and drove a forked stick into the ground on each side of it. When the flames died down to grey coals, Pierre ran a green stick through the birds. He laid the ends of the stick in the forked stakes.

Broken Knife washed the last mouthful of roasted bird down with cold water. "Until that beaver slapped the water, it has been hard not to turn around and go back to Jeannie. When it did, a dam burst inside of me, and any doubts were washed away. My life is here, not in a town. If it is all right, I will leave you tomorrow."

"Figured it was getting time," Pierre said with a grin. "Are you taking that little Crow girl back to her people?" he asked.

Broken Knife's words were hard. "I do not like the idea of her being spread-eagled between trees and shot full of arrows."

"I am glad. Gervias has fought that dirty business so long he will not even talk about it anymore."

Pierre tossed wood on the fire. In the firelight, he used a stick to draw a map of the Missouri River. "The Mandan and Hidatsa villages are here. A ways below them are three Arikara villages. Once you have the girl, stay clear of the Arikara. They and the Pawnee are related. At one time, both tribes practiced this Morning Star Ceremony. In those days, the ceremony included eating the victim."

"My Indian mother's tribe was a member of the Six Nations (Iroquois League). She mentioned her ancestors ate captives." Hesitating, he said, "When we were with Gervias, a few Pawnee words sounded similar to the words of her people. Do you suppose there is any relationship between the Tuscarora and the Pawnee?"

"Could be," Pierre replied. "I understand both tribes originally migrated out of the south. Wasn't the Iroquois League destroyed right after the Revolutionary War?"

"Yes," replied Broken Knife. "In 1779, President Washington sent General Sullivan with close to five thousand troops into Pennsylvania and New York. His orders were to destroy everything. Mrs. Walker said Sullivan burned forty villages and thousands of acres of orchards, as well as, destroying one hundred and sixty thousand bushels of corn and any other food supplies his troop could find. Many of the survivors of Washington's 'Devastation Policy' made their way into Canada."

Nodding, Pierre said, "I heard the hardest hit were the Cayuga and Seneca."

Broken Knife replied, "Most of the Seneca that survived Sullivan's attack made their way to Fort Niagara, but the British were short of rations and the vast majority of them either starved or froze to death that winter."

After considerable silence, Broken Knife went after more wood. When he returned, the aimless talk continued. Neither wanted to end what could be their last meeting.

Early the next morning, they checked the traps. All four held beaver. Pierre laid them on the bank. He examined the fur. "Prime pelts are taken late fall to early spring. For June, the thickness and sheen on these is not bad. I would say they are worth six, seven bucks apiece in St. Louis."

While Pierre skinned the last beaver, Broken Knife tied the traps on the sorrel packhorse. When he finished, he walked back to his friend. "If you do not mind, I will be off."

"Go ahead," Pierre said. "You watch your topknot around the Rees, or if you head northwest, the Cut Arms. I would hate telling Jeannie your hair is dangling from an Arikara or Cheyenne war lance."

Pierre held out his hand. "Arikara and Mandan traders come downriver every summer. You need anything send word."

A smile crossed Broken Knife's face. He gripped his friend's hand. "If you get tired of white man ways, come find me."

Broken Knife reached the Loup River the sixth night. In the light of early morning, he noticed a crack behind a clump of bushes. Riding closer, he saw the thick brush blocked a narrow opening into a deep wash. A hundred yards beyond the offset entrance, the walled passage opened into a grass-covered pocket with a spring at the far end.

Broken Knife hobbled the horses, then ate a handful of

parched corn. His hunger gone, he spread his sleeping robe under a rock overhang. It would stay shaded all during the day.

Wolves offering prayers to the Grandmother woke Broken Knife. Blocking out the howling wolves, he listened for any unusual sounds. Assured it was safe, he built a small fire.

Broken Knife dropped his white man clothes on the burning branches. When the fire died down, he straddled it and broke off small pieces of braided grass. A fragrant smoke rose over his body.

Walking into the moonlit clearing, Broken Knife reached toward the bright yellow ball. The Grandmother's rays bathed his muscular body. He tossed his prayer on the gentle breeze.

The euphoria of being Broken Knife surged through his veins.

Broken Knife rubbed rancid tallow on his legs. The strong tallow smell would fool the Pawnee's dogs. After checking on the horses, he blocked off the narrow entrance to the wash.

Crossing the river below the Pawnee village, Broken Knife stashed his bow and quiver in the willows. With a trade blanket draped over his shoulders, he strolled into the sleeping village.

Broken Knife went to where he had seen the Crow girl enter a lodge. Picking up a heavy stick, he stepped through the entrance. A dark form rose up. The club's knob end descended. The figure collapsed without a whimper. Pressing against the wall, he listened to the deep breathing of five people. Once his eyes adjusted to the dim light from glowing coals, he made out the longhaired girl.

He moved to her side. His hand covered her mouth. In his mother's language, he whispered, "Friend."

The girl's dark eyes stared into his face. A slender finger touched his lips. As his hand moved from her mouth, she stiffened. Her eyes locked on something behind him.

Broken Knife swung the stick. He heard a bone snap. Whirling, he hit the fallen warrior behind the ear.

The girl rose and touched his shoulder. She pointed at a walled off sleeping area.

Broken Knife stepped behind the hanging elk-hide where a man lie on his back snoring. A curled-up woman faced the wall. The Indian stiffened and sighed when Broken Knife drove the stick down. The sleeping woman did not change a breath.

He returned to the fire. The Crow girl held another girl's hand. Two captives had never crossed his mind. Broken Knife smiled. He motioned at two blankets on the floor then at the door.

Three blanket-wrapped figures walked out of the village. After retrieving his weapons, they waded downstream in ankle-deep water toward the secluded wash.

Broken Knife laid out jerky and corn. He motioned that he was going back to watch the village, and would be gone all day. The girls nodded.

On a low rocky knoll near the Pawnee village, Broken Knife moved rocks and cut prickly-pear cactus before lying down to blend into his surroundings. He lay there watching shadowy warriors running back and forth. A smile crossed his face. The Pawnee had missed the girls and believed the village was under attack.

The loud shriek of Pawnee warriors pouring from the village woke Broken Knife; emerging daylight had dispelled the fear of attack. The warriors milled about the village. Not finding tracks of the girls, or their abductors, small groups scattered in several directions. The largest group headed southwest. Thieving Comanche had the girls.

Broken Knife remained motionless throughout the day. By dusk, the small bands had returned, only the large group remained out. With no one looking east, there was no need to stay in the blind canyon.

The Grandmother had barely edged over the canyon rim when he reached the hideout. After a drink and a piece of jerky satisfied his gnawing hunger, he packed the horses. The girls rode double on his horse and led the two packhorses. He ran ahead keeping the North Star off his left shoulder. The night sky had turned light in the east when he turned into a deep arroyo, and they bedded down.

Sunrays spilling across the wash woke Broken Knife. With an easy motion, he shook off his blanket. He moved against the shaded bank and watched the horses. Satisfied that no danger lurked about, he glanced at the sleeping girls before leaving the wash.

Climbing onto a high ridge, he sat where the sun would warm his back. Below him, a small herd of buffalo, strung out in single file, headed for water. Overhead, hawks were looking for mice and gophers. Convinced no Pawnee were nearby, he returned to the arroyo.

The girls were huddled together under a rock overhang. Smiling at them, he laid out pemmican, sunflower seeds, and corn.

Broken Knife leaned against a rock and chewed a strip of dried meat. The girls were chattering like a pair of magpies. They were talking in Pawnee. It dawned on him that the girls must be from different tribes.

The little Crow girl finished eating and walked over. Smiling at her inquisitive look, he pointed at himself and said, "Broken Knife."

She raised her arms. Slowly she pulled her right arm back to shoot an imaginary arrow.

Broken Knife recalled her lack of fear at the Pawnee lodge. She had seen the arrow contest.

The Crow girl placed a hand on her chest. She rattled off three harsh words. One of the syllables had a strong T... sound.

Broken Knife tried. He could not form the words. Frustrated, he replied, "Teal....Teal."

109

The girl mouthed the sound several times then repeated her new name. Her eyes sparkled. She motioned to her friend. The girl looked to be a year or two older. As she came over, Teal pointed and motioned like a bird. She said something that sounded like Dove.

With gestures and a few simple words, Broken Knife learned Dove had been captured the previous summer and Teal that fall. He drew a crude map of the Smoky Water and the mountains. He used it to indicate he wanted to take them home.

Vigorously, Dove shook her head. With her index finger, she drew lines across her forearm. Confused, Broken Knife stared at her. She touched his belt knife and repeated the gestures.

His eyes widened. Cut Arm? Could she be a Cheyenne? In his excitement, a name popped out, "Suhtai?"

Dove's expression told him nothing. He changed the emphasis on the word. "Suh'tai?"

Dove danced up and down. She pointed north.

Broken Knife recalled Clark's chart placed the Cheyenne south of the Hidatsa and Mandan villages near an area marked Black Hills. What luck! Dove's return ensured a powerful Plains tribe's friendship.

He left the girls and went back to the same ridge. Propped against a rock, he surveyed a wide panorama without a sign of Indians anywhere. Then it hit him – Gervias! The trader must have talked warriors opposed to the ceremony into letting the girls go. He had probably steered the others south. Despite the reassuring thought, he decided it would be safer to travel at night.

While traveling toward the Cheyenne village, the conversation consisted of gestures and Pawnee words. With two eager teachers, Broken Knife soon made out most of what the girls said.

He was breaking camp on the ninth day, and in the hazy light of dusk, saw a thin ribbon of smoke. He caught and tied the horses before calling the girls. "There is smoke in the southwest. I am going to see what it is."

Tears filled Teal's eyes. "We do not want you to go."

He touched her cheek. "You and Dove go to bed. I will be back before you are awake." Broken Knife turned to Dove. She walked away with her head down. He heard faint sounds of sobbing.

At a trot, Broken Knife started a large circle. When it became too dark to see, he waited for the Grandmother's light to show the way. A stomping horse helped Broken Knife locate the camp. Nine warriors were sleeping around the fire ring. Ten horses stood tied to junipers in a nearby draw. He watched several minutes to make sure they had posted only one guard.

Working behind the dozing sentry, he hit him with a heavy piece of juniper. Broken Knife bridled one horse. He re-tied each horse to the horse's tail in front of it. Mounting the bridled horse, he led the string of horses out the draw onto the prairie.

Broken Knife rode into camp leading two horses. Teal's face beamed. She dragged several pieces of deer meat from the coals. She said, "We thought you would be hungry."

Despite her show of confidence, Broken Knife knew neither girl had been asleep. "It was Pawnee. I took their horses, and several miles away, turned seven loose. They will be a couple of days, or more, rounding them up. With more horses to ride, we will be long gone by then."

Two days later, Broken Knife climbed to the base of a high cliff. He searched the countryside. Not a thing appeared out of place. He had settled back against a boulder when a covey of quail took wing. Below where the birds flew up, a short-squat Indian came out of a dry wash. The Indian's hairstyle and adornments were not familiar to Broken Knife. The unsuspecting warrior climbed toward him. Broken Knife moved away from the rock. Terrified, the warrior fled back down the hill.

Broken Knife waited several minutes before following the Indian. A half-mile away, the warrior's tracks entered a deep arroyo. Broken Knife crept up to the rim, and saw five warriors hiding among scattered boulders. Above the warriors, a herd of horses fed near a catch basin of water. On the hunch they might be Cheyenne, or a related tribe, he went after the girls.

Dove peeked over the bank. She stiffened. Before Broken Knife could stop her, she jumped up. Half-crying, she screamed, "Ayah, Ayeeeeeeah."

A tall, slender warrior stared at the girl sliding down the bank. Dove threw herself into his outstretched arms. He held her head to his chest.

Teal and Broken Knife slid into the wash. A teary-eyed Dove said a few words. She then announced, "My father, Eagle Plume."

Eagle Plume placed an arm around Teal. He touched his new friend's shoulder. He did not try to say anything. The joy on his face expressed his happiness.

The girls stayed behind while Broken Knife went after the horses. He led the packhorses into the Cheyenne camp. The warriors watched as if they were hungry. Broken Knife motioned at Teal. They laid out smoked meat, parched corn, and sunflower seeds.

After the warriors quit eating, Dove's father spoke. She translated. "I thank you. We have been after Pawnee horses and not eaten for three days. After we smoke, let us leave. Today, my medicine is good."

Eagle Plume stopped in a box canyon. Black fire rings indicated the Cheyenne had used the canyon on many occasions. Dove rode up. She said, "My father says we will wait for the Grandmother to show the way. He also said that when the leaves change color, the villagers are going to a Hidatsa trade fair. The Hidatsa live across the river from the Mandans. He would like you to stay until then."

Since Drouillard would not be there until fall, Broken

Knife nodded his acceptance. "Tell your father we will wait."

Two days later, the Cheyenne village erupted with screaming people. One woman ran to Dove's horse. Tears streamed down her cheeks. Dove cried out. She jumped into the woman's outstretched arms.

Excited people sang and danced as the returning warriors moved through the village. Each one smiled and touched Broken Knife's leg.

Eagle Plume stopped in front of a skin lodge. He raised his arms. A hush settled over the crowd. He said a few words then led Broken Knife into the lodge.

Inside, Broken Knife saw the girls and the woman. He bowed slightly. "This must be your mother."

Dove beamed. "My mother's name is Waving Grass." She displayed an impish smile. "My mother has reminded me many times to express her gratitude for her lovely daughter's return."

Waving Grass smiled. She moved across the lodge with a dignity and grace that reminded Broken Knife of Bright Star. She pressed his hand to her cheek. Her tears flowed across his hand.

Broken Knife stammered, "Dove, please, ask your mother not to cry."

He glanced at Teal. "Let's look around the village while Dove talks to her parents."

Dove said, "My uncle is outside. He has a present for you. Tonight, there will be a feast and dance in your honor."

Bird Tail led them to a new tepee. He said a few words to Teal. A grin spread across her face as she said, "The lodge is a present from Waving Grass's clan."

BLACK HILLS CHEYENNE

Broken Knife lay with hands locked beneath his head. He could not remember being more at peace. The buffalo hide tepee had a feeling of warmth and coziness not found in dirt dwellings, or cabins. He had even gotten use to the camp herald. The old warrior came through the village each morning. He shouted any news and reminded everyone to swim. After all, water is blood – blood is life.

Laying there, his thoughts turned to Dove and Teal. The girls had fingered each trade good item several times before repacking each pannier. Not familiar with the Cheyenne custom of giving and receiving presents, he placed them in charge – giving and receiving presents was an integral part of Indian life. Now, the pixie pair managed him and the lodge like old mother hens, but he did not mind. It helped keep Jeannie from his thoughts.

The girls burst through the entrance flap. His reverie disappeared. Teal grabbed his hands as Dove cried, "My father has a present. The village warriors are there too."

"Whoa, not so fast," he said with a smile, "and speak Pawnee." Embarrassed, Dove repeated the message.

As Broken Knife and the girls approached the group of warriors, Eagle Plume held out a thirty-inch horn bow. "My father says a horn bow is best for buffalo."

Eagle Plume pointed at Bird Tail who held out a bundle of arrows with black, stone chipped points.

Broken Knife notched an arrow and shot at a nearby pine tree. The arrow wavered slightly. It missed the beetle blister. Despite missing the mark, he realized the value of a short, powerful horn bow. Power was more important than accuracy in shooting buffalo from a horse's back.

Dove touched Broken Knife's arm. "Four days ago, Cheyenne warriors returned from a Split Ears village. The Comanche, especially Many Horses, talked of nothing, except you, the medicine bow, and Lone Dog. My people are curious about the bow's medicine. It is considered bad manners to ask." She broke into a grin. "Sometimes curiosity wins over politeness. The warriors wish to see the medicine bow."

Broken Knife nodded. While Teal went after his bow and arrows, he watched several boys rolling a willow ring. When Teal returned, he said, "Dove, ask Slow Man's son to roll his hoop across the field."

Five arrows passed through the center of the ring before it had traveled twenty yards. A clamor of voices erupted among the Cheyenne. Broken Knife looked at the warriors then Dove. He asked, "What is wrong?"

"That ugly one says the arrows hit behind the ring."

Broken Knife chuckled at the furious expression on Dove's face. "Let's show them something they cannot argue over. Ask the boy to roll his ring down that steep bank."

The erratic speed of the hoop increased until it bounced in the air. The bow raised. The willow ring twirled like a top. When it hit the ground, another arrow appeared dead center in the round circle.

A deadly silence prevailed for several seconds before the excited warriors crowded about Broken Knife. Everyone waved their arms and talked at once. The girls finally pulled him away. "There is another surprise," Teal whispered, "and we helped."

Broken Knife followed the girls to Waving Grass's lodge. As they entered, Dove's mother held out two shirts. The first one, made from a lodge cover, would shed water like a duck's back. He hardly noticed it. His eyes were on the other shirt. Decorated with intricate designs of dyed porcupine quills, the pure white deerskin shirt was the most striking ceremonial shirt that he had seen. Broken Knife placed the shirts on the bed. Squeezing the girls to his side, he placed his cheek next to Waving Grass's cheek.

Eagle Plume called from outside the tepee.

Broken Knife pushed the entrance flap aside to see his friend and Bird Tail sitting on their horses. Bird Tail smiled. He held out the rein of a brown gelding. Riding toward a canyon called Spearfish, Broken Knife felt the horse respond to the slightest movement of his legs.

High rock ledges, large needle pines, scattered aspen, and a variety of bushes covered the sides of the winding canyon. Tall green grass and bright flowers filled the open spaces. On the canyon floor, water raced around boulders and rock outcroppings; narrow-leaf cottonwoods and red-river birch willows grew on the water-carved banks. Sounds of rushing water and swaying trees blended with the chatter of birds, squirrels, and chipmunks to enhance the beauty of the spectacular canyon.

At the head of the canyon, the riders rode into an open bowl. Eagle Plume gestured for Broken Knife to watch Bird Tail. The Cheyenne placed the bridle rein under his leg. He held a bow in one hand and an arrow in the other. The agile horse weaved around bushes, water puddles, speeded up, slowed down, stopped, and started again. The gelding did all of this without visible signals from the rider. Bird Tail's message was clear. Legs guided the horse. Hands held the weapons.

Bird Tail stopped. He gestured at Broken Knife. After two

passes across the meadow, Broken Knife found the horse moved right or left depending on which leg he used. To stop, he squeezed both legs and leaned slightly back. Pleased by his newfound knowledge, Broken Knife put the horse into a lope then jabbed the gelding with his right heel. The buffalo horse turned left. The rider went straight.

As Eagle Plume and Bird Tail rode up, Broken Knife wiped mud off his face and shirt. He spit out a mouth full of dirt. The jovial pair laughed until they nearly fell off their horses.

Still snickering, Bird Tail rode in front of his pupil. Using exaggerated motions, he squeezed the horse with his left leg, gripped tight with his right leg, and leaned into the right-hand turn.

Broken Knife shook his head. He climbed back on the brown gelding. After several tries, his nose had dug one more furrow, but he had the feel of a buffalo horse.

Eagle Plume grinned at the mud-covered rider. He gestured, "We swim, then go back."

Stretched out in the sun-warmed pool, Broken Knife wished Dove was with them. Sign language served for general conversation, but not for describing the training of a buffalo horse. He had asked Dove once why horses were picketed in the village at night. At the time, her response about buffalo horses and enemies stealing them had not meant much. Now, he understood the value of the buffalo horse.

Broken Knife woke the next morning hurting all over. His right shoulder and back from falling off. His legs from gripping the horse's side. Rolling out of bed, he used a lodge pole to pull himself erect. With short steps, he shuffled to the fire. Slowly, he lowered himself onto a backrest. He was still trying to find a comfortable position when Eagle Plume, the girls, and Waving Grass came through the entrance.

Waving Grass smiled. She held out a bowl of meat. As he reached toward it, his sore muscles produced a wince. Waving

Grass flew into a rage. She dropped the bowl. Whirling to face her husband, all she saw was his rear-end. Eagle Plume was going out the entrance on hands and knees.

Broken Knife held his sides to ease the pain. With tears rolling down his cheeks, he asked Dove what her mother had shouted.

Dove wiped her own eyes. "My sweet, gentle mother used words of a Comanche, or a Pawnee." Grinning, she continued, "She scolded him for not telling you how to ride a buffalo horse."

"How did she know I fell off?"

Dove smiled. "A favorite warrior prank is to put a new rider on a buffalo horse." When Waving Grass said something, Dove added, "My mother thinks a sweat lodge will be good for you."

Teal took Broken Knife to a small hide-covered hut. She raised the flap. "Dove is bringing hot stones and a kettle of water. Sit by the fire pit while I go after sagebrush."

Dove sprinkled water on the hot stones. She handed him the dipper. "Add water until the stones no longer steam. When they cool off, we will bring more."

Heat and moisture filled the willow-framed hut until Broken Knife could scarcely breath. He reached for the six-inch bundle of sagebrush leaves that Teal had brought. He held it under his nose. The strong fragrant odor cleared his nasal passages. Using the sagebrush, he wiped the sweat from his body. He started a soft melodious prayer for his parents and others that had gone to the other side. An hour later, Broken Knife walked from the sweat lodge. He felt rejuvenated both spiritually and physically.

Broken Knife and Bird Tail were coming out of Slow Man's lodge when they saw the girls and Eagle Plume. Slow Man, the village's largest horse owner, and Bird Tail walked away. Broken Knife went to meet Eagle Plume and the girls.

Dove said, "Scouts report buffalo to the south. My father

wants to know if you can ride?"

"I feel fine now." He hesitated. "My horse is not a buffalo horse. Dove, ask your father how those horses are trained."

Dove listened carefully before saying, "The most important thing is selecting the right horse. Geldings are best. The horse must be sure footed, have the courage to run beside a buffalo, and the heart to run many miles. Once the horse is selected, it must be trained to turn with pressure from your legs."

Eagle Plume started talking again. When he finished, she said, "My father wanted me to tell you that buffalo horses are of great value. Without them, the warriors could not provide meat for everyone in the village. He also said the highest Cheyenne war honor is to take a picketed buffalo horse from an enemy village."

Eagle Plume followed Dove's translation as best he could. When she finished, he nodded and spoke to her again. "My father says that if you pull the bow right-handed, the horse is trained to go to buffalo's right side. When the arrow hits it, the buffalo sometimes hooks at the horse, so be ready."

Dryly, Broken Knife said, "I already know about being ready."

Both girls broke into a giggle. Dove tried to keep a straight face when she said, "My father gives you the brown, buffalo...."

Eagle Plume interrupted. Teal and Dove started giggling again. "My courageous father told the horse to be careful. If it lets you fall off, it is the stew pot for them both."

Still laughing over the joke, Broken Knife took hold of the girls' hands. "Come with me. This time, I have the surprise."

Bird Tail came toward them leading two beautiful pintos. A woman's double-forked prairie chicken saddle sat on the back of each brown and white mare. Hands tightened on his. Broken Knife smiled. "Yes, they are yours."

Teal and Dove let out a squeal. Within minutes, they

disappeared over the hill on their new horses. That night the girls staked their mares outside the lodge by his new buffalo horse.

The next morning the entire village turned out for the buffalo hunt. Dove rode between Eagle Plume and Broken Knife. As her father talked, she explained his words. "When the buffalo run, stay on the edge or at the rear of the herd. Watch out for deep washes and prairie dog towns. If you fall off, hang on to the bridle rope, and get back on as quick as possible." Dove placed her hand on Broken Knife's arm. "Every year, warriors are killed, or crippled, during the chase. Teal and I want you to be careful."

The village riders approached the buffalo from downwind. They were within forty yards of the herd when a shaggy bull snorted. The bull's tail went up over its back. The massive herd responded instantly in a headlong dash.

For an instant, the rolling sea of black bumps held Broken Knife spellbound, and then, the gelding lunged forward. The horse put him along side a fat cow. Broken Knife buried an arrow in her side. The horse swerved then came back along side the same cow. A feathered arrow moved back and forth with each stride. The tip was buried in the cow's shoulder blade.

This time, Broken Knife waited until the front leg reached forward before releasing the arrow. The cow's front legs collapsed under her. He had killed his first buffalo from the back of a horse.

Broken Knife pulled the gelding away from an old bull. The horse moved beside another cow. The horse and young cow were running stride for stride when the terrified heifer lunged toward them.

The brown gelding swapped-ends. The horn bow flew from his hand. Desperate to hang on, Broken Knife's arms circled the short neck as his right heel hooked below the horse's hipbone. To Broken Knife, it seemed as if he hung that way for hours before the gelding stopped. He dropped to the ground.

Dust, heat, and the smell of buffalo sweat and manure permeated the air. He gasped for each breath. Struggling to his feet, he heard someone yell. Eagle Plume was riding toward him waving the dropped bow over his head.

Eagle Plume signed, "How was the chase?"

"Great," Broken Knife gestured, "but it ended too soon. I shot one cow and lost my bow."

Eagle Plume laughed then signed, "You have come a long ways. If your horse had not stopped, you would be in the gully with the Grandfather."

Broken Knife glanced at the Cheyenne. Eagle Plume must be kidding. They could not have come very far. When he looked over his shoulder, he forgot about time and distances. Forty yards away, a massive buffalo struggled out of a dry wash. Its left front leg twisted backwards.

The three-legged bull emitted low grumbling sounds. Its large black nostrils spewed blood-tinged mucus. The bull's red-streaked eyeballs focused on the two riders. Faced with a new danger, the monstrous head dropped and commenced swinging back and forth as if a clock's pendulum. Each moaning pass raised a small cloud of dust from the heavy tuft of chin whiskers dragging on the ground.

The two hunters watched in silence. Sign language could not express their feelings of sadness and pride at the Grandfather's defiance.

Eagle Plume urged his horse to one side. The shaggy beast turned to face the horse. With the bull's lathered side toward him, Broken Knife buried an arrow deep into its heart.

The bull hunched its back and grunted. Its massive head resumed the rhythmical swinging. Several minutes later, the bull dropped to its knees. Long, woeful sounds came from deep inside the bull. Finally, it toppled over.

The girls and Waving Grass rode up with two horse-drawn travois. Their laughter broke the respectful silence. "My people will fear this green-legged demon," Teal said as she handed Broken Knife a small round tin-backed mirror.

Broken Knife looked into the mirror and smiled. Except his white eyeballs, dirt blanketed his entire face. Looking down, he saw that dried, green manure covered his left leg.

Dove grinned. She pointed east. "There is a creek beyond that hill. Go swim. We will cut up and load the meat."

Sand-scrubbed clean, Broken Knife paused on top of the ridge, below him stretched out a panorama of Indians and dead buffalo. As he rode up to Teal, he saw a hoard of flies swarming about the old bull's white, vein-streaked carcass.

Teal smiled at the look on his face. "The others have gone to your cow."

"Eagle Plume did not take anything but the hide?" he asked.

"The thick hide makes strong parfleches and ropes," Teal replied. "Unless the people are hungry, it is all that is used on old bulls."

Broken Knife slid from his horse. He dug a hole with his hunting knife while Teal picked some grass. Arranging the grass in the deep hole, he gently laid the buffalo's heart on the soft bed of clean grass. Broken Knife used his knife to cut the palm of his hand. His blood dripped on the bull's heart. As the two bloods mixed, he sang a prayer asking the buffalo's spirit to share its boldness and courage.

Teal and Broken Knife weaved among dead buffalo on the way to find Eagle Plume. By one cow, an old man stopped sucking the teat and waved; warm milk dripped off his chin. A toothless woman beside the old man mouthed the soft yellow foot of an unborn calf. Another old couple drank pooled blood from the cow's body cavity. As he and Teal passed another group, a warrior motioned. He pointed at the opened skull of a yearling bull.

Teal smiled. "He wishes to share the brains."

"Thank him, but that is one thing I never liked."

Teal looked at Broken Knife. "Did your people eat after the kill?" she asked.

"Yes, the liver and sometimes the heart. The rest was cooked first."

Teal said, "My people believe uncooked parts have special powers. If you cannot make water – eat the kidney, or if you have yellow skin – the liver."

"Mine did too," Broken Knife replied.

Teal and Broken Knife rode up as the last of the meat was loaded on a travois. On the way back to the Cheyenne village, Broken Knife's curiosity made him ask Teal what Eagle Plume chewed on.

"He is thirsty," she replied. "Chewing on buffalo's nose gristle keeps the mouth wet."

The Cheyenne camp bustled with activity. The warriors were getting ready for the next day's hunt, while the women and girls took care of the meat and hides.

Meat was smoked for jerky, or after drying several days, it was pounded into a fine powder. Placed in clean two-foot sections of intestine, the powdered meat had melted fat poured over it. This boudin bagged pemmican kept for years.

Broken Knife watched the varied activities and wondered how the Plains Indian's culture could survive without the buffalo and the horses to chase them. Besides furnishing food, the buffalo provided hides for clothes, tent covers, moccasins, robes, ropes, horse hobbles, and the box-like parfleches. Sections of intestines, bladders, and stomachs provided containers for food and water. Tendons were separated for thread. Bones and horns provided eating utensils and scrapers.

Two months later, Broken Knife sat in his lodge. He realized that one day of excitement had blended into the next. With cooler nights and shorter days, it would soon be time for the Hidatsa Trade Fair. He was about to go find Eagle Plume when the Cheyenne came through the entrance. The girls were gone, but if they talked slow, Broken Knife understood most of the conversation. He nodded at a willow backrest.

"There are things I would ask my friend. Sit and let's smoke."

After several minutes, Broken Knife asked, "Where did the Cheyenne come from? How long have they had horses?"

"The old ones of our people lived along the Red River of the North in Canada. Many, many snows ago, the Ojibwa, Cree, and Assiniboine forced my people south to Minnesota and then the Smoky Water where they lived in dirt lodges and raised corn.

"The first Cheyenne traded Arikara for horses thirty-five winter counts ago." He paused at Broken Knife confusion. "It is a record of the single most important event in a village. Horses made it possible to move onto the Plains. This village crossed the Smoky Water twenty snows ago."

"Hadn't you hunted buffalo before that?"

Eagle Plume nodded. "Yes. Each year communal hunts were held. The people would drive a small herd over a cliff, or they would build a piskin." He hesitated. "Sometimes an old, or a young, buffalo was killed with a bow or a lance."

"What is a piskin?" Broken Knife asked.

"A pen made of piled trees to trap buffalo." He looked at Broken Knife. "Without the horse, we could never kill enough buffalo to live like we do now. Before my people had horses, many old people and some young ones died from starvation during bad winters."

Broken Knife was about to ask another question when the girls rushed through the entrance. Dove gasped, "Father, Bad Foot's track is below the village."

Eagle Plume shook his head. "I had hoped that bear was dead. In the morning, you can show us the tracks." He turned to Broken Knife. "This silver bear killed two warriors. Since then, many warriors are afraid of him."

"What makes you think it is the same bear?"

124

"He is missing three toes from the right front foot. Can the white man's gun kill Bad Foot?"

Broken Knife was surprised at mention of a gun. He said, "Yes. Do your people have guns?"

"A few. None of them make the loud noise anymore," Eagle Plume replied. "Does your gun?"

Broken Knife smiled. "It will shoot. Let's take Bird Tail and go after this bad-footed bear tomorrow."

The next morning, Broken Knife studied a bear track in the soft ground by the creek. His thumb and his little finger would not span the track. "How big is this thing, Bird Tail?"

"It is bigger than a small horse. When it stands up, it is much higher than I can reach. I have shot Bad Foot with arrows twice. The arrows do not hurt him. He sleeps in a deep canyon near the place where you first rode the buffalo horse."

Eagle Plume asked, "Where the soft yellow stones are in the water?"

"Yes, I have followed him to his cave."

The hunters worked separate paths through the narrow canyon. Broken Knife was a third of the way down on the right side when he heard a loud growl followed by something crashing through brush.

Broken Knife crossed the stream. He stopped behind a vertical rock ledge and peered around it. Just ahead Eagle Plume and Bird Tail were perched in a scraggly tree. A growling hump-backed bear paced back and forth beneath them.

Grinning, Broken Knife shouted, "Why are you in that bear's tree? He wants to climb it."

Eagle Plume edged higher. He yelled, "There is no room."

Bird Tail screamed, "Ayeeeah! Shoot!"

Broken Knife shook his head. "Let me go and get the girls and Waving Grass. They will want to see you two up a tree."

Bird Tail howled. "We sorry you fell from horse. This is no time for jokes. Bear will push tree over."

Broken Knife tamped the ball then checked the flash pan and flint. Satisfied, he threw a large rock at the silver bear. It whirled and charged the rock thrower.

The massive animal stopped twenty yards away. It raised up on its hind legs. Sniffing the air, the bear let forth a blood-curdling screech. Broken Knife aimed at the tooth-lined cavern. Pierre had told him when a grizzly stood and growled was the time to shoot. Broken Knife could not help thinking his friend better be right.

The spark of the flintlock ignited the powder. The gun roared. The enormous bear shook its head, dropped to all four feet, and charged. Halfway to the shooter, Bad Foot collapsed.

Broken Knife glanced at his two friends. "Grandfather bear does not want his tree anymore."

A pair of happy-faced Cheyenne crawled down. They used poles to roll the bear on its side. Eagle Plume circled the sprawling giant. He said, "Let's take the feet now. Tomorrow, we will bring a travois for the hide and fat."

A huge crowd gathered as they carried Bad Foot's paws into the village. The villagers were so excited that Broken Knife had trouble understanding what was said. From the admiring glances he received, his companions must be embellishing the killing of Bad Foot.

That night, the whole village danced around the displayed trophy. Despite the Cheyenne's strict, moral code, one young woman tried to flirt with Broken Knife. Not that it did her any good. Teal and Dove never left his side.

Eagle Plume and Broken Knife took a horse and travois after the bear. As they finished loading the fat and hide, Eagle Plume asked, "Can you make our guns shoot?"

"When we get back, bring them to my lodge. I will look at them." Broken Knife paused before asking, "Where did you get guns? Who taught you to shoot?"

"A white trader at the Mandan village showed us how to load and fire the guns, but we soon forgot what he said. After awhile, they would not make the noise anymore." Broken Knife had more questions, but decided to wait until he had seen the guns.

Warriors crowded around while he examined five North West trade guns. Bird Tail had the only muzzleloader with a serious problem. It had a split stock.

"Will the guns shoot again?" asked Eagle Plume.

"I need some flint arrow chippings. If Bird Tail will get a long strip of wet rawhide, I can fix his gun."

While his two friends were gone, Broken Knife tightened the screw on a loose hammer of one gun. He adjusted the flint on two other guns. Finished, he pulled the triggers. All three guns produced a good spark.

Bird Tail held out a strip of green rawhide.

Cutting off a piece, Broken Knife wrapped the wet rawhide tight around the stock. He handed the gun back. "Place this where the sun will shine on the stock all day. It will be good as new when the rawhide shrinks."

Eagle Plume came through the entrance with a handful of flint pieces. Broken Knife selected one. He adjusted it on the last gun. "Come on. Let's go try them out."

Broken Knife soon realized the warriors knew little about loading and firing. With Dove to translate, he spent the afternoon teaching the warriors how to measure powder, tamp the ball, and squeeze the trigger. The hardest part was convincing the shooters to keep their eyes open and not jerk when the powder ignited.

That night, Broken Knife gave Eagle Plume and Bird Tail a screwdriver. He explained how he had fixed the guns. Sure they understood everything, he said, "Remember these guns are not accurate beyond fifty paces. Another thing is the flint must be replaced after forty shots."

Eagle Plume touched Broken Knife's shoulder. "We will remember. What you have done for us is good. My people will not forget. Tomorrow, we will leave for the council at Nowawaste then to the Hidatsa village."

By mid-morning, the lodges were loaded on the travoises. Within an hour after the first lodge came down, the village started moving toward the council site. Broken Knife rode beside Dove. At the first opportunity, he asked, "What is Nowawaste."

Dove replied, "Nowawaste is where the shaman, Sweet Medicine, received the four sacred arrows and the Cheyenne code of conduct." After a pause, she added, "It is on the edge of a vast plain two days away. Other tribes call it Bear Butte."

Eagle Plume's village arrived at the council site late afternoon on the second day. Many Cheyenne lodges were already pitched and more coming all of the time.

The next morning, Eagle Plume sat in council. Broken Knife wandered through the large encampment. He started to count the number of lodges, but gave up after deciding there must be four to five hundred. He was going back to his lodge when he saw Teal and Dove running toward him.

Dove cried, "Come, we must hurry."

Teal added, "But first, you must get your best shirt."

"Why? What are you two doing now?" he asked.

"It is a surprise. We must hurry," they responded in unison. The girls barely gave him time to put on his ceremonial shirt before taking him to the center of the camp.

Bird Tail waited outside the council lodge. He smiled at Broken Knife. "You are invited to smoke."

Broken Knife entered the lodge. Bear Man, head Shaman of the Cheyenne, nodded to sit on his left.

The old Chief carefully tamped tobacco in the Sacred Pipe's bowl. The Pipe's four-foot stem was adorned with eagle feathers and leather bead work. Using a hot coal from the fire ring, the Shaman lit the Pipe. He blew a puff of smoke skyward. Bear Man then slowly pointed the stem toward the sky, the earth, the east, the south, the west, and the north. When he finished the ritual, he cupped the bowl in his hand, and held the stem while Broken Knife took a puff.

Broken Knife repeated the liturgy. He held it for the next man. As he watched the Sacred Pipe being passed, he noticed individuals handled the Pipe in slightly different ways. The way the Pipe was handled depended on the Chief's personal medicine.

The Chief next to the door smoked. The calumet was passed back around the circle to the person seated on the other side of the door. A Sacred Pipe is never passed across a lodge opening.

Looking around, Broken Knife wondered why he sat in the place of honor? Why was ceremonial tobacco being smoked? Normally a mixture of trade tobacco, sumac leaves, and willow bark called kinnik-kinnik was used. When the calumet came back to the Shaman, he placed it on the pipe stand.

Eagle Plume rose. He surveyed the assembled chiefs. "I speak about Broken Knife. He returned my daughter. He killed two Cheyenne enemies. He killed the silver bear. He fixed our guns. Broken Knife is my brother. Broken Knife is Cheyenne."

Shocked by Eagle Plume's announcement, Broken Knife looked at the gathered chiefs. Each nodded his approval. He stood and bowed his head toward his friend. "The honor is great. Broken Knife is proud to be your brother. He is proud to be Cheyenne."

HIDATSA TRADE FAIR

Drouillard and Big White (Shahaka), a Mandan Chief, watched a procession of mounted Indians trailing off the ridge. The two men strolled onto the flat where Cheyenne women were pitching tepees. They were about to go back when Drouillard felt a hand on his shoulder. He turned to see a grim-faced Cheyenne.

"White man trade Skunk Beads."

"Broken Knife!" Drouillard's face brightened at sight of his friend. "Am I glad to see you. Pierre spent a night with us on the river. He said you'd headed this way. When you weren't here, I started gettin' worried."

Broken Knife grinned mischievously. "I got side tracked."

"Don't tell me you have been rescuing distressed damsels again."

"Sort of, come meet them."

Drouillard gestured to Big White. "This is Broken Knife. The man I asked about."

Broken Knife greeted the Chief. When Big White left to go back to his village, Broken Knife led his friend through the Cheyenne camp. He stopped in front of a lodge. "Welcome to my humble home."

Drouillard went inside. Gazing at the neat, comfortable

interior, he said, "I suppose the prettiest woman in the Cheyenne nation takes care ah you."

Broken Knife held up two fingers.

"Two!" Before Drouillard could say anything else, the girls burst through the entrance.

"This is the pair. The smallest one is Teal, the other is Dove." In Cheyenne, he continued, "My friend, Drouillard."

Shyly, Dove looked at the floor.

Teal smiled and curtsied. "How do do Miter Drourd?"

Pleased, Broken Knife corrected her. "How do you do?"

Drouillard bowed with great fanfare. "I am fine. Thank you very much."

Confused by Drouillard's bow, Teal repeated the greeting. Broken Knife touched her cheek. His face beamed with pride, as he said, "No, Teal you say it once. Dove, would you get your parents?"

Drouillard enjoyed the easy banter between Broken Knife and his Cheyenne family. After they had eaten, he said, "Winter quarters is five miles downriver. Come with me to Fort Mandan. The Captains have been worried about you."

Broken Knife told the Captains about Jeannie and the Crow girl's rescue. He turned down an invitation to stay.

Nodding, Clark said, "If you change your mind, you and the Crow girl are welcome." He hesitated then said, "Coming upriver, we passed a couple of abandoned Cheyenne villages that had been raising corn. I would appreciate anything you can tell me about them."

"I will bring Eagle Plume. He can answer your questions better than I can."

The next morning Eagle Plume was busy trading, so Broken Knife rode through the Missouri River villages. There were two Mandan and three Hidatsa villages within a few miles of each other. The towns faced either the Missouri or Knife rivers with a stockade of upright poles around the other three sides to provide protection against enemies. He stopped several time to watch Hudson's Bay and North West traders barter guns and other trade goods for horses, furs, and robes.

After two days of the commotion, Broken Knife was glad when Drouillard stopped by and said, "Clark wants a check of the Knife River country. How about goin' with me?"

"How long will you be gone?" Broken Knife asked. "Eagle Plume leaves in five days."

"Shouldn't be more than ah couple ah days."

Broken Knife grabbed his bow.

That afternoon, he and Drouillard were following the Knife River, when ahead of them, they heard a low, grumbling noise. Both men dropped behind the closest willow bush. Within minutes, a silver-tipped, hump-backed grizzly bear ambled out of the willows onto a gravel bar. The bear waded in the river and stared at the water. The right front paw flashed. A fish flipped on the bank. The grizzly walked over and ate it. Finished, he went back after another one.

Drouillard shook his head. "We saw several grizzlies on the way up river, but not this close. I have a feelin' we are better off leavin' that critter alone."

"Eagle Plume said grizzlies are the worst animals on the plains, especially a female with cubs." Broken Knife hesitated then said, "Pierre said if you stand still a charging grizzly will stop about twenty yards away, raise on its hind legs, sniff the air, and growl. When it does, shoot it in the mouth. I killed one in the Black Hills and that is exactly what the bear did." He grinned. "However, I think your feeling is right. Leave them alone."

Drouillard and Broken Knife camped that night under a rock overhang three, four miles above where they had seen the bear. After eating, Broken Knife asked, "How was it coming up the Missouri?"

"The huntin' was easy once we got away from the settlements. The boatmen had the toughest time. Since there was seldom enough wind, they pulled or poled the boats upriver. It sure looked like a hard way to me, but the men preferred pullin' the boats with long ropes rather than usin' poles."

"From what I have seen of the Missouri, it must have been rough getting along the bank."

"You bet," Drouillard replied. "The men were in knee deep water, mud, heavy brush, or climbin' over rocks, and at the same time watchin' for snakes and other vermin as well as fightin' hordes of mosquitoes. Besides all those problems, it was either freezin' cold, rainin', or they were roastin' from the heat." Drouillard moved closer to the fire. "Several times, cavin' off riverbanks nearly hit one of the boats, but bein' out in the river was dangerous too because of planters and sawyers."

"What are they?" Broken Knife asked.

"A planter is a tree that has its roots attached to the river bottom with its top just below the surface. Out of the two, sawyers are the most dangerous. A sawyer is like a planter with its top bent deep underwater. When the tree trunk is bent too far, the top springs back up out of the water. Sawyers are powerful enough to wreck a boat when they come up. We might not have made it without Cruzatte and Labiche pilotin' the keelboat."

Broken Knife added wood to the fire. When he sit back down, Drouillard asked, "Did anyone tell you Sergeant Floyd died?"

"No."

"He got sick above the Platte, and died a few days later. Capt'n Lewis thought it was from a ruptured appendix."

"That is too bad. Everyone seemed to like him," Broken Knife said.

Drouillard nodded. "It was sure hard to leave him there. A few days later, we were camped across from a high bluff with a big pile of rocks on it. Cruzatte had traded among the Omaha, and he said a powerful chief named Blackbird was buried beneath the rock pile. He, along with two-thirds of the

Omaha nation, had died from smallpox in 1802. The old Chief asked to be buried in a cave near the top ah the bluff settin' on his favorite horse. That way, he could watch the traders goin' up the Missouri." Drouillard paused then said, "Hopin' to share in Blackbird's Medicine, Indians still leave gifts and tobacco ties on the pile of stones."

Broken Knife asked, "Did you have troubles with any of the tribes coming upriver?"

"Just the Sioux at the mouth of the Bad River. We had been there a couple of days when several chiefs came on the keelboat. One ah them named Partizan indicated that we could stay, or go back, but we could not take the boats upriver.

"An Osage slave had warned Cruzatte the Sioux were goin' to stop us, so we were ready for them. Captain Lewis drew his sword and cut the mooring rope which several Indians on shore were holding. Captain Clark was at the swivel gun, and the rest ah us were armed and ready to fight. After the chiefs looked around, Partizan decided if we gave them some tobacco, we could go on."

Drouillard got up to get more wood. On a nearby knoll, he saw a solitary Indian watching the camp. The warrior's dress and hair indicated he was Hidatsa. George moved away from the flames and gestured to come in and eat.

Walking up to the fire, the Hidatsa stared at Broken Knife before gesturing that his name was Little Man. He gestured that he was on his way home from visiting the Mountain Crow, when a Sioux war party stole his horses. He had killed one warrior and the rest had been too close behind him to stop and eat. He had not eaten for two days.

Broken Knife held out a strip of jerky then tossed a chunk of deer meat on the coals.

When Little Man finished eating, Drouillard offered tobacco. The Hidatsa shook his head. He gestured the Sioux were not the white man's problem. He must leave.

Drouillard held out the pipe.

While Drouillard and Little Man smoked, Broken Knife headed upriver. Satisfied the Sioux were not close, he returned to the night camp.

"There were no signs, but they will probably be here by morning." Hesitating, he said, "I will leave my gun. Even if Little Man cannot use one, have him hold it." After a nod from Drouillard, Broken Knife took his night robe and disappeared into the boulders.

Little Man and Drouillard were up at dawn. They were cooking deer meat when six Sioux rode into the camp. The leader gestured the white man could go, but not the Hidatsa dog.

Drouillard signed the Sioux were welcome to eat, but they could not have his friend. Moreover, as a gesture of friendship, the Sioux should return the Hidatsa's horses.

A warrior snarled. He raised his trade gun. From behind the warrior, Broken Knife put an arrow into the stock of his gun. The warriors whirled to face the new danger.

Drouillard and Little Man grabbed the rifles leaning against the rock.

Surrounded, the two warriors leading Little Man's horses dropped the lead ropes. Off in a hail of dirt and rocks, the Sioux struck their horses every stride with short leather crops.

Little Man took them to the highest point on the Knife River. He pointed out the surrounding country. Satisfied he had the lay of the land in mind, Drouillard said, "If we are goin' to make it back before dark, we best get goin'."

Little Man's dirt lodge sat on the outskirts of the Knife River village. He invited them to eat. Drouillard declined. Broken Knife accepted the invitation.

Broken Knife had seen Hidatsa women work and visit while sitting on the roofs of the conical-shaped dirt houses. This was his first time inside of one. The interior wall was a large circle of six-foot posts standing side by side. In from the post were four eight-foot logs holding a rectangular frame that supported angled poles coming off the circular posts. The ceiling poles laced with willows supported the dirt roof. At least fifty feet across, the floor was packed clay. Near the door was a small corral for a horse. Elk skins partitioned off sleeping area.

Broken Knife met Little Man's wives, Spring Run and Wilted Flower, his mother, Big Woman, and his daughter and son. The girl, Little Spring, and the boy, Hawk Wing, looked to be around nine and three.

Little Man's youngest wife brought bowls of rich stew. He pointed at a backrest. Finished eating, Little Man signed, "Why did his friend look and act like The People?"

Broken Knife gestured, "I was raised by Delaware Indians. I came here with the Cheyenne not the white men."

Little Man broke into a grin. "My brother is welcome."

Broken Knife stared. "You speak Delaware!"

"A warrior of your people called Big Hand stayed in my lodge two different winters. He came here with the French traders Jessaume and Charbonneau. Those two have lived with the Minnitaree and Mandan for many snows."

"Minnitaree?"

"My people's true name is Hidatsa, but the Mandan call us Minnitaree. Besides those two names, French trappers call us the Gros Ventre of the Missouri."

"That is a lot of names," Broken Knife said with a smile.

Nodding, Little Man continued, "Long before my grandfathers time, people from my village, the Awatixa, left the North Country and came here. Part of them settled near the Mandans (ca.1560). The rest followed the Yellow Rock and Big Horn Rivers to the mountains. They are called the Mountain Crow."

Broken Knife started to say something then stopped. Little Man grinned at his confusion. "There is more. Eventually, stronger tribes forced the Hidatsa proper and the Atsina out of the Red River Valley. They went up the Saskatchewan River toward the Blackfeet. French trappers called the Atsina, Gros Ventre, and since the Hidatsa traveled with them, they called the Hidatsa the same. The Atsina and the Hidatsa finally separated. Most of the Hidatsa come here. The rest went to where the Yellow Rock and Smoky Waters joined. They are the River Crow. The Hidatsa proper arrived here when I was a little boy."

"What happened to these Atsina or Gros Ventre?"

"The Gros Ventre live near the Blackfeet on the Milk River. The Gros Ventre are related to the Arapaho. The Arapaho had split off earlier and migrated toward the Black Hills. When the Cheyenne went there, the Arapaho moved into the country south and west of the Crow."

Rather than ask more questions, Broken Knife told about rescuing the girls and staying with the Cheyenne. When he said he was taking the Crow girl home, Little Man shook his head. "Her clan winters in the valley of the Wind River. By now, snow blocks the mountain passes. It would be better to wait until spring?"

"You know her?" Broken Knife asked.

"Only her father," he replied. "He was a great warrior. Returning his daughter will give you much honor among the Crow."

Broken Knife considered what Little Man had said before getting to his feet. "Thank you. I will talk with Teal about staying."

The next morning, Broken Knife went to Fort Mandan. He found the Captains going over charts. Captain Lewis glanced up. "How are you?"

"Fine, thanks." Broken Knife walked over to the chart table. "Little Man, who speaks Delaware, says we cannot reach the Crow until spring. He has asked us to spend the winter in his lodge."

Clark asked, "How did he learn Delaware?"

"A Delaware that traps for the North West spent two

different winters with him," Broken Knife replied.

Lewis looked pleased. "Good, find out what you can about the tribes between here and the Columbia, and if possible, have him draw a map of trails and rivers he knows about."

Chuckling, Broken Knife said, "I had a feeling you would say that. Eagle Plume is leaving today, so I had better get back. I will talk with Little Man and see you later."

As Broken Knife went out the door, Clark said, "Thank Eagle Plume again for the information on the Cheyenne villages."

A tearful Teal and Broken Knife watched their Cheyenne friends disappear over the ridge. He placed his arm around Teal's shoulders. Leading her away, Broken Knife said, "Do not cry. I promised Eagle Plume we would be here next year."

Spring Run and Teal took down the tepee and stored it, while Little Man and Broken Knife turned his horses in with Little Man's horses along the Missouri River bottoms. Riding back, Broken Knife said, "Coming here we passed through miles of burned prairie, and the grass around the village is burned. Why all this burning?"

Little Man frowned. "War parties burn it to hide their tracks. Villagers burn it to prevent a war party from sneaking up to close. The only hunting and pasture around here is along the river bottom."

The riders picketed their buffalo horses near Little Man's lodge. As he and Little Man went through the lodge entrance, Broken Knife said, "Tell me about Crow customs."

Little Man settled onto a backrest. "The Mountain Crow are composed of thirteen matriarchal clans. Clan taboos govern Crow life. For example, custom forbids clan members to marry within the clan, and sometimes, anyone from a closely allied clan. After marriage, the husband never speaks directly to his wife's mother, or her to him." Setting his bowl down, he continued, "If there is a disagreement, or dispute between clan members, the women meet and try to solve the problem. The women may decide the guilty person must give a horse, an elk-tooth shirt, or anything else they deem appropriate to the wronged person. If the guilty party does not accept the women's ruling, the elder men may ban him from the village."

"With the Delaware, the Chief and elders handled such problems," Broken Knife said.

"Being a Crow Chief does not mean a governing role. Only the Camp Chief has any authority." He paused. "His role is limited to selecting the next campsite and deciding when the camp will move there. The only times the Crow use a regulatory force is during camp moves and communal hunts. For instance if a village hunt is to take place, no one can go out by himself. If anyone sneaks out, the military club members whip him, break his weapons, and take away any game he has killed."

"If you are not appointed, how do you become a chief?" Broken Knife asked.

"The Crow have four requirements. The warrior must lead a successful war party, steal a picketed buffalo horse, count first coup on a live foe, and take an enemy's gun or bow."

When Broken Knife asked about the military clubs, Little Man smiled. "It is late. We have all winter to talk."

The next morning, Broken Knife told Little Man that Captain Lewis would like information about the country upriver.

"I have been to where three streams join to become the Smoky Water. We can talk to other warriors and make him an elk-hide map."

The leather map was finished a week later. Broken Knife took it to Fort Mandan. He spread the map out on a table. Pointing out the main features, he said, "This area is called the Three Forks. Here three streams join to form the Missouri. Little Man has not been above the Three Forks. He said Snakes coming from the Lemhi valley to hunt use the right-hand fork. They will have made a good trail across the mountains."

"We have heard some about the Snakes," Clark said. "What about other tribes?"

"To the north and east of the Lemhi is the Bitterroot Valley. The Flathead live there. North across the mountains is the Nez Perce. These tribes are friendly and have many horses."

Clark went to the corner of the room. He returned with a gun, powder, and lead. "Give this to Little Man. Tell him we hope to thank him personally before we leave." He pointed at a large pack. "We want you to take that. Besides trade goods and a brass bucket, I had Shannon put in an ax, shovel, adze, files, several knives, and a crosscut saw. Do you need anything else?" he asked. "How about powder and lead?"

"No, I have plenty of both, but thanks."

Now that they were finished with the map, Broken Knife and Little Man talked about the Crow, the mountain ranges, and the rivers in the Big Horn and Wind River country.

With a storm raging outside, Broken Knife asked Little Man about the Mandans. Many of them were light skinned, had blue or hazel eyes, and had different colors of hair. He had seen one woman with auburn hair and several with salt-and-peppered grey hair.

Little Man replied, "During my father's boyhood, a white man called Verendrye came here (1738). Verendrye and others since him have wondered if the Mandans are true Indians."

"If they are not, who are they?" Broken Knife asked.

"A man named John Evans came here a few snows ago. He claimed a Welsh Prince named Madoc crossed the Big Salt Water with three shiploads of people. This was long before other white settlers crossed the Big Salt Water. Powerful tribes forced these people up the Father of Rivers to the Smoky Water and Ohio rivers. Evans hoped to find a connection between the Mandans and the lost Welsh people."

"What did he find out?" Broken Knife asked.

"Evans did not have time," said Little Man with a shake of

his head. "He claimed this country belonged to Spain, and French traders had no business here. When Jessaume went to kill him, some Mandans put Evans in a bullboat. The last anyone saw of him, he was bobbing up and down the Big Smoky."

"Evans reached St. Louis because he gave Captain Lewis information concerning this country." He paused before adding, "He must have decided the story was not true, or it would have been all over St. Louis."

The next morning dawned bright and clear. The storm had left two foot of snow on the ground and eight- to ten-foot drifts. That night a warm wind started and by the next day, only part of the drifts remained. The Hidatsa called the wind, a Chinook.

Little Man brought out three pack boards with a buffalo robe and wolf hide on each one. He suggested they take Drouillard and go hunting. Shortly after mid-day, the hunters saw a small buffalo herd. With wolf hides across their shoulders, they crawled close enough to kill eight buffalo.

The sun dropped below the horizon as the hunters finished skinning the last buffalo. While Drouillard gathered buffalo chips, Broken Knife began digging a shelter in a snow filled gully for the night.

Little Man helped get the snow cave started then went back to the buffalo. He cut the two largest ribs from three carcasses. After scraping off the flesh, he forced the rib ends into the pack boards' corner holes. Little Man set aside two buffalo hides for the snow cave's entrance and floor. The rest he folded and placed on the sleighs.

Finished stuffing themselves on roasted buffalo tongues and hump-ribs, Drouillard asked about the Plains tribes.

"When my people first settled on the Smoky Water, Apaches, Padoucas, and other tribes lived here. As stronger tribes moved on the plains, the Apache migrated south. The Padouca and many smaller tribes were wiped out." Pausing, he said, "The stronger tribes killed the warriors and old people

141

of the weaker tribes. To make their own tribe stronger the children and any willing women were taken into the tribe. The rest were kept, or traded off, as slaves. Now that most villages have at least a few guns, this kind of raiding is not as frequent as it was before guns."

Broken Knife shook his head. "How did guns change anything? Eagle Plume's village had five guns, and none of them worked. Even if they had worked, the warriors could not load them or hit anything."

Little Man replied, "After the traders show how to load the gun, most warriors do not have powder and lead to practice with, so they soon forget what the trader tells them." He paused. "Besides that, if anything goes wrong with their guns, the warriors cannot fix them."

Drouillard said, "Many of the eastern tribes now stipulate in a treaty with the government that a gunsmith live at a nearby settlement or post."

Little Man said, "Plains Indians fear and respect lightning, thunder, and the round winds. Guns make the thunder noise. Many warriors are more concerned about the noise than whether the gun actually shoots a ball."

Drouillard nodded in agreement. "A warrior with a bow could shoot several times while one gun is being loaded. The Teton Sioux outnumbered us thirty to one but when we pointed the deck gun at them, they backed down."

"What about horses?" Broken Knife asked.

"The Snake tribe brought the first horses onto the Plains about seventy-five snows ago. They got them from their cousins the Ute and Comanche. These southwest tribes traded for, or stole, horses from the Spanish. With horses and stone war clubs called Pukamoggran, the Snakes ruled the Three Forks area. The warriors raided as far south and east as the Black Hills."

A little confused Drouillard said, "Word around St. Louis is Plains tribes catch wild horses."

"During my grandfathers time, there were no wild horses on the Plains. After the small pox outbreaks, many horses no longer had owners. These horses started the wild herds."

"How long have the Crow had horses?" Broken Knife asked.

"Maybe sixty-five snows (1740). Crow horses came from the Snake and Arapaho. About that same time, the Blackfeet traded with the Flathead and Nez Perce for horses." Little Man hesitated. "I have wondered why the Nez Perce had horses before the Blackfeet. Another thing is many of the Nez Perce horses are spotted. I have never seen a spotted horse from the Spanish. Could these horses come from the north?" he asked.

"Could be," Broken Knife replied. "The Russian settlements would have horses."

Little Man said, "Thirty snows ago (1775), the Sioux and Cheyenne traded with the Arikara for horses. Now, all of the Plains tribes raise horses as well as take them from their enemies."

Little Man went outside and relieved himself before changing the subject to warfare. "Old men say it is better to die in battle, but few young men agree. For Indians, there is more honor in counting a first coup, or even a second coup, than in killing an enemy. The highest war honor with all Plains tribes is to take a picketed buffalo horse out of an enemy village.

"In the beginning, horse tribes were the most powerful, but once guns reached the plains, the power shifted. The Blackfeet obtained guns from the Cree and drove the Snakes off the plains and into the mountains. Now, the Snakes must sneak onto the Three Forks area to kill enough meat to survive the winter." He paused at the look on Drouillard's face. "The Spanish will trade horses, not guns. Guns come from the British and French traders."

Broken Knife said, "With the Cheyenne a war party was usually five or six men out to steal horses. Not fight."

With a nod, Little Man replied, "Warriors go on foot

because horses leave too many signs for the enemy to see. The warriors take large dogs with them to carry pemmican, extra moccasins, and ropes." He paused before adding, "Young men join a war party only after the leader has had a spiritual vision promising success. The last thing a war party leader wants is to have any of his party killed. If a member is killed, it shows he has poor medicine, and no one will follow him again." Little Man stared at his friends. "The average lodge contains eight inhabitants with two of these being warriors. Most villages are ten to twelve lodges, so it is a serious matter for the village to have any warrior killed."

Finished with guns, horses, and warfare, Little Man talked about an extensive trading system among the Plains Indians. Because the Arikara, Mandan, and Hidatsa lived in permanent villages on the Missouri and had gardens, their villages served as the trade centers. Roving Plains tribes brought buffalo robes, furs, and horses. Canadian traders brought guns, pots, beads, and other goods. All the Plains tribes participated in this trade except the Sioux and Blackfeet. The Sioux traded with the British in Minnesota. The Blackfeet traded in Canada.

Now, Little Man thought Americans might change a trade system that had gone on for decades. The Trade Fairs would stop if the Americans traded directly with the various tribes. Little Man went on to say only the Sioux had caused problems with the Missouri riverboats because they did not want traders bringing guns to their enemies. Eventually, he thought the Arikara would cause the most trouble. Many Arikara warriors were too shiftless to hunt and lived off their wives garden trade. When Little Man finished, no one said anything.

Morning dawned clear and crisp making the frozen hides on the sleighs easy to pull across the snow. There was little conversation on the way back. Drouillard and Broken Knife were still pondering over what Little Man had said.

NORTH WEST TRADERS

A week after the hunting trip, storm clouds formed in the northwest. That night, it snowed six inches. The next morning when Little Man looked out, he said, "There will be tracks along the river, let's go find a deer."

A couple of miles upriver were signs where several deer had fed that morning. Picking a likely spot, the hunters waited. Broken Knife studied Little Man's horn bow. "What kind of horn works best?" he asked.

"Any thick piece will do, but mountain sheep or elk horns make the strongest ones. Sections of bone are glue together in the rough shape of a bow and then smoothed with rubbing stones. When the bow is finished, it can be carved and painted." He glanced at his bow and smiled. "Sometimes that takes longer."

Broken Knife grinned. "How do you get the glue?"

"By boiling buffalo hooves," replied Little Man.

Two bucks stepped out of the willows about thirty paces away. Broken Knife motioned for Little Man to shoot the closest one. When his friend shook his head, Broken Knife realized it was too far for a horn bow. He shot one, and when the second buck hesitated, he killed it too.

Impressed, Little Man said, "Eagle Plume said you possessed a Medicine Bow." He pointed northwest at the black

145

storm clouds. "You can tell me about it later. We better cut them up and get out of here."

The wind started to blow and with it came small, biting snow pellets. The hunters wrapped the warm wet hides around their shoulders. With the choice pieces of meat on pack boards, they started for the lodge. It was not long before Little Man turned his back to the raging blizzard. He held out his bow. He shouted over the howling storm. "Hang on and do not let go. If we are separated, you will die."

Blocking out everything, Broken Knife placed one foot ahead of the other. With each step that got harder. Cold penetrated his bones. Leg joints refused to bend. He did not know how long the frozen nightmare lasted. In pure white surroundings time and distance lost meaning. Only numbing cold persisted.

Little Man pulled Broken Knife through the lodge entrance. Broken Knife's hands were locked on the bow. Hanging from his eyebrows and hair, icicles covered his gaunt, blue face.

Half-moaning, half-crying, Teal tried to pry loose his stiff fingers. Big Woman threw a robe at Teal's feet as she went outside after a kettle of snow while Spring Run and Wilted Flower cut the pack straps. They were prying off the frozen deer hide when Big Woman returned with the snow. Big Woman glanced at the panic-stricken Teal. She motioned to rub his hands and feet with snow.

As Broken Knife's face turned red, he started to shiver. Spring Run moved him closer to the fire and rubbed a thick coat of bear grease on his hands and feet. She forced him to drink warm water until he fell into a deep sleep.

Broken Knife woke with a hot tingling sensation. He hobbled over and sit beside Little Man. "I do not remember getting here. Is Teal all right?"

"She has not left your side for two days. A little while ago, I made her go lie down. How do you feel?"

"My fingers and toes feel as if they are on fire; otherwise all right." Broken Knife's voice softened. "I am grateful. I owe my friend a life."

Spring Run came over with a brass bucket of bear grease. She ran her fingers over Broken Knife's face then talked to Little Man. He said, "She wants you to keep your hands and feet covered with this until the stinging is gone." Little Man sighed to himself as much as to Broken Knife. "You must learn to live with blizzards here and in the mountains."

The first warm day after the storm, Broken Knife went out to practice with his knife and bow. Finished with the knife, he was shooting the bow when he sensed movement. He whirled. A white man was coming off the ridge.

The man held out his hand. "Antoine Larocque, you are the Delaware staying with Little Man?"

"Yes."

"I am a North West trader out of Fort Assiniboine."

"Where is that?" Broken Knee asked.

"It is almost straight north of here where the Souris River flows into the Assiniboine. I hear you are headed for Crow country." When Broken Knife nodded, he said, "I plan to visit there this summer. Since they live in the mountains, I am hoping to get prime beaver pelts and robes."

"You trade for the robes?"

"Robes that have been worn for eighteen months or so bring a premium. They make the very best hats. I am taking some iron traps, but convincing warriors to trap is hard." Smiling, he added, "Most Indians would rather chase buffalo."

Broken Knife grinned. He would rather chase buffalo too.

After he and Larocque talked about the past winter and the coming of spring, Broken Knife said, "A couple of weeks ago, Little Man talked about Plains Indian warfare. I still have some questions about it. Have you heard of any big battles between the tribes?"

With a nod, Larocque replied, "I summered a couple of

years ago with David Thompson. He is a North West Company surveyor and explorer. He spent the winter of 1787-88 with an old Cree Indian called Saukamapee. This Cree helped the Blackfeet in two battles against the Snakes. Thompson figured the first battle occurred between 1723 and 1728. In that fight, Saukamapee told him as the warriors approached each other both sides shouted, leaped, and sang. About a hundred yards apart, each group stopped and sat behind shields. The warriors arrows could not penetrate the thick rawhide shields, but having smaller shields, a few Blackfeet were wounded. At dusk the fighting stopped and the participants went home." Larocque smiled and added, "During a battle that lasted most of the day, there were only a few minor wounds. Not a single warrior was killed.

"The second battle occurred ten years later. Saukamapee and nine other Cree happened to be at the Blackfeet camp and offered to help. The Cree had guns. The battle started the same, but when the Cree fired the muzzleloaders, the noise panicked the Snakes. When the warriors fled, several were killed with bows and lances."

Larocque went on to say, "Saukamapee told Thompson that horses were not used in this battle; however, a few days later, a Snake and his horse were killed. Despite the horse being dead, the people were afraid and would not get too close. The strange animal had carried a man and his possessions, so the people called it a Big Dog. Later, mainly because of its size, they changed the name to Elk Dog."

"Who is David Thompson? I have never heard of him."

"Thompson has seen and mapped more of Canada than any other man. He started with Hudson's Bay at York Factory when he was fourteen. When his twelve-year apprenticeship was up, he joined the North West. His first assignment with the North West was to determine the longitude and latitude of the Mandan villages and the North West's posts. In 1797, he traveled over four thousand miles carrying out his assignment.

His goal is to map all of Canada."

"Is he a Canadian?"

"No, he is a Welshman," Larocque replied.

Broken Knife said, "I understand Hudson's Bay Company was chartered in 1670. Were they granted all the country that drains into Hudson Bay?"

"That is right. The Company of Adventurers, as they are called, controls an area equal to the tenth- or twelfth-largest country in the known world. A mistake Hudson's Bay made was building posts around Hudson Bay then waiting for Indians to come there." Larocque paused then said, "North West traders built their posts near the Indians. By doing this, the North West Company put pressure on the older company right away. Now, Hudson's Bay sends out traders to the villages. Did you meet those that were here a couple of months ago."

"Yes, that reminds me of another question. One of them mentioned pemmican posts. What are they?"

"Let me explain the North West Company first. When Simon McTavish set it up, he and Joseph Frobisher were the managing partners in Montreal and London. Except McTavish and Frobisher, the company partners all winter in the "pays d'en haut" which is the country beyond Lake Superior. The company men that live and work there are the North Men. The North West partners and clerks rendezvous once a year at Grand Portage. Besides this meeting, a mail system goes to all the posts twice a year.

"With the scattered post, a problem the North West Company faced was food supplies. From Lachine to Grand Portage on Lake Superior is about two thousand miles. It takes around fifty days to paddle that distance. Going upriver, the canoe men live on lyed corn and grease (buffalo tallow). From Rainy Lake to Lake Winnipeg, the traders live on wild rice and grease. Getting something to sustain the men traveling to the northern trading posts was the problem."

"No hunting at all?"

"Not unless there is game along the river; otherwise, there is never enough time. North Men take the winters catch by canoe to Grand Portage and have to be back before the rivers freeze that fall. Peter Pond solved the problem with pemmican. Around two pounds of pemmican is the equivalent of eight pounds of meat. Once the North Men reach the wintering posts, they can hunt and fish. Whitefish are used in great quantities at these posts."

"Is it the same as Indian pemmican?"

"Pretty much, there is forty pounds of fat and fifty pounds of dried meat per pack. Anyway, to answer your question. Posts were setup in the buffalo country where men made pemmican. The pemmican goes to the Cumberland House on the Saskatchewan River. From there, it is distributed to the other North West posts. Leaving the Cumberland House, men with canoes can reach the Arctic Ocean, Hudson Bay, Gulf of St. Lawrence, Gulf of Mexico, and without too much more trouble, the Pacific Ocean. There are many portages on the water routes, but none of them takes more than a day.

"Alexander Henry (the younger) is the wintering-partner at the Pembina Post. He sends in over three ton of pemmican and two ton of grease a year, and his post is not in prime buffalo country."

At Broken Knife's blank look, he added, "It is north of here where the Pembina River flows into the Red River."

"How long have you been a trader?"

"About five years. After some college and spending time around Philadelphia to learn English, I started as a clerk with the XY Company. After a couple of years, I quit and joined the North West." Larocque paused. "Word came a couple of weeks ago that Simon McTavish has died. I imagine the XY and North West will merge now. With McTavish dead, the North West and Hudson's Bay will more than likely join forces too. Since all the furs go to England, it would be easier and cheaper to ship them from Hudson Bay rather than Montreal."

"You mention Peter Pond awhile back. I heard he was responsible for the route that Mackenzie and his men took to the Pacific."

Larocque nodded in agreement. "At that time, he had mapped and knew more about the North Country than anyone. In a round about way, he is responsible for the North West Company. One of his men killed John Ross, an important Hudson's Bay trader, in an argument over fishnets. Simon McTavish used this to pull Montreal's independent traders together to form the North West Company. He argued, if they did not stop feuding with Hudson's Bay, the government would prevent them from going to the North Country." He hesitated. "Despite all he accomplished, Pond has been kicked out of the fur trade. He lives in Connecticut now."

Broken Knife held out his hand. "I better be getting back. Thanks for all the information."

Larocque gripped his hand. As he started to turn away, Broken Knife said, "Oh, by the way. Have you seen any hardwood around here? I need a couple of pieces about six feet long."

"Would a hickory oar do?" Larocque asked. "I have a couple of extra ones."

"Thanks, what do I owe you?"

"Nothing, when I get to the Crow country, you can help me convince them to trap. Come with me. I will get it for you now."

Chunks of ice floating on the river signaled the coming of spring. Besides chunks of ice, bobbing carcasses of buffalo drowned while crossing on thin ice filled the river. These swollen, putrefied buffalo were considered a delicacy. The villagers pulled them out of the river, and with horn ladles, scooped out the green, decayed flesh.

Once the ice and dead buffalo were gone from the river, the Captains were anxious to leave. The captains hired Touissant Charbonneau as an interrupter, and a trader named Baptiste LaPage to replace the discharged Newman. The Shoshone Indian wife of Charbonneau and her six-weeks-old son were going too. The woman's name was Sakakawea (Sacagawea, Sacajawea).

On April 7, 1805, the Lewis and Clark expedition started out for the Pacific Ocean in two pirogues and six small hollowed out tree canoes. Drouillard had headed upriver the day before with a hunting party.

The morning the expedition left, Broken Knife and Teal stood on the bank and waved good-bye. It seemed hard to believe the expedition had suffered only one death and two serious disciplinary problems: Sergeant Floyd died (near Sioux City, Iowa); Reed deserted; Newman had been insubordinate to Lewis. After Reed was caught, a court of enlisted men sentenced Reed and Newman to run a gauntlet (Reed four times), and then be drummed out of the service. Except the death of Sergeant Floyd, these problems were insignificant compared to the courage and dedication shown by the cheerful men starting into the vast expanse of plains, mountains, and rivers.

The day the main body started upriver, Corporal Warfington with five soldiers, the two discharged men, and several French traders headed downriver with the keelboat.

The keelboat held: two live animals (a prairie dog and a magpie); thirty-nine pressed plants; a skin and skeleton of each species of animal that was trapped or shot coming up the Missouri.

AUTHOR'S NOTE: Broken Knife learned several years later that nineteen of the plants, the prairie dog, mule deer, antelope, jack rabbit, elk, bighorn sheep, badger, coyote, and sharp-tail grouse were new species, or not thought to have existed in America. In addition to the plant and animal specimens, there were detailed river maps, weather charts, and information on the location, numbers, strengths, and habits of fifty-three Indian tribes.

Clark was a Second Lieutenant. President Jefferson had promised him a captaincy, but the War Department made him a Second Lieutenant and the President did not force a change of orders. To Captain Lewis's credit, he shared the command equally as he had promised. None of the men knew Clark was not a Captain.

After his criminal and mutinous expressions to Lewis, the conduct of Newman was exemplary; however, Lewis could not reverse the court martial ruling. When he returned to St. Louis, Captain Lewis petitioned Congress on behalf of the enlisted men. On the 3rd of March 1807, Congress authorized double pay and three hundred and twenty acres of land for each man, including John Newman and Richard Warfington. Lewis and Clark received double pay and sixteen hundred acres of land each. Despite their contributions, York and Sakakawea received nothing.

MOUNTAIN CROW

Broken Knife and Little Man were returning from checking on the horses. Little Man said, "The mountain passes should be clear by now."

A solemn Broken Knife said, "I have been thinking about going since Drouillard left. It is hard to leave my Hidatsa friends."

"It has been a good winter. We have learned much from each other." Pausing, he added, "You speak Crow and Hidatsa well. The Crow will be surprised at a white man who knows their language and customs."

Sadness hung over Little Man's lodge. Nobody wanted Broken Knife and Teal to leave. The gloomy faces were too much. Broken Knife went to his bed. Underneath it were two hardwood bows that he had made from Larocque's oars. There was also a pack containing colored cloth, beads, awls, and mirrors. He set the presents down as Big Woman brought out a beaded gun scabbard and a shoulder bag for Teal. The gifts brightened everyone's mood.

After the excitement died down, Little Man said, "We better go to bed. There is a lot to do before Broken Knife and Teal leave."

Little Man's wives loaded robes, extra moccasins, and food in the pack bags. By noon, only five of the six horses were packed. As Spring Run brought out the last pannier, Hawk Wing and Little Man disappeared.

Broken Knife finished tying the pack. Hawk Wing hollered. "Look what I have. Look at this! It is yours." He set a black furry ball down. The pup yipped and jumped on his leg.

Little Man said, "The pup's mother is the best dog in the village. Its father is Captain Lewis's dog, Scannon."

Broken Knife handed the pup to Teal. He smiled at Hawk Wing. "It is a fine pup, thank you." Good-byes and promises to return said, he and Teal started up the Smoky Water.

The first night, Teal and Broken Knife stopped by a small stream. They camped near rock ledges covered with stick-dried hawk nests. The dry branches would burn without smoke. Broken Knife unpacked and picketed the horses. Building a fire, he laid out something to eat.

Chewing on a strip of jerky, he watched Teal play with the pup. "Its father's name is Scannon. What if we call the pup Scamp?"

Teal rolled the playful pup over. "Black Dog is a better name," she said.

Broken Knife nodded. He laid out two robes near the fire. "Teal, I am going up on that bluff to look around. Do you want to come?"

"No, I will play with Black Dog."

Little Man had warned him about Assiniboine and Sioux war parties. He saw no movement or smoke in the clear air. It was dark when he returned to the camp.

The next seven days of travel were without incident. Where the Yellowstone flowed into the Smoky Water, the riders turned up the Yellowstone. Near the junction of the Big Horn and Yellowstone, there was a camp of River Crow. Broken Knife stopped. He fired his gun then tossed a blanket in the air.

Several warriors rode out and escorted them into the village. Broken Knife stared at some of the men's long hair. On many, it hung below the waist. He saw one old man carrying

155

his hair rolled up in a ball. The warriors led them through the village to a lodge where Rotten Belly, the Camp Chief waited. "Word arrived three days ago that you were coming. We will eat and smoke."

Finished eating, Broken Knife asked, "Do you know the girl's family?"

"Yes, her grandparents, and her mother's sister and brother are on the Stinkingwater (Shoshone River)." He hesitated then added, "What you have done is good. Before you go, my people would hold a feast and dance."

Broken Knife shook his head. "The family has mourned enough. We must go."

"That is true," Rotten Belly said. "There is a good trail to the Whistling Water camp, but if you want, warriors will show you the way."

Broken Knife said, "Thanks, we will be fine."

The travelers followed the Big Horn River for several miles before stopping for the night. With a half-sun peeking over the horizon, they broke camp and continued along the river.

Following the river, the Big Horn country changed from open grass-covered plains, to rolling hills with scattered evergreens. In the distance, there loomed mountains. Pine trees covered the summits on most of the mountains. A few ended in austere peaks covered by snow. Four days after leaving the River Crow, the riders reached the junction of the Stinkingwater and Big Horn rivers.

Word of Teal's coming had reached the village. A boy of fourteen or fifteen forced his way through the excited crowd. He said, "I am Redfeather. Come with me."

The young man led them to a tattered lodge. A man and two women stood beside the entrance. Redfeather shouted, "My father, Grey Wolf, my mother, Owl Woman, and my sister, Whispering Wind." Barking dogs, excited villagers, and crying over Teal made it hard for Broken Knife to hear the names.

The older man smiled. He motioned at the entrance. Broken Knife handed the packhorses' lead rope to Redfeather. The condition of the buffalo-skin lodge surprised Broken Knife. Everything was clean, but old and worn.

Grey Wolf saw the look on Broken Knife's face. With downcast eyes, he said, "After the Pawnee came, we cut our hair and gave everything away. You are welcome to share what we have."

Broken Knife nodded his acceptance. He went outside and removed a parfleche from one of the horses. He set the box in front of Owl Woman. "Teal is back. Two Pawnee are dead. Your mourning can end." Touching Owl Woman's hand, he said. "Reestablish your lodge with these."

Grey Wolf appeared confused by the name, Teal. Broken Knife smiled and said, "At first, I could not say her name, so I have called her Teal."

Grey Wolf returned the smile. "A good name, we will call her the same."

Owl Woman opened the parfleche. She stared at the box, her eyes filled with tears. In a quivering voice, she said, "You have returned life to my family."

The packhorses were unloaded, and the packs opened. For the first time, Broken Knife understood why Little Man's wives had taken so long to pack the bags. The corn, squash, beans, and dried meat would last months. No one had said anything, but the women knew Teal's family would be mourning their loss.

Owl Woman and the village women erected a new lodge. Teal and Whispering Wind pitched Broken Knife's Cheyenne lodge beside it. Two days later Grey Wolf's war shield sat on a tripod in front of his lodge. The shield faced the rising Grandfather.

Broken Knife was arranging packs in his lodge when Grey Wolf poked his head under the entrance flap. "My wife and daughter are preparing a feast. There are things I must know. Let's take a swim."

The two men walked through the village. Several warriors invited them to eat, but Grey Wolf made excuses. Out of the village, they followed the river to a deep pool. Grey Wolf said, "We will swim here, then talk."

Sitting on a rock to dry off, Grey Wolf said, "The people wish to hold a dance in your honor. At such gatherings, it is customary for the guest to recite his war deeds. How do you feel about this? When I asked Teal, she said you did not like talking about your feats."

Broken Knife skipped a stone across the water. "I do not like visiting the past."

Grey Wolf nodded his understanding. "Redfeather and Whispering Wind will not be satisfied until they know all about you. With the villagers there is a way."

"How?" asked Broken Knife.

"A few days ago, a warrior returned from the Comanche. He told about the arrow game and your medicine bow. If asked about your deeds, say your medicine prevents you from talking about them. The people will respect this."

Grey Wolf glanced at the sun. "We better go."

As they entered the lodge, Broken Knife froze in mid-stride. He could do nothing but stare. The girl by the fire astounded him. Her dark eyes set above high cheekbones, along with her slender nose, full lips, and fine jaw line formed an incredibly beautiful face. Whispering Wind's black lustrous shoulder-length hair had a red ochre line down the part. The multi-colored skunk bead necklace hanging from her graceful neck, and a pure white, elk-tooth dress added to her natural beauty.

She stepped toward him. The belted dress and her fluid movements revealed her reed-like body to perfection. Wind's eyes sparkled. "Broken Knife stares. Do I displease him?"

"Oh, no! You are beautiful."

Redfeather's laughter broke the trance. Broken Knife

flushed. Grey Wolf and Owl Woman grinned with approval. Broken Knife made the mistake of saying, "Is it hot in here?"

Everyone roared except Whispering Wind. A whisper of a smile crossed her face.

The dinner consisted of buffalo tongue, herb-seasoned hump-ribs, boiled squash, and corn meal fry bread. When Broken Knife complimented Owl Woman, she smiled and nodded at her daughter. "Wind fixed most of it."

"Well, thank you both. I hope we do not eat like this often, I will look like Fat Boy."

Teal asked, "Who is Fat Boy?"

"Someone I once knew. There are things my new family should know that I do not wish to tell the village."

In a firm voice Grey Wolf replied, "What you say will not be mentioned again."

Broken Knife told of his Delaware life, the Pawnees, the Cheyenne, and some about the Walkers and the expedition. When Broken Knife paused, Redfeather asked, "Who are Shawnee and Delaware?"

"Indian tribes in the land where the Grandfather rises. Now warriors of both tribes trap for the North West Company." He hesitated, "It would be big medicine for a Shawnee to kill Wind-of-Death's son."

An excited, Redfeather asked, "How many warriors have you killed?"

Owl Woman interrupted. "That is not polite. If Broken Knife wants you to know, he will tell you."

Broken Knife smiled at Redfeather. "Four Shawnee, three white men, and two Pawnee. I do not wish to walk this way again. Ask any question now."

Grey Wolf promptly said, "White men!"

"Two of them killed my Delaware mother. The other one took my gun. When I tried to take it back, he pulled a pistol."

"Pistol? What is that?" Grey Wolf asked.

Broken Knife held his hands twelve-inches apart. "A gun

159

this long." His voice lowered. "Not even Little Man knows what I am going to show you." As he finished speaking, a knife vibrated in a lodge pole.

Wide-eyed, Grey Wolf and Redfeather stared. Smiling, Broken Knife said, "The knife is carried on my back. Soon, I will need a larger shirt."

Grey Wolf looked at Broken Knife. "It is wise to say nothing concerning your past. The older warriors will think you boast. The young braves may wish to find out if what you say is true."

Broken Knife looked at Redfeather and Whispering Wind. "There is another thing. I will not enter any Crow shooting or running contests. Some will say Broken Knife is afraid, but the quickest way to make enemies is to win. For you to remain quiet will be hard."

Wind touched his hand. "We understand."

Eagerly, Redfeather asked, "Will you show me how to throw a knife?"

"Yes, if you will teach me how to train a buffalo horse," replied Broken Knife.

Grey Wolf's pride reflected in his smile. "My son has broken many horses. Speaking of horses, we better move them to the night pasture if we are going to the feast."

The family was getting ready for the celebration when Broken Knife tied an inch band of red print cloth on Wind's forehead. When Teal and Owl Woman looked envious, he put pieces around their heads. The distinguished looking Grey Wolf would have the handsomest and proudest family at the dance.

Grey Wolf's family arrived at the large fire in the center of the village just as the dance started. The drum beaters faced the opening of the lodge circle. The circle always faces east. The young men stood in rows facing north. The young women were in rows ten feet away facing the men. Older men and women stood below the young people facing west. The

160

drummers started a rhythmic beat. The women sang in low two- or three-note monotones. Then, they began moving back and forth in a line. The young men circled behind the drummers to the girls' side of the square. Each one stood behind a girl. Putting his arm through one of her arms, he moved back and forth with her. After dancing awhile, the men returned to reform the rows facing the women. The dance was repeated then several other were danced.

The precise movements of the dancers were strange to Broken Knife. He did not join the fun. Despite his not taking part, several young women flirted with him. Wind stayed away the entire night.

During the dance, Grey Wolf told several warriors that if Broken Knife talked about his war deeds, he would lose his medicine. Since medicine was involved, no one asked about his exploits.

The next morning, Grey Wolf and Broken Knife were looking at the horses he had brought with him. "Only one is a buffalo horse?" Grey Wolf asked.

"I have never ridden the others," Broken Knife replied.

"Good buffalo horses are hard to trade for. We will need more if we are to have enough meat for winter," Grey Wolf said in a solemn tone.

Broken Knife was thoughtful for a minute. "Let's go back. There is something I would like to ask you and Owl Woman."

At the lodge, Whispering Wind handed her father and Broken Knife a bowl of meat. "We decided how to hide the knife."

"That is not all they decided," Redfeather said with a grin. "Broken Knife better be careful."

Wind scowled and threw a bone scrapper that barely missed her brother's head. Broken Knife chuckled at her stern look then announced that he was going after horses.

Redfeather jumped to his feet. "Warriors will not follow you until you have had a spiritual vision, but I will."

The boy's eagerness brought a smile to Broken Knife's

161

face. "Take the horses to water. We will talk about your going when you get back." As their son went out the door, he looked at Grey Wolf and Owl Woman. "I would like to take Redfeather with me. There will be little danger if he does as I say."

Grey Wolf nodded. "I went on my first war party at his age. This time of year there is always a Piegan village on the Musselshell River. It will be a good place."

Owl Woman sighed, "The time has come."

"Good, we will leave in the morning. Who are the Piegans?" Broken Knife asked.

"The Blackfeet Nation is composed of three tribes the Bloods, Blackfoot, and Piegan. The Blackfeet and the Crow are bitter enemies. Be careful once you cross the Elk River (Yellowstone)."

Whispering Wind pulled out a tanned hide. "We will make moccasins and pack the dogs."

Teal's eyes filled with tears. Broken Knife took her hand and led her outside. They walked along the river. Her tiny hand in his. With a slight squeeze, he said, "You must not be afraid. I will be careful."

She forced a smile. "Sometimes, I wish things were as before."

"I know," he said, "But now, you have a family that loves you as I do. When I get back, we will take the horses and go somewhere. How does that sound?" Teal smiled as they started back to the lodge.

The Grandfather's rays faced Broken Knife and Redfeather as they left the lodge. Grey Wolf met them at the village outskirts. He held out a four-foot stick with a carved knob and two eagle feathers on one end. "I prayed this coup stick will serve Broken Knife well. The feathers show you have counted two first coups on Crow enemies. Do they displease you?"

Broken Knife's finger and thumb barely circled the hardwood stick. "No, I will carry it with pride."

Grey Wolf nodded and walked away.

Redfeather and Broken Knife headed northwest. The three dogs trotting behind them carried extra moccasins, pemmican, and bridle ropes. Redfeather was a strong runner. By late afternoon of the third day, they had reached the Elk River.

Redfeather turned upriver to where Stillwater Creek flowed into it. He pulled a bullboat out of the rushes. Floating across the Elk, they found a sheltered place to tie the dogs and build a fire.

Pleased at the progress thus far, Broken Knife said, "Let's lay over a day and hunt. The dogs are hungry, and we need meat. If you want to go upriver, I will go down. Maybe one of us can kill a deer."

Broken Knife went a couple of miles without seeing any deer tracks. In the distance, he did see several antelope. Returning to camp, he kindled a small fire and waited.

Redfeather returned at dusk. After grabbing a handful of parched corn, he dropped by the fire. "Not a single deer track, but plenty of antelope and buffalo signs." Redfeather held out the corn. "This may have to do. Buffalo are hard to kill when you are on foot, and you cannot get close to antelope. We need the gun."

"Guns make too much noise. Tomorrow, I will show you something Drouillard taught me."

Early the next morning, they went to where Redfeather had seen a herd of antelope drinking. Near the water, Broken Knife tied a strip of red cloth on a stick. He pushed the stick into the ground. Returning to the rock ledge where Redfeather waited, he said, "We will not have to wait long. Antelope are full of curiosity."

Several antelope approached the fluttering cloth but none came close enough to shoot. Finally, two bucks' and a doe's curiosity was too much.

Broken Knife whispered, "Take one of the bucks, I will

163

shoot the doe."

While Redfeather built a willow smoke rack, Broken Knife fed the dogs and cooked several strips of meat. When the first stars appeared, they added wet wood to the fire and smoked strips of antelope meat. They had more than enough jerky to reach the Piegan camp.

Eight days later, Redfeather and Broken Knife were on a juniper-covered hill overlooking a valley containing several hundred horses. They had watched the village and horses for two days. Just before dark, several owners took their horses to small secluded areas. Twice they watched a large bunch of horses being taken to a blind canyon two miles from the village. Broken Knife decided they were the ones to take.

In the darkness of pre-star light, Broken Knife rose. "I will go after two buffalo horses from the village. You catch and tie the nursing mares to trees."

Redfeather nodded. Without a word, he disappeared into the night.

Broken Knife crouched in a stand of willows between the river and the Piegan lodges. Several couples came by, but he waited for a single warrior. When one came down the path with a blanket on his shoulder, Broken Knife tapped him on the head with the coup stick then pulled him deep into the bushes. He gagged and tied the warrior before putting on his moccasins.

With the Piegan's blanket draped over his shoulders, Broken Knife walked into the village. Careful to stay in the shadows of the campfires' light, he strolled through the village twice trying to decide which were the two best picketed buffalo horses.

The campfires were darkened coals, and the lodge noises had ceased when he led the first horse out of the village. A half-mile away, he picketed the horse on green grass and went back after the second horse.

Free of the village, Broken Knife rode one horse and led

the other one across the meadow toward Redfeather. He could not help but think how easy it had been. Not one dog or Piegan had paid any attention to him.

"Any problems?" Broken Knife asked as he rode up to Redfeather. Behind Redfeather, he saw several tied mares.

"No, there was a boy about my age guarding ten horses between here and the river." Redfeather held up the Piegan's bow. "He is bound to a tree."

"Good, did he know you were a Crow?"

"No, I hit him from behind," said Redfeather.

Broken Knife thought a minute. "If they were being guarded, they must be good horses."

Redfeather broke into a grin. "I think you are right. We are taking at least thirty horses now, but if the Piegan catch us, I would rather die over a whole herd of horses than a lot of horses." A big smile covered his face. "Songs are written about such things."

Broken Knife smiled. He held out the rein. "Ride this horse and lead the old, hobbled mare. Head toward the Smoky Water."

Redfeather appeared confused by the direction. Without a word, he unhobbled the mare and headed north. As the horses left the canyon, the tied mares whinnied. The foals ran to their mothers. The other horses followed the old mare. A short time later, the second bunch joined the herd. With Redfeather on a fast trot, they had covered five or six miles when Redfeather stopped.

Over his shoulder, he shouted, "There are buffalo ahead."

Broken Knife rode beside him. "Turn and head east. Bear back toward the Elk River crossing. I will drive the buffalo over the horse tracks to hide the change of direction." Turning to go, he added, "When it gets light, watch for a place to hole up until tonight."

Broken Knife circled the small buffalo herd. At first, a few bulls snorted and trotted off. Deciding the rider presented no danger, the bulls re-joined the herd. Slowly, he rode back and forth behind the herd until the buffalo fed in the direction Redfeather had taken.

Two hours later Broken Knife located the horses in a deep wash. As he rode up, Redfeather pointed. "With brush across here, the horses cannot get out. There is plenty of feed, but no water."

"That is fine," Broken Knife said. "They can go without water until tonight. Let's close it off and crawl up on those high ledges. One of us can sleep while the other keeps watch."

After settling down in a shallow cave, Redfeather looked at Broken Knife. He asked, "Why toward the Smoky Water. Our village is the other way?"

Reminded of his own curiosity with Lame Bear, Broken Knife smiled. "The Piegans will see the horse tracks headed toward the Smoky Water. The buffalo covered the tracks when you turned this way, so the warriors will think the Assiniboine, or Cree, stole their horses. With luck, it will be a long time before the Piegan find out two Crow took them." He paused. "I am pleased you did not kill the boy. Never kill anyone unless you are threatened."

Redfeather smiled with pleasure then shook his head. "If all white men are this sneaky, I must fast and pray for Old Man Coyote to protect his poor red children."

Broken Knife grinned. "Lie down and sleep. I will keep watch."

While Redfeather slept, Broken Knife's mind wandered. He pictured the Piegan dropping like a lead weight when struck by the coup stick – Chouteau's library and the picture of men jousting. He picked up the hardwood stick and balanced it in his hand. A smile crossed his face. Up close, it would be better than a bow or knife. He watched several hours without any sign of pursuit before closing his eyes and going to sleep.

Broken Knife and Redfeather inspected the horses. There were twenty-two fillies and mares, twelve geldings, and nine

166

stallions. One filly caught Broken Knife's eye. "Let's give Wind that red and white one."

Redfeather chuckled. "Do you know what you are doing?"

Broken Knife ignored the remark. "Tonight, we will switch riding horses and cover more ground."

By riding nights and hiding out days, they reached the Elk River in four days. Camped where they had cached the antelope meat, Broken Knife fixed something to eat while Redfeather hunted a place on the Elk River where the horses could cross without swimming.

Redfeather rode into camp at dusk. He announced, "We are three miles below the ford."

Broken Knife smiled. "It is a good thing you were leading. If it had been me, we would probably be at the junction of the Elk River and Smoky Water."

Redfeather picked up a piece of meat. "Somehow, you being lost is hard to imagine." With a grin still on his face, he added, "Let's wait until morning and cross just before the Grandfather's rays reflect off the water?"

"It is fine by me," Broken Knife said. "If they are thirsty, it will be easier to get them in the water."

Redfeather reached the ford, and without hesitating, led the mare into the river. The others anxious to drink followed. Redfeather moved the lead mare further out while Broken Knife nudged the others from behind. When the horses were full of water and started to look around, they were halfway across. A couple whirled and bolted for the bank. When Broken Knife cut them off, they returned to the herd.

Once across the river, Redfeather held a fast, steady pace toward his village. Returning from a successful war party with a first coup and an enemy's bow, he wanted his friends and everybody else to know it.

Two days later, Redfeather stopped not far from the village. He painted his face black. The sign of a successful war party.

WHISPERING WIND

Broken Knife hoped Wind would be at the lodge. It was empty. He was filling a bowl with stew when Wind walked through the entrance.

"I am surprised Broken Knife is not celebrating," she said. "The night of the dance, he liked the young women to look at him."

"Is Whispering Wind jealous?" he asked with a grin.

Wind scowled. She stomped toward the entrance.

Broken Knife jumped to his feet. "Wait! I am sorry. Please, do not be mad. I have something to show you."

Wind hesitated then turned. She looked as if she were about to cry. "I am sorry too, I am jealous. Not of the women, but because you enjoyed it." The next instant her face changed to one of excitement. "What do you want to show me?"

On the way to the horse pasture, Broken Knife marveled at the girl that walked beside him. At the flick of an eyelash, her face displayed every emotion. Happiness, sadness, defiance were all there. One minute she looked as if she could lick Red McCloud. The next a little girl to protect.

Broken Knife was glad no one else was with the horses. He did not want to share Wind with anyone. When he pointed out the filly, she cried out, "Oh! She is beautiful."

Wind held out her hand and walked toward the young mare. She rubbed the filly's nose then her ears. When the filly stretched her neck out and nibbled at Wind's hair, she glanced over her shoulder. "Please, do not trade her off."

Mischievously, Broken Knife replied, "She is not mine."

"Oh, whose is she?" she asked walking toward him.

"She belongs to a pretty girl that should not be jealous." He stared deep into her eyes. "Tomorrow, your brother will ride her. Soon, we can go on a picnic like the Walkers did."

Whispering Wind squealed. Her arms circled his neck. With her cheek next to his, she whispered, "Oh! Thank you." She pulled back slightly. "What is this picnic?"

Too flustered to answer, Broken Knife thought about what her dumb brother said about giving Wind a horse. "You will see when we go on one. If I get a hug for each horse, you can have them all, one day at a time."

Wind stepped back. She pulled a face. The sparkle in her eyes thrilled him from head to toe. Her voice soft and warm, she whispered, "We better go. The others will be waiting."

Owl Woman and Teal met them at the lodge entrance. Teal's arms circled Broken Knife's waist. Owl Woman's fingers touched his cheek. In an emotion-filled voice, she said, "Thank you for restoring my husband's pride and making my son the village hero."

Half-smiling, Grey Wolf growled, "Leave Broken Knife alone. How can we find out what happened with you two blubbering all over him?"

Broken Knife glanced at Grey Wolf. "There is not much to tell that you do not already know. Your son did most of it. He will want to tell you about it."

"Not much!" cried out the leader of many war parties. "Two first coups, an enemy's bow, two picketed buffalo horses, forty-one other horses and you return without losing a horse. Never has a Crow war party been this successful. What do you mean not much? The medicine bow excuse works outside this

169

lodge, not in it. Talk."

Broken Knife told about his part of the raid. When he mentioned using the buffalo to cover the horses' tracks, Grey Wolf chuckled. "It would have been good to see Piegan warriors racing toward the Smoky Water, while their horses were going in the opposite direction." Grey Wolf hesitated. "To lead the herd mare and have the others follow is good too. Crow warriors have always driven the horses. If any scattered, they were left behind." He smiled. "The owners were too close to round them up."

When the talk turned to individual horses, Broken Knife yawned and mentioned how good his bed would feel. He did not want to explain about giving Wind the filly.

The next morning, Teal asked Broken Knife to show her the horses. As they walked among the lodges on the way to the horse herd, many warriors hailed greetings, but no one asked about the Piegan raid. They were about to go back when Redfeather arrived with most of the village men. The Piegan horses had brought great honor to the village, and everyone wanted to be part of it.

Despite plenty of help, the men could not catch fourteen of the horses. This led to a heated disagreement among the bystanders. Some argued that, with the exception of one old mare, it did not matter whether the others were caught or not. The horses were too young to break anyway. The ensuing argument, over how young to break horses, lasted the whole afternoon and into the night. Broken Knife decided one thing for sure. They were not going to suffer from lack of horse advice.

Redfeather rode the geldings and stallions before declaring ten gelding and three stallions were well broke.

Pleased by the news, Broken Knife asked, "Would you ride Wind's paint filly now?"

Redfeather shook his head. "Are you sure about this?" he asked with a mischievous smile. When Broken Knife scowled,

Redfeather said, "Catch your brown buffalo horse and meet us at the sandbar."

When Broken Knife got to the creek, Grey Wolf held out the filly's bridle rope. With the lead rope in hand, Broken Knife looked over his shoulder. Redfeather crawled on behind him. He said, "Lead her in the water."

Redfeather slid onto the paint filly's back. Her muscles tensed. Her eyes bulged, but she did not offer to buck. After a couple of tugs on the war bridle rein, the filly bent her neck into the turn. Redfeather circled right and left in the knee-deep water until she responded to a light pull and release of the rein. Satisfied, he left the water.

"The filly is kind and responsive which may not be the best thing for you." Redfeather chuckled at Broken Knife's blank look. "If the filly threw my sister off, she would be furious and not think you are so great."

Walking back to the lodge, Broken Knife considered what Redfeather had said. He had often wondered why Wind was not married. He had asked Redfeather, but all he would say was to ask his sister. For some reason, Broken Knife did not quite dare do that.

Broken Knife entered the lodge to find Teal waiting. She grabbed his hand and sat him down on a backrest. Wind, who stood beside it, laid a new buckskin shirt across his lap. The shirt had beautiful, yet simple, porcupine quill work across the front. A six-inch strip of leather fringe hung from the shoulders.

Wind smiled at the pleased look in his eyes. "We stretched the leather where the knife lays. If this one fits, we will make a heavier one not as light colored." With a coquettish smile, she whispered, "This is for special occasions – like courting songs."

Redfeather and Broken Knife spent the next few weeks working horses. Finished riding early one afternoon, Grey Wolf said, "How about soaking in a hot pool."

"A good idea," Broken Knife replied. "We need to talk

about our horse herd."

As they rode toward the hot pool, an acrid smell filled the air. Broken Knife sniffed. He glanced around. "Is the sulfur odor why the river is called Stinkingwater?" he asked.

"Yes, it gets stronger the farther upriver you go," responded Redfeather. "In many places, there are yellow mounds with steam coming out of the ground. Some of our people are afraid to go there."

Filled with curiosity, Broken Knife said, "I would like to see this place sometime. Now, there are more important things to decide." He glanced at Grey Wolf. "There are twenty-two mares and fillies, and most of the mares are probably with foal. Before long, fur traders will come here and trade for horses. What if we keep the best stallion, the mares and fillies, and raise horses?" he asked.

"It is not for us to decide," Grey Wolf replied. "The horses are yours." Broken Knife appeared confused. Grey Wolf continued, "A war party leader is not required to give any horses away. Braves and warriors go for glory, not horses. After all, the leader's medicine made the raid successful."

"No!" Broken Knife replied shaking his head. "The horses belong to the family. Redfeather, if you want your own, take as many as you like."

When Redfeather declined, Grey Wolf beamed at his son. "Generosity is a sign of true leaders. I can trade the other stallions and any geldings we do not want for another twenty-five or thirty mares."

Redfeather said, "Broken Knife is not dumb. With Wind making calf-eyes at him, he can give the horses now or later."

Broken Knife scowled. "Be serious. What do you think?"

"The big, brown stallion is the best one, but before trading any off, we should try them on buffalo."

Grey Wolf nodded in agreement. "Scouts report a herd near Spirit Mountain. We could leave in two days."

The three men reached the lodge after dark. They were eating by the fire when Wind asked about riding her horse.

Redfeather shook his head back and forth. "You cannot even eat in peace around here without some pesky girl asking questions." At Wind's black look, he quickly grinned. "Anytime my dear sister wants to ride she can."

She smiled at Broken Knife. "Can we go on this picnic tomorrow?"

Teal broke in with, "What is a picnic? Can I go?"

Broken Knife nodded. "It is taking food to a pretty place and eating on the ground." A perplexed look crossed his face. "We do that everyday."

Wind laughed. "It will be fun."

Broken Knife and Wind were ready to leave for the picnic when Teal took hold of his hand. "I do not feel very good. Can I go another time?"

"Of course," concern filled his voice, "do you hurt any-where?"

Teal shook her head. Turning away, she smiled at Wind.

Wind and Broken Knife rode to a lake three miles from the village. While he tied the horses near a shaded cove, Wind sat on the green grass with her long legs curled under her. Smiling, she said, "It is a beautiful day. Despite the consequences, I am glad we came."

Not understanding her comment, Broken Knife asked, "What do you mean?"

Wind blushed. "Someday I will tell you. Not now."

Realizing she would say no more, he said, "In a few years, it would be good if Teal lived with Jeannie, or the Walkers, and learned the white man ways. Before then, she should learn their language. I would be pleased if you learned it too.

Whispering Wind stared at her lap. Her sad eyes raised to his face. In a voice he could barely hear, she said, "This is the first you have mentioned Jeannie since you talked of your past. You care about Mrs. Walker and Jeannie in different ways. Is

Jeannie your wife?"

"No, my life is here with you."

"Your words please me." Her hand covered his. "If I learn the white man talk can I go too?" Then, her face changed. "What if they do not like me?"

"Jeannie and Mrs. Walker could not help but like you." Pausing, he touched her cheek. "White men claim the land from these mountains to where the Grandfather rises. With treaties and trade goods, they will take Crow land as they did Delaware lands. It would be good if you and Grey Wolf understood what they say."

Wind looked puzzled. "I do not understand your words. How can the white man own land? Old Man Coyote put us here to share Mother Earth."

"The white man makes laws that permit it," replied Broken Knife. "When white men want Indian ground, their government in Washington proposes a treaty. If the tribe refuses, the government declares war and forces the Indians to mark a paper. This new paper treaty becomes law." He hesitated. "All dealings with the white man's government means the same thing – Indians lose ground."

"I do not understand any of this. If you think it is important, we will learn." Her eyes twinkled. A warm smile crossed her face. She murmured softly, "Teach me something now."

He smiled. "Try this: Wind—is—elegant." After a couple of attempts, he smiled again. "That sounds good and I agree. Wind is elegant."

"The words have no meaning for me. Your eyes say I am pretty."

"The words mean more than just pretty," he replied with an emotion-filled sigh. A serene look crossed her radiant face. The urge to take her in his arms nearly overwhelmed him. He forced his eyes away.

"Little Man mentioned a taboo about a brother and sister

talking together more than is absolutely necessary, and yet, you and Redfeather talk and joke."

Wind smiled. "My family breaks several taboos, but only in the tepee, or when no clan members are around."

Nodding, Broken Knife said, "I heard a woman say she could not do something because she has a hole in her moccasin. Does that mean something?"

Wind's eyes twinkled. "She is admitting that she is not a virgin, or if married, has been unfaithful to her husband. Does the white man have such women?"

"There are wanton women, but they are regarded as bad, especially by other women. What do the Crow men do with unfaithful wives?" he asked.

"It depends," she replied. "A husband might offer a wife to a visitor, or a friend, but if she is unfaithful without his knowledge, he may beat her, or tell her to go and find another husband. My people do not consider a loose woman bad, just weak in matters of the flesh." Wind hesitated before saying, "A man and a woman may live together, but that does not mean there is affection between them. Many men treat wives worse than slaves. Still, there is no place in our clan for an unmarried woman. During a bad hunting season, the hunters of a lodge may not find enough meat to feed a woman that should have her own husband. Since my people have had horses, it is better. Before then, many of our people starved to death each winter."

"A Delaware gave gifts to the parents of the woman he wished to marry," Broken Knife said. "Is it the same with the Crow?"

"Yes and no. A man may offer a present, even a horse, to gain a loose woman's favor. If she accepts and spends the night with him, she is his wife. If a man seeks a chaste woman for his wife, he must offer presents to her family. This in turn gives him the right to marry her sisters.

"Marriage is essential for the well being of my people. The woman has children to strengthen the tribe and maintains a lodge for her husband. He must provide food and hides and protect his family. A husband cannot do this if he is doing woman's work, and his weapons are in the lodge. The husband and wife have their duties. Each is necessary for the other's survival."

"Little Man mentioned that in some Crow clans a warrior must count a coup, or have seen twenty-five snows, before he can marry."

"Yes, this also strengthens the tribe by insuring the young man is brave and healthy."

Wind took his hand. "To answer your question about the moccasin. Only a virtuous woman can participate in a religious ceremony. The chosen woman will be asked if she is morally good. If she is not, the woman will say there is a hole in her moccasin, and she cannot take part. The woman dares not lie because someone will expose her. Since more women have low morals than high ones, a pure woman is greatly revered by my people."

He started again to ask why she had never married, but recalling her reaction about being jealous, he decided against it. Instead, he said, "Grey Wolf would not give Owl Woman as a present."

"No, and my mother has never been unfaithful. Since you will not ask, I will tell you. There are no holes in my moccasins."

"You are right." His fingers touched her cheek. "I would not have asked. My giving you a horse and bringing you on a picnic is what you meant earlier?"

Wind's eyes reflected her smoldering love. "Yes, some may gossip. I do not care."

Broken Knife felt a warm rush of blood. He placed his hands on her shoulders. As they searched the depth of each other's eyes, a flock of squawking ducks rose off the lake.

Broken Knife jumped to his feet. He could kick himself for being careless, but how did he know a big eyed, long-legged girl with a soothing voice would be so distracting? Grabbing his bow

176

and Wind's hand, Broken Knife led her to the horses. Untying them, he handed her the lead ropes. "Stay behind this rock."

Not daring to go too far, he walked a short distance and listened. If Indians had scared those ducks, they were probably after horses. When the ducks landed in the same area, he went back. He boosted Wind onto the filly.

"Stay on the edge of the meadow. If I holler, go to Grey Wolf as fast as you can."

At the edge of the village, Wind slowed her horse to a walk. Broken Knife rode beside her. She took his hand. "I showed you how I feel. You did not answer."

Broken Knife pressed her hand to his cheek. He gazed deep into her eyes. "You know how I feel. Since the day your beauty took my breath away, it should have been obvious. My eyes see only you."

Whispering Wind sighed. "For me, it is the same."

"Tell Grey Wolf and Redfeather to watch our horses. I am going back to look around."

Broken Knife went after his coup stick. Following the Piegan horse raid, he had removed the feathers and practiced until he could use it with speed and dexterity. He had even named it, Matilda.

Near a spring where the ducks flew up, Broken Knife found a partial track. Not far away was a broken twig and crushed grass. Satisfied he had the direction of travel, he went to where the creek emerged from a deep canyon. He waited behind a boulder. Broken Knife had not been there long when a Cheyenne come out of the trees. The warrior carried a water bladder in his hand. Filling the bag, he went back into the trees. Broken Knife followed him to where the tops of several pines were tied together – a war lodge.

Four Cheyenne stood outside the lodge. One was Bird Tail.

Broken Knife smiled. He stepped from behind a tree.

A young brave grabbed his bow. Bird Tail knocked it

down. "Excuse Walking Rabbit. This is his first war party. He is nervous."

After exchanging the news since parting at the Hidatsa village, Broken Knife said, "It is late. Crow warriors will be coming." He ginned at his friend. "The Crow are meaner than a silver bear. My brother should try for Pawnee or Arapaho horses."

Bird Tail laughed. "It is good advice. Eagle Plume says you are coming to the fall trade fair. We will see you then."

Reaching the outlet of the lake, Broken Knife saw Redfeather and several warriors racing across the meadow. Redfeather slid his horse to a stop. "We were worried."

"There was nothing around here, so I checked up the creek."

When Broken Knife entered the lodge, Wind threw herself into his arms. She buried her head in his shoulder.

Broken Knife kissed her forehead. He pressed her soft hair to his cheek. "Grey Wolf, I wish to speak with Wind."

Grey Wolf nodded his approval.

Outside, he and Wind walked hand in hand to a log overlooking the moonlit river. He sat and stared at the shimmering water instead of facing her. "I want you for my wife more than the sacred breath within me." He sighed. "I am afraid."

Wind snuggled closer. She laid her head on his shoulder. She asked, "Why are you afraid? "It is certainly not of me."

"I wish us to walk life's journey together, but that may not be possible. A Cheyenne war party was above the lake. What if it was Pawnee, or Shawnee, looking for me? If my enemies find me, they find you." He touched her cheek. "My fear is for you."

Wind kneeled before him. The Grandmother's rays bounced off her tears. She held his hands, and looking longingly into his eyes, she whispered, "Life itself is fear – fear of starving, fear of freezing, fear of enemies – but you should not fear life. The Spirits decides if a human's walk through life is a long or short journey." Warm moist lips brushed his cheek. "Our walk should start now."

Broken Knife buried his head in her shoulder. Anguish and joy flooded his senses. He straightened up and pulled her onto the log. "The white people have a custom where two people pledge to marry, but wait awhile. Could we do that?"

Wind sighed, "It is a bad custom. I warn you now. You are the one that wishes to wait."

"What do you mean?"

"Do not worry. You will find out," she said as she pressed closer.

He placed a hand on each side of her head. "At the lake, I started to show you another custom." Gently, his lips touched hers.

Wind stiffened. Confused, she started to pull back. Then, she relaxed and soft warm lips parted. When Broken Knife raised his head, she smiled. "I am glad the white man has one good custom."

Back at the lodge, Broken Knife explained their decision. He apologized for not offering presents first.

Grey Wolf laughed. "Since the first day, my daughter's eyes have seen only you. The problem my daughter and conniving wife had was making sure you felt the same. Why do you think they spent half a day dressing her for your first feast with us?" he asked.

Teal ran over. She gave him a big hug. "I helped too. I was not really sick." After a playful spat on the bottom, he kissed her cheek. He took Owl Woman's hand in his. "About the mother-in-law taboo...."

Redfeather interrupted. "That has been decided. If no one is around, you can talk to each other. However, there is a very good and old Crow custom never to be violated. You must treat your brother-in-law with respect and kindness."

Broken Knife cuffed him side the head. "You are not my brother yet."

Sitting by the fire with Wind snuggled beside him, Broken Knife thoughts turned to Bright Star and Jeannie. A few nights ago, he had looked into one of the green stone and told them of his love for Whispering Wind.

THE VALLEY

Dew clung to the grass when Broken Knife, Grey Wolf, and Redfeather left to roundup the horses. On the way, Broken Knife told about the Cheyenne war party.

Grey Wolf said, "You were wise to say nothing. Two warriors with my son lost relatives to the Cheyenne. Wind said you wanted her and Teal to learn the white man tongue. Would it be good if we all learned?"

"Yes, the white man will come. Many of them do not speak straight. Our people should understand their words," Broken Knife replied.

It was mid-morning before the travoises were loaded. With the prospective buffalo horses and seven travoises, it looked as if a village was moving, not a single family. The hunters passed small buffalo herds, but Grey Wolf kept going. Near the forks of the Stinkingwater River, Broken Knife saw yellow sulfur mounds along the banks. Several places, yellow mud flowed into the water (Cody, Wyoming, Colter's Hell).

Grey Wolf stopped above the mud pots on the south fork of the Stinkingwater. Sitting around the night fire, Grey Wolf talked about the mountain behind the mud pots. His people called it the Mountain of Spirits. Many believed evil spirits lived there.

Grey Wolf led the procession several miles up the south fork to a broad green valley where they would hunt. As soon as they pitched the lodges, Teal and Wind gathered wood. Owl Woman used the shoulder blade from an elk to scrape a fire pit.

Broken Knife picketed his horse then took a shovel from one of the travois. Walking over to Owl Woman, he placed a hand on her shoulder. With a smile he said, "I will do this." When he began digging in the soft ground, Owl Woman stared at the shovel. By the time he finished the two- by six-foot pit, everyone had gathered around.

Grey Wolf's voice was full of scorn. "My son is right. The white man is devious. He takes horses and blames it on the Assiniboine. Now, he corrupts our women." He cracked a smile. "Soon Indians will have fat wives and no horses."

Owl Woman snapped back, "If the husband complains, he better learn to make his own moccasins."

Broken Knife chuckled. He touched her cheek. "I have many things to make work easier. Now that there is a pit, Wind can help me build a meat smoking table over it." With a saw and ax, he and Wind went into a nearby stand of pines. They were barely out of sight before he felt Wind walking on his heels. Her firm breasts rubbed against his back. He turned to stare across the top of her head.

"Wind, stop this. You are driving me crazy."

She tilted her head back. "Stop what?"

He did his best to sound angry. "You know very well what I mean."

Wind raised on tiptoes. She gave him a soft, lingering kiss. Pulling back, she said, "I have no idea what you are talking about."

Broken Knife showed Wind how to hold and work a crosscut saw. They cut four posts, four short crosspieces, and a pile of seven-foot poles. Back at the camp, he set the four corner posts. Wind helped him lash the poles in place. When they finished, a double-decked table covered the new fire pit.

After three days of hunting, Grey Wolf took Broken Knife aside. "We are about through trying the horses on buffalo. There is enough meat, but we need salt. Four days journey from here is a salt pit," stoically, he went on, "Wind can show you the way."

Broken Knife studied Grey Wolf. Why Wind instead of Redfeather? He shrugged his shoulders. If he could have her alone for eight days, who cared.

Wind and Broken Knife started upriver with three packhorses. As they followed the stream, the surrounding country changed. Rolling hills turned into mountains; tall pines replaced junipers and aspen.

Broken Knife stopped his horse. When Wind rode beside him, his hand found her hand. Ahead of them were gray, snow-capped peaks beneath a deep blue, cloudless sky. These were the Stony Mountains. Speechless, he and Wind viewed the spectacular surroundings for several minutes.

Camp was setup on a bend of the stream. A majestic granite peak stood beyond the running water. Broken Knife added wood to the night fire before sitting beside Wind. He asked, "Why did Grey Wolf send you?"

Wind recoiled as if he had hit her.

"Oh! Wind," he moaned, "I am sorry."

She nestled on his lap. Her bottom lip quivered. She whimpered, "You did not want me to come?"

Broken Knife's voice cracked. "Not want you! I never want us apart."

Wind pecked his cheek. She jumped to her feet.

Frowning, he growled, "Wind, if you do not stop this teasing, I will paddle you."

Wind stood between him and the riverbank. Framed by brilliant stars, the vivid peak, and moonlit water, her feet moved slightly. Narrow hips swayed. The doeskin dress slowly settled to her ankles. Bathed in the Grandmother's luminous

183

light, she held out her hands.

Broken Knife moaned. He stepped forward. With the full length of Wind's warm body pressed against his, the fears, the doubts vanished. Nothing mattered except the beauty that Wind alone possessed.

The Grandfather's rays lit the snow-covered peak before Broken Knife stirred. Suddenly, he raised up. Wind was gone. He jumped to his feet and called her name. There was no answer.

Grabbing his bow and a handful of arrows, he raced to the river. She was not there. Frantic, he ran down the trail. At the first river bend, he heard laughter. Wind stood in a pool of water.

Giggling, she asked, "Why the bow? As you see, I hide nothing."

Broken Knife flung the bow and arrows aside. With one stride and a long jump, he pushed Wind's head under water. When he let her up, she gasped for breath. Before she could protest, his mouth covered hers.

Wind lay on the grassy riverbank. Her head on Broken Knife's chest. Idly, her hand roamed the inside of his leg. She raised her head and softly kissed him. "What a strange husband. He tries to drown me, then smothers me, and then so gentle."

His lips conveyed all of the love and tenderness he had to give. "Please, never do that again. When I saw you were gone, the image of my father and the vultures returned."

Wind touched his face. Her voice softened. "I am sorry to have frightened you."

He gave her bare bottom a playful spat. "It is getting late, we better go."

She snuggled closer. "My father is worse than my mother. The salt cave is three river bends away."

Before he could respond, she said, "I am sorry we tricked you. You wanted us to wait, but my father does not understand waiting. Neither do I. Life's breath is a gift to be taken away at anytime – now, tonight, tomorrow – a Shawnee, a Pawnee, a silver bear, or many other things could kill us. Why wait for what the Spirits decide?"

Broken Knife pulled her into his arms.

That afternoon, Broken Knife walked to a nearby creek. The creek appeared to come directly out of the distant mountain. Deciding the water must come from a big spring, or out of an angled canyon, he went back to see if Wind wanted to ride over and look.

The riders followed the creek to where the water came out of a narrow, steep-walled canyon. Intrigued by the canyon entrance, they tied the horses and walked up the winding streambed. They had gone a good half-mile when the narrow canyon made a sharp turn and opened into a broad, green valley.

The valley looked to be a mile wide and nine- or ten-miles long. Beaver dams dotted the willow-lined stream as it meandered through the lush meadow.

Wind and Broken Knife climbed onto a flat bench that run along the West Side. Across the meadow, the ground rose in a gentle slope. The slope ended at a rock ledge that stretched the full length of the valley. Scattered stands of aspen and an occasional pine covered the side hill.

Broken Knife took Wind's hand. He led her along a small stream toward a vertical rock outcropping. At its base, water bubbled out of a shallow depression. Dense dark timber covered the steep slope behind the spring.

Wind let go of his hand and picked a pale-blue lupine blossom. "My husband is silent." When he did not respond, she sighed, "It is beautiful, but we better go. It will soon be dark."

Broken Knife said little on the way back. After eating, he sat by the fire. Tired of his silence, Wind nibbled his ear. "What a husband! One night and he is tired of me."

He pulled her onto his lap. "The valley is in my thoughts." Hesitating, he added, "Before coming to the Crow, I stood across from where the Smoky Water empties into the Father of Rivers. As I stood there, I felt a force drawing me toward these mountains. Standing by the spring with you beside me, a deep inner peace surged through me. I felt at home." He pulled her head on his shoulder. "The valley is to be our home."

"Live there instead of going to the Wind River?" she asked.

"Yes, everything we need is there." Broken Knife rose with Wind in his arms. He shook her playfully. Lying her on the soft robe, he whispered, "Now, let's see who is tired."

Broken Knife tossed out the last of his morning coffee. He picked up his bow. "There were deer tracks along the river. Let's go after one?"

Crouched behind a large rock, Broken Knife and Wind were above a brushy gully with deer tracks going into it. They had not been there long when Wind touched his shoulder. A four-point buck stood below her. With Wind between him and the deer, he could not shoot without standing up.

Wind took the bow from his hand and notched an arrow. Slowly twisting sideways, she shot. The deer bounded into the brush. Growling, she said, "I missed."

Broken Knife could only stare.

Wind's face clouded. "You are angry because I can shoot?"

"Angry, I could not be happier."

Wind's voice softened. "We were afraid you might not want a wife that shoots better than most warriors."

"I still cannot believe it. How did you learn?"

"My father let me shoot Redfeather's first bow. After that, I coaxed until he made me one. At first, the boys laughed, but finally, they let me enter the contests." She hesitated. "When I started to win, the boys were angry and chased me away."

186

In English, he blurted out, "That is why young men have not been lined up ten-deep outside your lodge."

Wind stared at the ground. "I do not know the words."

Broken Knife raised her chin. "I am sorry." His eyes beamed with pride. "Now, I understand why you are not married."

The look on Wind's face made him go warm all over. She sighed, "I waited for you."

Broken Knife held her a long time then said, "You did not miss."

The buck lay under a bush. Its mouth and nose full of pink, frothy blood. After they cleaned the deer, Broken Knife buried its heart. He held Wind's hand and thanked the deer's spirit not only for food, but for the honor of witnessing his wife shoot.

Broken Knife lay on his back. He stared at countless bright stars. His thoughts were on the remarkable girl beside him. Overcome by a deep, powerful surge of emotion, he raised his left hand toward the yellow ball. Silently, he asked the Grandmother to watch over the best of all possible things – Wind.

"My husband cannot sleep?" Wind asked as she raised her head off his shoulder.

Gently, he pulled her head back down. "My love for you blocks out the dangers. If I forget Lame Bear's teachings, you could be taken away. I asked the Grandmother to protect you."

Wind adjusted to the curve of his body. "No one hunts here except our people. Only the Crow and Shoshone use the salt cave. Now, go to sleep." She slid up before he could close his eyes. Her lips covered his. "That is for caring." About to lay back down, she whispered, "In case you start worrying again, the Snakes are not a danger. They reach the salt pit by coming down the canyon." With a titter, she settled down beside him.

Where the salt-pit trail left the river, Broken Knife saw horse tracks and day-old manure. He waited for Wind to ride beside him. He held out his bow and quiver. "Someone is at the salt pit. Hang these on your saddle and stay close. If there is trouble, go straight to Grey Wolf. I will meet you there."

A short ways up the trail, Broken Knife saw two men and a woman seated by a fire. He raised his hand, then signed that they had come for salt.

One of the warriors stepped away from the fire. He gestured that they were welcome.

Wind rode closer. She whispered, "Snakes." Motioning her to wait, he clasped his neck and rode forward.

The warrior smiled. "You are the white man that took the Crow girl home."

"Yes, my name is Broken Knife. You speak Hidatsa well."

"My brother, Slow Fox, and I were Hidatsa captives for many years. I am Black Brush. We must leave, but you are welcome to our fire."

"Thanks." Broken Knife hesitated before asking, "Have you heard anything about white men going to the Big Salt Water?"

Black Brush replied, "A few weeks ago, Bannock warriors visited our village. One of them said the whites had reached Cameahwait's band on the Lemhi River. He is the brother of Charbonneau's woman, Sakakawea. Cameahwait furnished horses and a guide to take them through the mountains to the Nez Perce."

Broken Knife smiled. "Thank you. It is good the white men found friends among your people."

Pointed sticks and round stones were scattered around the salt pit. Generations of Indians had used them to pry out and crush chunks of salt into fine granules. Finished loading the horses, Broken Knife asked, "Could we head straight back? I am anxious to tell Grey Wolf about the valley."

With first a pout then a smile, Wind nodded.

The stillness of early evening had arrived when Wind and Broken Knife rode into the camp. Grey Wolf walked out to meet them. "We are happy you are back, but not this quick." With concern, he asked, "Did everything go well?"

Broken Knife's scowl broke into a grin. "Just as you planned, Father."

Owl Woman left the drying racks. She hugged Wind. With a sly grin, she said, "My son looks well. How is your wife?"

"She is just fine," he replied with a chuckle.

Redfeather and Broken Knife went to turn out the horses. As soon as they were out of sight, Broken Knife cuffed him side the head. "You should have told me Wind could shoot a bow."

"I wanted to, but my sister and mother said slow death by starvation was my fate if I did." He broke into a grin. "I will give you one warning. Watch out for her temper."

Broken Knife looked skeptical. "How can anyone so gentle have a temper?"

Redfeather chuckled. He did not answer the question.

"Did Redfeather tell you about the horses?" Grey Wolf asked.

"No, we discussed other things," Broken Knife replied.

"Only two would not run beside the buffalo," said Redfeather.

The news pleased Broken Knife. After talking about the horses for a few minutes, he told Grey Wolf and Redfeather about the valley. When Grey Wolf mentioned he would like to see it, Broken Knife said, "Let's go in the morning."

The riders sat on the bench and looked over the meadow before riding toward the far end. Where the bench merged into the meadow, they saw flattened grass. A good-sized elk herd had bedded down there. Fresh tracks showed the elk had gone into the heavy timber. Riding on toward the end of the valley, they heard elk calves barking for their mothers.

The stream entered the valley through a narrow gorge. Water flowed around and under huge boulders. It would be impossible to get in the valley from this end. Grey Wolf pointed toward the East Side. He said, "Strong winds blow pine trees over, roots and all. Deep snow bends aspen trees. There are few signs of this happening here." He paused to look further. "Winters are mild in this valley. Have you seen signs of anyone being here?"

Broken Knife shook his head. "Eventually, my enemies will find me. In open country, we are all in danger. Here with only one entrance to guard, it would be safer. What if we leave some of the horses now, and after the trade fair, move here?"

Grey Wolf considered the idea. "It is a serious matter. The family should see this place then decide."

Pleased, Broken Knife replied, "That is wise."

Three days later they moved the camp to where Broken Knife and Wind had spent the first night. Grey Wolf and Redfeather tied heavy pieces of sagebrush to the ends of the travois poles. The irregular marks left by the brush would disappear with the first rain.

Broken Knife and Redfeather went ahead to roll rocks, move others, and free driftwood. Where two different rock ledges ran into the water, they cleared a trail on the opposite bank. By the time they reached the valley entrance, a good trail, wide enough for three- to four-foot wide travoises, weaved in and out of the streambed.

Owl Woman looked across the valley. She smiled at Broken Knife. "My husband is right. With water and wood this close, there will be fat wives."

Broken Knife was helping unload the travois when Teal and Black Dog came running up. She had found a cave. She insisted they come and see it. Broken Knife saw what she had found was a twenty foot deep rock overhang. With a solid wall and door across the narrow front, it would make an ideal storage room.

He explained what he had in mind. The whole family was anxious to help, but mostly, they watched. Tools to cut and flatten logs were unknown to his helpers. After the wall was up, Broken Knife used thick leather straps to hang a pole door.

When he finished, not even a field mouse could get inside.

Sitting around the night fire, the family was proud of what they had accomplished, but a little sad to be leaving the next morning.

Arriving at the Whistling Water village four days later, Broken Knife learned a party of white men had come. When Broken Knife found Larocque, he had just finished trading for a stack of buffalo robes. Broken Knife said, "It is good to see you."

Larocque jerked about. He broke into a grin at sight of Broken Knife. "The English words scared me. I hoped you would be back before we left. How are you?"

"Fine, how is the trading?"

"All right, but not many beaver robes or plews."

"Plews?" Broken Knife asked.

Smiling, Larocque replied, "Beaver pelts. I will be through in a few minutes. Could we talk later?"

"Our lodge is straight across the village. Come over when you finish."

Broken Knife met Grey Wolf and Redfeather coming from checking on the mares. "Larocque will be here in awhile. If he needs horses, we can trade for guns, powder, lead, and anything the women want."

"That would be good," Grey Wolf said.

The three of them were discussing what horses to trade when Larocque walked up. Broken Knife smiled. "This is Grey Wolf and Redfeather. My wife's father and brother."

The trader broke into a grin. "A wife already?" he asked.

"Yes, wait until you meet her. She and her mother are inside the lodge. Are you hungry?"

"No, I ate before coming over."

Larocque shook his head at sight of Wind. "I have never seen such a beautiful girl."

Broken Knife smiled his thanks. He turned to Wind and Owl Woman. "This is Larocque, a trader from the North."

When they both said hello, a surprised Larocque bowed. Broken Knife grinned at the trader's face. "They are learning English and can say quite a few words already." He pointed at a backrest. "You did not sound enthusiastic about the trading."

"I just wish there were more robes and plews. The ones I am getting are the best quality I have seen. If you can get some of the warriors to trap, I will leave five traps and send more back." Grinning, he added, "I understand the Piegan are missing horses and that you have plenty. Would you like to trade off a few packhorses?" he asked.

Broken Knife looked surprised. "That is the first I have heard of missing horses. I found ours wandering on the plains."

Calling Grey Wolf over, he explained what Larocque wanted. When Grey Wolf finished talking, Broken Knife said, "Grey Wolf will talk to his clansmen about trapping. As for horses, take all you want." He broke into a grin. "I can always find more."

Smiling, Larocque nodded his thanks. "I brought you some bow wood. What else do you need?"

"Guns, powder, lead. I will ask Wind about lodge things and make a list."

"Most of my goods are gone, but there is plenty of everything at the Hidatsa village. Would it be possible to get six horses now? We are leaving for the Yellowstone tomorrow."

"Redfeather can bring them to your lodge early in the morning. Are you sure that is enough?" Broken Knife asked. "You can have more if you need them."

"Six should be plenty, but thanks for the offer." Larocque bowed to the women. He held out his hand to Grey Wolf. When Grey Wolf looked surprised, Broken Knife laughed. He explained shaking hands was the white man's sign of friendship.

Owl Woman watched the trader walk out. "He is different from Jessaume and Charbonneau. Hidatsa women say they think that Indian women are for the taking. Wind must be careful if those two are at the trade fair."

ARIKARA WARRIORS

Broken Knife and Wind rode ahead of the slower moving travoises. Topping a low rise, they saw Little Man riding toward them. As he rode up, Little Man said, "Yesterday, hunters reported you would be here by noon." He smiled at Wind. "My friend has new responsibilities."

A silly grin crossed Broken Knife's face. "It is good to see you. This is my wife, Whispering Wind."

"You are Grey Wolf's daughter?" Little Man asked.

"Yes," Wind replied. "My parents and brother are coming behind us. I want to thank you for the many presents of food your wives sent us."

Despite the teasing, Broken Knife was glad to see Little Man's family, but sad to learn that Wilted Flower and her newborn son had died during childbirth. When Wind said they had a horse and salt for them, Little Man looked at Broken Knife. "The Piegan declared war on the Assiniboine for stealing their best horses. The Assiniboine swear they did not steal the Piegan horses. Now your wife gives one away."

Broken Knife smiled. "Do not worry. This one came from the Pawnee."

Wind and Owl Woman pitched their tepees close to Little

194

Man's lodge. Nearby were Crow, Assiniboine, River Crow, and Cheyenne tepees. Broken Knife asked Cheyenne friends about Eagle Plume and Bird Tail. Warriors said they were coming by way of the Heart River.

After two days of the trade fair hubbub, Broken Knife could not stand the commotion any longer. He sat in the lodge sanding a new bow when he heard Teal scream. She burst through the entrance. Teal sobbed, "White men have Wind."

Broken Knife grabbed his coup stick. He followed Teal to the other side of the Hidatsa village. Forcing his way through a group of bystanders, he saw his wife backed against a dirt walled lodge.

Wind faced three traders. She held her skinning knife low and ready. Her dark defiant eyes begged the traders to come closer.

"You filthy Pork Eaters. Leave her alone."

The men whirled. Two of the traders held knives. The other one gripped his wrist. His shirt was covered with blood.

The shortest trader glared at Broken Knife. "Ya're thet guy w'at lives wit' 'ese filthy beggars, ain't ya? Looky w'at she did ta Jock just fer touchin' 'er. We'll fix 'is 'ere up'ity bitch, 'hen settle wit' ya fer callin' us Pork Eaters."

Broken Knife's eyes turned to stone. "Try me first!"

Snarling, the short trader stepped forward. Matilda's knobbed-end broke his forearm. As the trader fell, the other knife-holder lunged over him. Broken Knife moved aside. Sliding his hands together, he laid the coup stick across the man's broad back. The last trader dropped his useless hand. He pulled a knife. Broken Knife hit him beside the head.

Before he could turn, Wind was at his side. Her skinning knife still held low and ready.

Redfeather and several armed Crow and Cheyenne warriors pushed through the crowd. He touched his sister's shoulder. "Are you all right?"

Wind's eyes softened, she nodded.

Redfeather looked at Broken Knife. He broke into a grin. "I warned you about making her mad." He glanced at the coup stick then at the traders. "My brother does not understand counting coup. You touch the enemy, not kill him."

Broken Knife ignored Redfeather's remark. He went to the whimpering man. Yanking him to his feet, he said, "You touch an Indian woman again. I will kill you." To make sure the trader understood, he rested Matilda on the protruding bone.

The man's eyes rolled back. The moaning stopped.

A tall Indian stepped out of the crowd. "I am Big Hand. I would talk with my Delaware brother."

Surprised, Broken Knife nodded. "I will meet you at the river crossing in a few minutes."

As the Delaware walked away, Teal asked, "What did you call those men?"

"The canoe men that work for the North West are called Pork Eaters because they live on lyed corn and grease. To call a trader a Pork Eater is the worst insult. It is like saying to a Crow that he has no relatives."

With an arm around Teal, he smiled at Wind. "Now that you have spoiled my peaceful afternoon, let's go home." Wind grimaced then smiled. She took his hand.

Soon after the three of them reached the tepee, Grey Wolf and Little Man came through the entrance. Gasping for breath, Grey Wolf asked, "What happened?"

Wind scowled. "One of those men touched me."

Broken Knife answered his question. "She was about to carve up three traders." His eyes twinkled. "If you had told me how mean a daughter you raised, I would have stayed here."

Grey Wolf beamed at his daughter. He glanced at Broken Knife. "For someone that hates crowds and talk, you are always in trouble."

"Do not blame me. Your daughter started it."

Broken Knife turned to Little Man. "I am going to meet

Big Hand at the river." He pecked Wind's cheek. Jumping back, he asked, "Will you help Grey Wolf keep Wind out of trouble while I am gone?"

A moccasin hit him in the back before he reached the door. Glancing over his shoulder, he chuckled at the scowl on his wife's face.

Big Hand greeted Broken Knife. He said, "Three Shawnee are here. They wish to smoke with Wind-of-Death's son."

On the way to the Shawnee's lodge, they saw Larocque coming toward them. He asked, "Is Wind all right?"

"Mad as a wet hen, but not hurt," Broken Knife replied. "I had no idea she could be such a hell-cat."

Larocque grinned at Big Hand and Broken Knife. "I have heard it said, 'the prettier they are, the meaner they are'." The grin left his face. His voice turned flat. "It might have been better to have killed them. Wind severed the tendons in Jock's wrist. You crushed his jaw. The one you hit across the back can only mumble and roll his head. That shattered arm will have to come off. They will be lucky to reach Fort Assiniboine alive."

Broken Knife's eyes turned hard. "There is a difference in Indian women. Traders better learn to recognize it. If Wind had been hurt, Crow and Cheyenne warriors would have killed every white man here, and with the exception of you, I would have helped." Displaying a broad grin, he clapped his friend's shoulder. "Come with us. We are on our way to meet some Shawnee."

Broken Knife greeted the three warriors. When he said Lame Bear's vendetta died with him, the Shawnee called Fast Elk nodded. "Drouillard sent word you want peace with my people." He held out his pipe. "What you did today is good for all Indian women."

After smoking, Larocque and Broken Knife left Big Hand with the Shawnee. They went to the trader's lodge. Larocque pointed at several packs. "Everything Wind wanted is there. I am leaving tomorrow afternoon. You can pick those up anytime today or in the morning. He paused. "I might not be back again; whoever takes my place will find you."

"Are you quitting the fur trade?"

"I am thinking about it."

Broken Knife glanced at the four guns leaning against the packs. Larocque smiled. "Those are Pennsylvania rifles, not trade guns. I had to borrow a couple from other traders."

"I am glad horses are worth this much," Broken Knife said. "It looks as if raising them will be profitable."

"Are you considering that?" Larocque asked.

"We have thirty-five mares and a stallion now. From the looks of the mares, we will have at least thirty foals in the spring."

Larocque's voice expressed his interest. "Most traders prefer packhorses to using the Souris River, but there is never enough horses here. If the Indians quit burning the grass, they could keep more." The trader went to a trunk. He returned carrying a pistol. "You mentioned Wind could shoot a bow. Maybe, she would like this."

Broken Knife balanced the pistol in his hand. "Thanks for the pistol and getting us rifles. Someone at the Crow village will get word to us if you come next summer." He held out his hand. "You have been a good friend."

Broken Knife returned to see Wind flitting about as if nothing had happened. He and Grey Wolf were talking about leaving when Redfeather burst through the entrance. "Hidatsa warriors say three Shawnee are here."

"I have already smoked with them," Broken Knife replied. "Larocque has our goods ready. We were just talking about going home." He paused. "I hate to leave until Eagle Plume gets here."

"A few more days will not matter," Grey Wolf said. With a smile, he added, "It is good about the Shawnee."

"It does not mean I can be careless," said Broken Knife. "There are always hotheads seeking glory."

"Redfeather and I will get the things from Larocque's. We will see you in the morning," Grey Wolf said.

Under the robes that night, Broken Knife felt Wind's slender body quiver, and he realized the traders had bothered her more than she let on.

He pressed her head to his cheek. "Larocque is sorry about today."

Tears were close to the surface when she whispered, "Why did that man touch me where only you have?"

"Remember when you said many women are weak in matters of the flesh, and some men give their wives or daughters to visitors?" He felt her nod. "That is the Indian women traders have seen. They assume all Indian women are that way." Gently kissing her, he continued, "If you went to St. Louis and saw only the white women in saloons, you would think all white women were that way. Do you understand what I am trying to say?"

Wind sighed. "I think so." When he placed his lips on her forehead, she raised her head. "Anyone touches me again, I will say my jealous husband goes a little crazy." As eager lips met, the day's problems floated away on the night breeze.

The next morning when Grey Wolf came into the lodge, Broken Knife asked if he had heard anything concerning Eagle Plume. "No, but the talk is about yesterday," Grey Wolf replied. "Every warrior here wants to call you friend."

Broken Knife looked thoughtful. "That is good. I thought it best to tell only Little Man and Eagle Plume about the valley. Maybe, a few others should know. The Piegan will eventually find out that we took the horses. It would be good to have a warning if our enemies come after us."

"I saw the Snake, Black Brush. He is a good man. I will tell him and a couple of others."

Broken Knife went to the entrance and looked out. "I am getting worried. If Eagle Plume is not here by in the morning, I am going to find him." He glanced over his shoulder. "Let's try out the new guns?"

"Can I shoot too?" Wind asked.

Broken Knife smiled. "Everyone should learn. If Owl Woman does not want to shoot, she and Teal can learn to load them."

Grey Wolf started toward the entrance. "I will find Redfeather. We will meet you by the big, lightning-scarred cottonwood tree."

Broken Knife showed them how to measure the powder and tamp the ball properly. Once they could load the guns, Owl Woman and Teal went back to the lodge. As they left, Broken Knife setup several targets for Grey Wolf and Redfeather. Taking Wind down by the river, he handed her the present from Larocque.

Not sure the pistol was real, she asked, "Does this shoot?"

Laughing, he took the pistol. After loading it, he showed her how to aim it then said, "Try it and see."

Wind shot at a piece of driftwood caught on a rock. The ball missed the stick, but it chipped off a big hunk of rock. She broke into a big smile. "By the time we reach the Stinkingwater, I will hit the mark." She rubbed the shiny barrel. "Why did Larocque give this to me?" she asked.

He touched her cheek. "Larocque wanted you to know all white men are not alike."

Wind started to re-load the pistol when someone yelled. Turning, they saw Little Man coming toward them. He shouted, "Eagle Plume is hurt."

Running behind Little Man, Wind and Broken Knife followed him to his lodge. Entering the lodge, Broken Knife glanced at Big Woman. "How is he? Where are Dove and Waving Grass? What about Bird Tail?"

"A ball passed through Eagle Plume's shoulder. Another one went through his leg, but it did not break the bone. He sleeps from loss of blood." Pausing, Big Woman said, "The Arikara have his wife and daughter. Bird Tail is dead."

Broken Knife stared at the wall. "I must go after them."

Wind put her arm around his shoulder. "I am going too." Broken Knife started to object. Wind's eyes hardened. "You are my husband. I am going. Dove and her mother will need me."

Little Man grinned at the look on Wind's face. "Hidatsa hunters saw Arikara not far from where they found Eagle Plume. The Arikara were from the middle village on the Smoky Water. We can be there in six days."

"I suppose saying you are not coming is the same as telling Wind she cannot."

Little Man started to answer. Wind beat him to it. "We are both coming. Little Man and I can hold the horses while you go into the village after them."

"What makes you think I am going into the village?"

Confidently, she replied, "You will take them as you did the Piegan buffalo horses."

Broken Knife looked gruff. "Little Man, a Delaware beats a wife that gets bossy. What would you do?"

Little Man shook his head. "Occasionally, a wife may need a beating, but after what Wind did to that trader, I do not want to be around if you try it."

Broken Knife grinned at his friend's remark. "We will talk to the Cheyenne and get them to let us go alone."

Teal hugged Broken Knife's waist. She sobbed, "Where is Dove?"

"Do not cry, honey. We will find her." He turned to Grey Wolf. "In the morning, Wind and Little Man are going with me after Dove and Waving Grass."

Grey Wolf nodded. "We did not see you leave. When two Cheyenne came looking for you, the warriors told us what happened."

Broken Knife rummaged in a pile of robes. He pulled out two bows. He held out the longest one toward Redfeather. "I would like to take my brother, but Grey Wolf needs you more."

Redfeather nodded his understanding. "We will be careful," he said as he and Grey Wolf went out the entrance.

Broken Knife handed the other bow to Wind. She pulled back the string. "It is easier to pull than my horn bow. I will take it and my pistol with us."

Wind was too excited to sleep. She wiggled closer. "Please do not be angry, or worry. Several different Crow women have gone on war parties. I promise to do exactly as you say."

He kissed her softly. "I am glad you are coming. Now, go to sleep."

The travelers stopped at dusk the first couple of nights, so Wind could shoot her pistol. After the second night, she hit the tree every time. Broken Knife watched her close and soon understood why. She had stopped sighting down the barrel. As the gun came level, she fired.

Little Man led them to a ravine three miles from the Arikara village. After the evening meal, Little Man described the village and the surrounding ground. When he finished, Broken Knife decided to leave. He could lay on the nearby knoll and watch the village until he found out where Dove and Waving Grass were being held. Little Man held out a bag of bear grease. "This will keep mosquitoes and flies away. Around Arikara villages, they are bad."

"Thanks, I will bring Dove and Waving Grass upriver tomorrow night. If you hear shots, meet us along the river bank."

Wind walked out of the camp with him. "Do you want my pistol?" she asked.

"It makes too much noise. Matilda will be better." He held her tight. "Please, do not worry. You are in more danger. Warriors watch closer away from villages than in them."

After a lingering kiss, she whispered, "I am glad we did not follow that silly white man custom and wait."

He touched her cheek. "So am I."

Above the village, Broken Knife hid his bow on the riverbank. He pushed a log into the water and floated past the dirt lodges. Swimming ashore, he crawled on top of the nearby knoll. Within minutes, he was asleep.

The buzz and bites of mosquitoes woke him. He quickly rubbed on the bear grease. Circling above the Arikara village, he saw black swarms of mosquitoes and blow flies. The paths between the lodges had built up by walking over animal carcasses and accumulated filth. The strong odor of the bear grease did not block out the pungent smell coming from the village. It was the dirtiest place he had ever seen.

The sun was high overhead when Broken Knife heard a loud screech. Below him, an old woman sitting on a lodge roof screamed at a young girl. The girl rolled off the roof and went in the lodge. It was Dove.

The cloud-darkened village had been quiet several hours. Rubbing on more bear grease, Broken Knife walked through the stockade gate. He stopped outside the lodge Dove had entered. Standing by the entryway, he listened several minutes before going inside.

Coals from the fire pit gave off enough light to see Dove. She slept tied to a lodge pole. Broken Knife covered her mouth until she recognized him. Cutting the ropes, he took her outside. He asked, "Where is your mother?"

"She was sent to a trader's lodge," Dove replied. "I know where it is."

Broken Knife recognized the sounds coming from within the lodge. He made Dove wait by the entrance.

A blazing fire lit the lodge interior. Two men and Waving Grass were on a buffalo robe.

Broken Knife stepped forward. A back and forth swing of Matilda crushed each man's skull.

Waving Grass gasped. Squirming from under the dead man, she curled herself into a ball. Broken Knife lifted her chin. She moaned softly. Her pitiful sounds and forlorn face brought on an overwhelming rage. It was several seconds before he said, "It is me, Broken Knife." Waving Grass cringed. He touched her shoulder. "Broken Knife, it is Broken Knife."

She cried, "Oh! Broken Knife."

Helping Waving Grass up, he held out her dress. "We must go."

Dove gasped at sight of her mother.

Broken Knife's finger touched her lips. "Be still. Take your mother and walk toward the stockade gate. If anything happens, run. Little Man is waiting for us upriver."

At the gate, an Arikara stepped in front of Waving Grass. As his gun came up, the warrior fell to the ground. The gun went off.

Broken Knife pulled his knife out of the dead man's chest. Straightening up, something knocked him down. He jumped to his feet. A huge dog with yellow eyes and exposed fangs growled. The dog leaped again. Broken Knife stepped aside. He laid Matilda across the dog's back. Between the gun going off and the yelping dog, the village was awake. Sounds of alarm come from every direction. Screaming the Cheyenne battle cry, Broken Knife ran through the gate.

Catching up with Waving Grass, he put his arm around her waist. She gasped, "Leave me! Save Dove."

"Be quiet, save your strength. When I stop for my bow, you keep going."

Broken Knife grabbed his bow. He tilted his head to listen. The village turmoil made it hard to hear anything. It sounded as if the Arikara were behind the stockade waiting for the Cheyenne attack. He caught up with Dove and her mother just as Wind and Little Man rode out of the willows.

Wind smiled with relief. "We heard the shot."

Little Man boosted Waving Grass on the extra horse. Broken Knife lifted Dove on his. He squeezed Wind's hand. "Walk upriver until you reach thick willows then turn and head for the camp, I will meet you there."

Broken Knife crawled into a large clump of willows. Just

before sunrise, thirty-five to forty riders passed. They were too busy hitting their horses to see any tracks. He watched until they rode out of sight.

Wind held out a bag of water and a piece of jerky. Between gulps, he asked, "How are they?"

"Nothing serious, only bad bruises."

"We are safe for awhile," he said. "The Arikara warriors went upriver." Smiling, he gave her a big hug. "You hid the trail well."

Broken Knife started toward Waving Grass. Wind stopped him. "She told her captor that she would give herself if he would spare Dove. He gave her to those traders for the night. When she fought, they took turns holding her down."

Tears filled Wind's eyes. "She is ashamed you saw her."

"What about Dove?" he asked.

"She was not hurt." Hesitating, Wind said, "Waving Grass has washed herself twice. Still every few minutes, she wipes her hands and face with bunches of grass. Those traders must have treated her awful."

As they walked over, Wind said, "The warrior at the gate killed Bird Tail and took them prisoner."

Dove threw herself into Broken Knife's arms. She sobbed as if her heart would break. Crying herself out, she stepped back. "How did you find me?"

"I heard the old woman hollering at you."

A trace of a smile appeared on her face. Dove said, "I was thinking of you lying on the hill at the Pawnee village, and did not hear the old woman tell me to fetch water."

Broken Knife kneeled in front of Waving Grass. He raised her quivering chin. He gasped at sight of her swollen eyes and bruised face. His throat filled. He could not speak. When his hand started to shake, he reached out to Wind. She led him to a grassy place beneath a tree. Holding him until the quivering stopped, she asked, "What is it?"

"I saw my mother last night," he replied, "and again just

now."

Wind touched his cheek. "You were not there for Bright Star. Her spirit is pleased you were for Waving Grass." She cradled his head on her lap. "Go to sleep, I will watch."

Broken Knife woke with the Grandfather high overhead. He raised up. Little Man was asleep under the next tree. "There is nothing moving," Wind said with a reassuring smile.

"Bright Star appeared while I slept. She is pleased about Waving Grass. Mostly, she is happy to have such a wise daughter." He squeezed her hand then said, "I will watch while you get them ready. We will leave soon as it is dark."

Little Man and Wind were saddling the horses. Broken Knife was about to join them when he saw an Arikara in the next swale. The warrior looked around then turned and went back.

Broken Knife hurried to the horses. "Let's get out of here. An Arikara was just over the hill."

"Do you think he saw us?" Little Man asked.

"I could not tell for sure. Take the lead. I will bring up the rear."

After a couple of miles, Broken Knife rode beside Little Man. "Keep going, I will see if they are camped for the night or following us."

Little Man said, "It will not be long until rain washes out our tracks."

Broken Knife glanced at the clouds. "Are you sure?"

"Yes, but maybe not until morning," Little Man replied. "Straight ahead is a flat butte with ledges around it. On the west side is a rock cave. There are several deep overhangs near it. We can wait out the storm there."

Broken Knife pulled up his horse. "See you at the cave." As he rode by Wind, he growled, "Do not argue. Follow me."

Wind's curiosity got the better of her. She asked, "Why did you let me come?"

Pleased, Broken Knife grinned. "If I had said you could

not come, we would have argued, and you would have come. It is nice to surprise you."

"You really did." Wind squeezed his hand. She shook her head. "Just when I had decided my husband was a slow learner." Broken Knife tried to push Wind off her horse. Laughing, she fell in behind.

Close to where he had seen the Arikara, he handed his horse's bridle rein to Wind. "Wait in the trees. I will look around."

A pawing horse led Broken Knife to sleeping Indians. There were twenty-two. The Arikara warriors had not posted a guard. He cut the horse's picket ropes. Riding one horse and leading another one, he screamed the Cheyenne battle cry. When he trotted away, the loose Arikara horses followed.

A heavy overcast dimmed the morning light. Glancing over his shoulder, Broken Knife could make out the Arikara horses following them. He smiled at Wind. "Let's separate. One of us might see a deer."

In the distance, he saw Wind wave. As he rode up, she said, "Over the rise, five buffalo are in a mud wallow." Wind lowered her eyes. She said, "Like a dutiful wife, I will hold my husband's horse."

Broken Knife buried an arrow in a yearling's heart. Wrapping the hump-ribs and tongue in a piece of hide, he tied the bundle across Wind's saddle. As he finished, the clouds opened. Rain poured down in sheets. They hurried toward the caves. The loose Arikara horses turned their backs to the storm.

Broken Knife heard Little Man yell over the pelting rain. Little Man cried, "You two look like drowned rats." He led them to a deep rock overhang. "The cave is just ahead. Go stand by the fire while I tie your horses with mine."

Little Man entered the cave shaking his head. "You find more horses."

Laughing, Broken Knife said, "There were twenty more, but they stopped when the storm hit."

Broken Knife told Little Man about the sleeping Arikara. When he mentioned the Cheyenne war cry, Little Man smiled. "Arikara are a cowardly bunch. Those warriors are probably praying for the Cheyenne to go away."

It rained that day and most of the night, but there was dry wood under the overhangs and plenty to eat. Leaving the cave, Broken Knife saw the twenty Arikara horses with the ones Little Man picketed the previous night.

Waving Grass looked like a different person. The swelling had left her eyes. The yellowish bruises were fading out. She even had an occasional smile.

The fifth night after leaving the cave, Little Man pulled Broken Knife aside. "We will be at the village by noon tomorrow. I can find out about Eagle Plume and bring back dresses."

"Good," Broken Knife said, "before you go, I want to thank you."

In a somber voice, Little Man replied, "Why? If it had been Little Spring and Spring Run, you would have done the same, and Eagle Plume would have helped."

Broken Knife walked to the fire. He smiled at Wind. "Take Dove for a walk while I speak with her mother."

Sitting beside Waving Grass, he said, "No one will hear how I found you."

Tears filled her eyes. "Some women say they would die before being taken captive."

Broken Knife took hold of her hand. He said, "Women who say that have never faced the choice. The brave ones would have done as you did. You were a mother protecting her daughter, nothing more. Any man would be proud to have a wife with such courage."

Waving Grass laid her head on his shoulder. She unleashed a dam of tears.

With the early light of dawn bathing the hills, Little Man rode into camp. He handed a bundle to Waving Grass. "You

208

and your daughter must look nice when you see your husband."

Crying with happiness, Waving Grass and Dove run to the creek.

Little Man smiled at his friend. "Eagle Plume can walk with a forked stick." He glanced at the Arikara horses. "Several Cheyenne braves are coming to drive the horses into the village."

"Good," Broken Knife said. "They were all here this morning."

To the exuberant Hidatsa, it did not matter it was Cheyenne women. All that mattered was their village had achieved a victory over another Indian village. Everyone shared the glory. To the Cheyenne leaning on a forked stick, it mattered a great deal.

ABSAROKA WINTER

Eagle Plume could barely hobble about, and Broken Knife did not want to leave him. Staring into the fire, he thought about the valley and all that needed to be done. Wind came through the entrance and dropped down beside him.

"Let's put Eagle Plume on a travois and take him with us?" Before he could reply, she said, "It would be good for Waving Grass too."

Pleased by the suggestion, he pecked her cheek. "You always know when I am worried. Have you mentioned this to Waving Grass?"

"She wishes to go," replied Wind.

Broken Knife drove fifteen Arikara geldings out of the Hidatsa village. He had given the other five to Little Man. Behind him, Wind and Dove each led a packhorse. Waving Grass walked beside the horse pulling Eagle Plume.

Between the Little Missouri and Powder rivers, Crow hunting parties were seen almost everyday. The hunters kept them supplied with liver, tongues, and hump-ribs. Not having to hunt, it took fifteen days to reach the valley entrance.

Grey Wolf, Owl Woman, and Teal waited at the last bend in the narrow canyon. After a tearful reunion, Teal and Dove ran ahead. Broken Knife saw the girls go into a new lodge. He glanced at Owl Woman.

"It is for Eagle Plume," she said. "Redfeather's friend White Cloud brought word four days ago you were coming. He and my son went upriver. They should be back before long."

Broken Knife and Grey Wolf drove the Arikara horses into the meadow. Tails over their backs, the geldings ran toward the other horses.

Broken Knife asked, "Can you trade them for more mares?"

Grey Wolf shook his head. "Why mares? Every time you go away, you come back with more horses. That is better than raising them." Smiling, Grey Wolf replied, "Usually a good gelding is worth two mares. My son and White Cloud can ride them before we decide on the ones to trade off." Perching on a nearby rock, he asked, "What about the Arikara?"

When Broken Knife finished telling what happened, Grey Wolf nodded. "It is good you brought Eagle Plume here."

"Waving Grass needs time to heal also," said Broken Knife. "Have you been able to hunt?"

"With two or three more hunts, there will be enough pemmican and smoked meat for winter." Broken Knife glanced toward the horses. Grey Wolf said, "The horses stay in the upper end of the valley. If any come this way, Black Dog chases them back. At first, I did not understand giving away our dogs." Pausing, he said, "One dog is better than many."

"It is good Black Dog keeps the horses back," said Broken Knife. "But, we should still block off the canyon."

Perplexed, Grey Wolf asked, "Why? The horses cannot get near it."

"Keeping enemies out is more important. The Arikara do not worry me. The Piegan are a different matter. When they find out where their horses are, they will be after them."

"Could we pile rocks and driftwood between those big boulders?" asked Grey Wolf.

"A wall and gate would be better," replied Broken Knife. "I can make a harness out of thick leather. We can use the grey mare to pull logs there and build one."

Grey Wolf shook his head. "What is this harness?"

"It is hard to explain. After I make one, you will understand how it works."

"Will this take long?" asked Grey Wolf. He had a worried tone to his voice. "The buffalo are drifting toward the Plains."

"A day or two." Broken Knife hesitated. "If White Cloud would help hunt, Wind and I could build the gate."

White Cloud agreed to stay, and the hunting party left the next morning. Besides the three hunters, Teal, Dove, and Owl Woman went too.

As soon as the hunters left, Broken Knife started on the harness. He used two-inch wide strips of heavy leather to make a breast collar, belly band, and tugs. He adjusted the harness to fit the grey mare then fastened a thirty-inch pole between the tugs. Finished, he showed Wind how to tie a log to the makeshift singletree.

Wind drove the mare and pulled logs to the canyon. Broken Knife joined them together to form a strong barricade. When they were through, a six-foot wall with gun ports and a gate blocked the trail.

Broken Knife wiped a smudge off Wind's face. He gave her a squeeze. "Now we need a place to store guns and powder."

"Leave the guns here?" she asked.

"Yes, then if there is trouble, we can come straight here," he replied.

The entrance gate finished, Broken Knife and Wind used the mare to drag downed trees from behind the spring onto the bench. Wind cut and burned branches, while Broken Knife sawed the trimmed trees into fourteen-inch blocks. Not long after they started, Waving Grass came over. She watched awhile then asked if she could help. It was the first time she had shown an interest in anything.

Under the robes that night, Wind asked, "Do all white men gather wood?"

"Most do," he replied. "Tomorrow, I will split the blocks into smaller pieces. My frail wife needs wood close to the lodge."

Wind poked him. "Wood is a serious matter. One winter, the Camp Chief chose a bad place, and three mothers froze to death hunting enough wood to keep their babies warm. In the dead of winter, the Camp Chief moved the village to a better wood place."

He kissed her tenderly. "This winter you can burn all you want."

Broken Knife split the blocks into four or five pieces. Waving Grass and Wind stacked the cut wood under rock overhangs and big branched pine trees. The three of them had worked a couple of hours when Eagle Plume hobbled over and sat under a nearby tree. "Is this for winter?" he asked.

"Yes," replied Broken Knife. "Waving Grass, do you want to show Eagle Plume the storeroom?"

Eagle Plume returned from the cave. He watched a long time. "These are things white men do?" Eagle Plume asked. Broken Knife nodded. His Cheyenne brother lapsed back into his silence.

The split wood was stacked and still no Grey Wolf. Broken Knife was about to go look for the hunters when Black Dog barked. Running to the gate, Broken Knife and Wind saw Grey Wolf coming around the bend. Wind opened the gate. As the riders passed, she smiled at the curious expressions.

After answering many questions, Broken Knife said, "Grey Wolf, let Wind take your horse. There is something else." As the others rode into the valley, he showed Grey Wolf the gun and powder box. "With Black Dog's warning and extra guns here, a war party will not get beyond this wall."

Grey Wolf nodded. He opened and closed the gate several

times. "You said a wall and gate. I did not see it this way."

A thoughtful Grey Wolf did not say anything on the way back. When he and Broken Knife walked up on the bench, Grey Wolf stopped. He stared at the stacked split wood. Grey Wolf looked back at the gate. He looked up the valley at the horses. He looked back at the wood. In a solemn voice, he said, "The path we walk here is no longer the path of my fathers and those that walked before. I believe it is a good path."

Touched by Grey Wolf's words, Broken Knife did not reply.

On the way to his tepee, Grey Wolf said, "Tomorrow, we should go after serviceberry branches. We will need snow-shoes. This winter, we can straighten the rest for arrow shafts."

"How about making a fish trap first?" asked Broken Knife.

"What is that?"

"To catch fish with." Puzzled, Broken Knife asked, "What do the Crow use?"

"Crow do not eat fish," replied Grey Wolf. "My people believe fish are unclean." He broke into a grin. "Since fish live in water, I have never understood this."

"We can catch a few. If you like the taste, we can smoke more for winter."

Grey Wolf cut slender willows while Broken Knife weaved the sticks into a strong circular trap. "How does that catch fish?" asked Grey Wolf with skepticism.

"You will see." Setting the woven-willow trap in shallow water, he yelled for Wind to bring the girls and a bag of salt.

Broken Knife explained what he wanted. Dove, Teal, and Wind piled rocks on each side of the trap. Going upstream, they dragged heavy sticks beneath the undercut banks driving the fish toward the trap.

Several large trout turned back at the narrow opening of the trap. Trying to stop them, Wind and the girls became so excited Owl Woman jumped in the water to help.

Soaked fish-chasers watched Broken Knife lift out the trap. It was full of fish. While he showed Wind and Owl Woman how to clean fish, Grey Wolf built a fire and the girls cut forked willows.

Dove and Teal placed pieces of fish on the forked sticks and held them over the coals. When the pieces turned a golden brown, Broken Knife sprinkled on salt. He passed the fish around. Another trap full was eaten before everyone had enough fish.

On the way back, Wind picked a handful of yellow flowers. At the lodge, she put the petals and some dried herbs in a kettle of boiling water. Broken Knife asked what she was doing. Wind looked at him with sorrowful eyes. "I am making a herb tea for Waving Grass. This morning, I saw her crying. At first, she would not say why, but I coaxed until she told me." Her voice softened. "The Arikara gave her the pox."

Broken Knife's eyes reflected his sadness. "She has suffered enough without this. Will the herbs clear it up?"

"Yes, but not the shame."

After hauling a travois load of serviceberry and chokecherry branches into camp, Redfeather and Broken Knife checked on the horses. Two stallions had been fighting. Watching both horses limping, Redfeather suggested they geld the bald-faced one. "You catch him," Broken Knife said. "I will get Grey Wolf and a rope."

Redfeather led the stallion to a clean grassy area. Using the rope, Redfeather and Broken Knife pulled the stallion to the ground. After tying the legs up, Grey Wolf reached over the hip and cut out both testicles. "Was that deer sinew you tied the blood vessels with?" Broken Knife asked.

Grey Wolf replied, "Deer and antelope sinew are used the most, but some warriors squeeze the cord between two sticks then cut below the sticks. The Gros Ventre warrior that showed the River Crow how to geld believed tying the cord was the best. He thought if the ends were tied with antelope sinew, the horse run like the antelope."

Eagle Plume hobbled around without the crutch. He looked better, but he said his leg throbbed at night. Finally, a firm voiced Owl Woman told him to stop trying to walk so much.

A few days later, she scolded him again. He replied in a dry voice. "It is no wonder Crow husbands fight hard. With such bossy wives, they are afraid to go home if they lose."

Everyone, but Waving Grass roared. She frowned. "Owl Woman is teaching me to be a Crow wife. My husband better pay attention." She glanced at Wind and grinned.

A warm smile passed between Wind and Broken Knife. It was good to hear Waving Grass joke.

As the Grandfather peeped over the mountain, Broken Knife woke Wind. "Get ready. It is time to practice. I will go after Redfeather."

Redfeather and Broken Knife used the knife. Wind her wooden bow. When Redfeather switched to his bow, Broken Knife watched Wind. He marveled at how fast she released the arrow. His voice full of pride, he said, "You are really good."

"This new wooden bow is easier to pull." A faint smile covered her face. Looking deep into his eyes, she said, "Teach me to throw the knife."

The look on her face tightened his stomach muscles. How could he refuse her anything? He showed her how to hold the knife and talked about being relaxed. As he droned on, Wind took the knife. Balancing it in her hand, she threw at a nearby tree. The knife stuck.

Broken Knife tried to look black. He growled, "It took me two footraces and an hour's lecture before I hit the tree."

Wind broke into a smile. "Remember, you are a slow learner. Besides, men try too hard." She kissed his cheek. "And beside that, I had a better teacher." Not knowing what else to say, Broken Knife retrieved the knife.

The arrival of shorter days and morning ice brought bright colors to the valley. Aspen trees and maple bushes glowed with brilliant colors. Within one stand of aspen, the leaves ranged from dark to pale green, light to bright yellow, and an occasional tree of varying shades of orange. The maples were brownish to bright orange and red. The brilliance of a few bushes appeared as if the bushes were on fire. Surrounded by dull-brown grass, pale yellow willows, and green pine trees, the vivid leaf colors were spectacular.

The halcyon days of a mountain fall hung over the valley, still Eagle Plume stayed near the lodge. Broken Knife decided it must be his shoulder. He found Eagle Plume sitting on the sunny side of the tepee. "Wind and I are going to the stream. You and Waving Grass come along."

Eagle Plume smiled. "Are you a bossy Crow woman now?"

"Never mind, come on."

Eagle Plume looked surprised to see Wind carrying a bow and arrows. He said nothing. At the stream, Eagle Plume dropped on the first log they saw.

Broken Knife squeezed Wind's hand. "Take Waving Grass after some willow grouse." Wind and Waving Grass went up the trail. Broken Knife looked at Eagle Plume. "Does your shoulder bother you?" he asked.

Eagle Plume stared at the ground. "I cannot pull my bow." His voice full of anguish, he asked. "How will I feed and protect my family?"

It was several minutes before Broken Knife said, "When Wind returns, you can try her wooden bow. It pulls easier than a horn bow."

The two men had talked sometime when Eagle Plume saw Wind and Waving Grass coming toward them. They both carried chickens. "Does she shoot so well?" he asked.

"Yes, and they will be shot in the head." Broken Knife paused. "I have often wondered what Lame Bear would think of her."

Wind laid the birds down. Broken Knife pointed at a

nearby stump. "Let Eagle Plume try your bow."

Eagle Plume notched an arrow. He tried to draw the bow, but his shoulder gave way. The arrow dropped to the ground.

Broken Knife said, "That is all right. We practice with the knife, bow, and gun every morning. Tomorrow, you can try a gun."

Eagle Plume shook his head. "Even after you showed us, I could not hit anything."

"Ours are not trade guns. These shoot straight."

The next day, Broken Knife took Eagle Plume to the entrance gate. Eagle Plume studied each detail of the gate. He asked, "This keeps enemies out?"

"Yes," Broken Knife replied. Removing a gun and powder from the storage box, he said, "We can shoot through those holes, and in this narrow canyon, no one will be able to get by here." He held out the gun. "Hit that branch in the stream."

Eagle Plume balanced the gun barrel on his left hand. With the gun butt firm against his right shoulder, he pulled the trigger. He missed the target, but he did not care. The recoil of the gun had not hurt the injured shoulder. After a half-hour of practice, Eagle Plume had hit the branch several times.

Grinning from ear to ear, Broken Knife said, "Tomorrow, you can try Wind's pistol."

Eagle Plume shook his head. "Not tomorrow." He pointed up the valley. "Lodge smoke lays across the meadow. Tonight, snow will come." He asked, "What is a pistol?"

Broken Knife held his hands twelve-inches apart. "It is a gun this long. You can hold it with one hand. If shooting the rifle had hurt your shoulder, Wind was going to give you her pistol."

Eagle Plume touched Broken Knife's arm. "I am grateful to you and Wind."

"Why? We are brothers."

Large, white flakes floated on lifeless air. As if a little kid, Broken Knife held out his hand. He watched drops of moisture

218

cover his palm. Going inside, he broke into a wide grin. He placed his cold, wet hand on Wind's bare back.

Wind yelped. She threw off the sleeping robes. Snickering at her black look, he said, "Come and see how pretty the snow is."

Wind scowled and tried to wiggle under the warm robes. Laughing, he scooped her up as if a baby. He carried her outside. She kicked and screamed while he offered his Morning Prayer. Beads of moisture clung to her brown body. Going inside, he set her by the fire.

Wind rested her chin on drawn up knees. Her lip quivered. She whimpered, "Why did you do that?"

With a twinge of guilt, he was about to go after a blanket when he saw Wind's eyes sparkle. The guilt quickly passed. He replied, "Because you are an old grouch."

Sweetness covered her innocent face. "Me! How can you say such a mean thing?"

The lazy snowstorm turned into a raging blizzard. Looking outside, Broken Knife could not see the other lodges.

Wind sat beside her husband. Her head rested on his shoulder. "When we have beaver, I will make fur-lined mittens and laced moccasins."

"As soon as the storm breaks, Redfeather and I will start a trap line. Besides what we need, I would like enough for a beaver pack."

Wind looked up. "What is that?"

"Sixty pelts pressed into a bundle," he replied. "Limit the number we trap, and there will always be beaver here."

Wind touched his hand. "My husband is happier here than in the Stinkingwater village."

It was some time before he said, "After living with the white man, an Indian village did not feel the same."

Wind touched his cheek. "I miss my aunts and uncles, but life here is better. There is stacked wood to burn, a storeroom full of food, and tables instead of flat rocks to work on. These are all good things."

Broken Knife said, "Here, our path is between the paths of the Indian and white man. As Grey Wolf said, it is a good path for us to walk. Still, deep inside there is something missing."

Wind laid her head on his shoulder. "You are my husband. That is all that matters."

Evening light crept into the lodge, and Broken Knife realized they had talked the day away. He added wood to the fire. The flames gained new life. Dancing shadows flitted across the skin wall of the tepee. When two joined, he looked at his beautiful wife. Her eyes reflected his desires. He gently carried her to the robes.

The new day began crisp and cloudless. Broken Knife stepped out into crystal-clear air. Covering his eyes with his hand, he waited for his pupils to accept the dazzling light. Pure white snow blanketed the valley. Twelve- to fourteen-inches of snow buried willows and bushes and bowed the pine tree limbs. Not a track or sound marred the white splendor.

Broken Knife shouted for Redfeather to bring snowshoes. He went back inside after the beaver traps. Leaving the traps and sharpened stakes at the first beaver dam, Redfeather and Broken Knife went to check on the horses. In a sheltered aspen grove, the horses pawed two foot of snow to uncover thick tufts of grass.

Broken Knife showed Redfeather how to set a trap. Finished setting the tenth trap, they waded out of the water. The frigid air froze their buckskin leggins solid.

Wind gasped at sight of her stiff-legged husband waddling through the entrance. She tossed wood on the fire. Helping him move near the flames, she pulled off the board-stiff leggins. Wind wrapped him in a buffalo robe then handed him a bowl of herb tea. He could not stop shaking long enough to take a sip.

Wind kissed his cheek. She giggled. "The Grandmother punishes you for taking her favorite daughter out in the snow."

Scowling, Broken Knife tried to answer. His clicking teeth and Wind's laughter were the only lodge sounds.

With bright stars overhead, the snow crusted. The next day, Redfeather cleared a slide through the trees, across the bench, and onto the meadow. Teal and Dove slid down the steep slope on an elk hide. The girls were having so much fun that Eagle Plume and Gray Wolf tried it.

On stormy days, the men straightened arrow shafts and talked. One of the first questions was about the white man building things. When Broken Knife said white men fenced fields, and even built wood lodges for horses and cows, it went beyond their understanding.

"Why build for animals?" Grey Wolf asked.

"White men do not share land," Broken Knife replied.

Eagle Plume looked puzzled. "The ground is Mother Earth for all to share."

"That is the Indian belief, not the white man. If need be, groups of men fight to protect white man lands. These men are soldiers. Right now, the government claims the land from this valley to the Father of Rivers."

Eagle Plume bristled. "The Cheyenne will fight."

"So will the Crow," added Grey Wolf.

"You can fight, but as the Delaware and Shawnee are finding out, you cannot win. White men have been fighting thousands of years. Despite always clamoring for peace, they are efficient killers." Broken Knife looked intently at his father-in-law and brother. "An army chief receives many honors if he destroys an Indian village. He would be disgraced, even punished, if he touched an enemy, or took an enemy's bow, and went home. Count coup on a white man, and he will shoot you in the back as you walk away. The white man fights to win." Pausing, he said, "He does not leave the battle because it is a bad day, or he wants to hunt."

Grey Wolf and Eagle Plume busied themselves running arrow shafts over grinding stones. Neither one spoke the rest of the day.

During the worst cold spells, snow squeaked when they walked on it. With plenty of wood, the lodges stayed warm. A day or two after a bad storm, it usually warmed up, and in the afternoons, water dripped off the tree branches. With fast flowing water and abundant grass under the snow, the horses did not lose weight, and most of the mares appeared to be with foal.

By mid-winter, sixty beaver skins were pressed into a pack. The day after they finished trapping, Redfeather and Broken Knife snowshoed out of the valley. Four cows and two yearling buffalo were eating the grass between the water and the snow-covered riverbank. They shot the two yearlings. The choice cuts of meat were pulled across the crusted snow on the hides.

Eagle Plume and Grey Wolf met them at the gate. Grey Wolf smiled at the meat bundles. "I am surprised you found buffalo."

"The buffalo were on the Stinkingwater not far from the entrance," replied Redfeather. "Broken Knife thinks maybe a few winter near the boiling mud pots where the ground is warm."

As he helped pull the meat across the frozen snow, Grey Wolf shook his head. "No one has gone to the mud pots in the winter to see."

Redfeather and Broken Knife hung the meat bundles in trees near the storeroom. Come morning, the meat was frozen solid, and it was moved inside. The storeroom held beaver tails, ducks, grouse, buffalo, and elk meat. Salt put out for the horses kept a small elk herd in the valley. Killing an occasional elk with a bow and arrow did not scare the others away.

Winter left almost as fast as it came. The first day that robins chirped the arrival of spring, bare ground appeared on the side hill.

Wind and Broken Knife checked on the horses, and on the way back, stopped to watch the Grandmother rise above the

East Rim. Her rays flooded the valley with soft light. It was a warm evening and with the chores done, they sit on a boulder. Wind's head rested on her husband's shoulder. A herd of elk fed out on the bare slope. She snuggled closer. "It has been a good winter."

"The next one will be better," replied Broken Knife. "I am going to build us a cabin."

Puzzled, Wind straightened. "What is that?"

"A cabin is made of logs. Inside, it stays warm and dry no matter what the weather is outside. You can have a place to cook along one wall."

"Not use our lodge anymore?" Wind asked.

"We can have both," he replied. A summer lodge and a winter cabin."

Slowly, she rubbed against him. She whispered, "There are things you might forget in a cabin. We better go practice."

SHINING MOUNTAINS

The valley filled with the birth and growth of a new season. Broken Knife and Wind watched two foals play. He reached for her hand. Squeezing it, he said, "I am getting restless. What if we go see the country to the West of here?"

"I would like that," Wind replied with a squeeze of his hand. She asked, "While we are gone, could we speak English?"

"Why?" he asked. "You speak better than many whites now?"

An innocent smile crossed her face. "When we visit Jeannie and Mrs. Walker, I wish to speak properly." The look on her face made him nervous. He gave her a wary look. What was she up to now?

Wind said, "Let's talk to my father then go see Eagle Plume and Waving Grass."

"How about visiting Black Brush?" asked Grey Wolf. "His people know the Wind River and Teewinot country the best." He drew a map on the ground. "Above where we come in the valley is a good trail to the Big Horn River. Follow the Big Horn to a deep gorge in the Owl Creek Mountains. Across those mountains is the Wind River valley. Not far from where the Wind River turns into a gorge is the Popo Agie River. The

Shoshone camp along the Popo Agie. From there, Black Brush can tell you where to go."

Wind and Broken Knife left the next day. The riders with two packhorses followed Grey Wolf's trail into Boulder Basin where snow covered the north-facing slopes. Occasionally, drifts covered the trail. Reaching the Greybull River near a place Grey Wolf had called Meeteetse, Broken Knife shot an elk for camp meat. The next morning, the travelers headed southeast to where a hot spring emptied into the Big Horn River.

Near a large pool of water, Broken Knife unpacked the horses while Wind fixed something to eat. After eating, they soaked in the warm water. Above them, the water bubbled out of the ground boiling hot.

Broken Knife and Wind rode out of the morning mist into bright blue sky. Following the Big Horn River to a narrow walled canyon, they forded the river. A winding trail took them to the head of a red canyon. From the ridgeline, the riders overlooked a long green valley. A solid wall of granite peaks bordered the valley on the west. Far to the left, the river below them made a sharp bend and disappeared. Grey Wolf had mentioned that when the Wind River came out of the narrow canyon it was called the Big Horn River. Not far from where the river turned into the gorge were the hazy outlines of smoke columns, an Indian village.

Wind and Broken Knife stopped a half-mile from the village. Firing his gun, he tossed a blanket in the air.

Several warriors rode out to meet them. One rider held up his hand. It was Black Brush. While they ate, Black Brush told them news of Lewis and Clark. The expedition had reached the Big Salt Water. By now Black Brush thought, the expedition should be back among the Nez Perce.

Broken Knife nodded his appreciation. "Have any been hurt or killed?"

"No," he replied. "But, last fall the men had a hard time crossing the Bitterroot Mountains." Pausing, he said, "The guide that Cameahwait sent with them lost the snow-covered trail over Lolo Pass. Finally, Clark took some men and went ahead to find something to eat."

Broken Knife set his bowl down. "Can you tell us about the Seeds-kee-dee? Does it flow to a bay of salt water? Are there other names for it?" he asked.

"Black Brush nodded. He replied, "Bearded men followed it here long ago. Since then, some have called it Rio Spanish, or River of the Spanish. The Spaniards called it Rio Verde."

While the men talked, Wind and Black Brush's wife fixed a wikiup near Black Brush's lodge. Wind was in bed when Broken Knife entered the traveling lodge. She listened patiently as he began telling her what he had learned. When he started on how the Seeds-kee-dee must join the Colorado. She wiggled her warm body against his. "Hush, there are better things."

The next three days rain came in sheets and torrents. Bad weather gave Broken Knife ample opportunity to learn about the trails and rivers of the Wind River and Teewinot ranges.

Before Broken Knife and Wind left, Black Brush said, "Our village and the Crow are friendly. Some Snake tribes, especially the Bannock, are not. When you leave the Seeds-kee-dee and head for the Snake River, watch out for Gros Ventres. The Big Bellies travel through that country to visit their cousins the Arapaho whose territory is southwest of here."

The riders followed the Wind River. Sagebrush and junipers covered the slopes on the right. To the left were low mountains with rock ledges and pines. Behind these, an occasional granite peak was seen. The travelers crossed the Wind River where a stream from the south end of the Absaroka Mountains joined it. Turning south towards the head of the Seeds-kee-dee, Wind mentioned game might be scarce higher up, and they should stop and hunt.

A faint look of fear crossed Broken Knife's face. He said, "Do not kid me. You want to pester me in that warm-water

226

pool below here."

Wind scowled. She stuck her tongue out before stopping in a small grassy meadow.

Broken Knife and Wind separated to hunt. The hunters had not gone far when Wind shot a spike elk. The young bull was on a steep game trail in thick pines.

Broken Knife crossed the creek. He helped her cut out the choice pieces. After leaving an offering to the elk's spirit, he said, "If you had been a Delaware, Lame Bear might have taken you instead of me. If he had, I would have been jealous, and your poor mother would have been stuck with you."

Wind gave him a coquettish look that gave him butterflies in the stomach. "You did not seem to mind last night. Tonight, you can watch the horses while I swim."

Grinning, he said, "You know I will."

Broken Knife and Wind followed a steep trail through heavy timber and rock ledges. At timberline, the travelers rested the horses. They were on the edge of a vast mountain park. Blue, red, and pink flowers, low-growing willows, and green grass covered the broad open ground. At the far end of the park, a sheer-walled mountain towered above the alpine meadows. Beyond the flat-topped mountain of granite were the peaks and pinnacles of the Wind River Mountains.

The riders rode to a nearby lake. The placid water reflected every detail of a nearby pine. Broken Knife said, "Larocque talked about a lake in Canada that was like this one. He said it was called Lake of the Woods."

Wind sighed, "It is beautiful. Let's stay here tonight?" After erecting a brush shelter, Wind pointed at a high ridge. "We could ride over there and see the country to the West."

Broken Knife and Wind weaved up the sagebrush slope. Ahead of them, a dark point appeared on the skyline. As the riders continued, the spot grew larger and larger. Reaching the crest, the riders sat spellbound. Across from them ten granite peaks with many small spires and pinnacles rose off the floor of a pristine valley. A winding river flowed along the foot of the peaks. Two deep, rock-lined canyons not more than eight- to ten-miles apart separated the imposing group from other mountains in the snow-capped range. First seen as a small dot on the skyline, the tallest glacier-carved peak dominated the other nine.

Broken Knife's words broke the spell. He said, "That has to be the Teewinots and the Snake River."

Wind nodded. She did not comment. Viewing one of the Grandfather's finest creations, what was there to say?

The riders turned to go back. Before them was an equally impressive sight. They were on the rim of a gigantic bowl formed by rock-crested mountains. To the north was the Absaroka Range. To the south was Wind River Range. On the right was the Gros Ventre Range.

Broken Knife shook his head. "This country is unbelievable."

Wind said, "The Indian name for the pass we came over means joining or union."

He pointed across the bowl. "Look at that mountain straight ahead. From the way it slopes, water must drain east into the Wind River, west into the Seeds-kee-dee, and this way into the Snake River. With water flowing east and into drainages of the West, we must be on or near the heighth of land dividing the continent." Filled by awe-inspiring grandeur, he said, "Yes, Union Pass is a good name."

Wind suddenly pulled up. She pointed southwest of the lake. "Something moved over there."

Wind and Broken Knife rode behind a small stand of scrub pines. Before long, two separate groups of Indians rode out of the trees. He glanced at Wind. "We better re-pack the horses."

Broken Knife finished tying on the last pack as a Shoshone with a woman and two girls rounded the lake. Not far behind were four young braves.

With his gun under his arm, Broken Knife walked out to meet them. As he passed Wind, he said, "Keep your bow handy."

Broken Knife recognized the Shoshone. It was Black Brush's brother. The warrior looked at Broken Knife and tipped his head. The four Indians stopped. The braves did not pay any attention to Broken Knife. They stared at Wind. Raising his rifle, he grunted. The warriors glared at the gun then turned and rode back along the lakeshore.

Broken Knife went back to the camp. In Hidatsa, the Shoshone said, "I am Slow Fox. Those are young Bannocks after horses and glory."

"You were at the salt pit with Black Brush last summer."

When Slow Fox nodded, Broken Knife glanced at Wind. "We better finish this, or they will come after us tonight." He said to Slow Fox. "Stay by your family."

Broken Knife leaned his gun against a tree. He picked up his quiver. Removing all but three arrows, he placed it on his back. With bow in hand, he walked toward the lake.

Slow Fox started to follow. Wind touched his arm, she shook her head.

The Bannocks stood just inside the tree line. When they saw Broken Knife coming toward them, the braves tied the horses and went to meet him. Thirty feet separated Broken Knife and the Bannocks. The biggest one grinned. He signed this must be his lucky day. Tonight, the Crow woman would keep his bed warm.

The smile left Broken Knife's face. He gestured boys should not brag.

The braggart and the one on his left wilted to the ground. Arrows protruded from their chests. Broken Knife grabbed the third arrow. It hung up in the quiver. Instinctively, his hand released it, and he threw the knife. He reached for the arrow again.

The remaining Bannock pulled back his bowstring. The warrior's arrow dug into the ground. Feathers of an arrow

229

shaft protruded from the Bannock's armpit. Broken Knife looked at Wind. Her face held the same defiant look he had seen at the Hidatsa village.

Wind walked over beside him. "You said to keep my bow handy."

"For a second there, I thought Lame Bear wanted me to join him." He hugged her hard. "I must give your mother more presents."

The Shoshones stared at the dead Bannocks. Slow Fox shook his head. "My brother has told and re-told the story of Whispering Wind and the white traders." He stared at Wind's bow. "Wait until he hears this."

"She is a sweetie," Broken Knife said with a twinkle in his eye. "Our wives can fix something to eat. Let's hide the bodies."

The four Bannocks were carried to a deep crevice and covered with rocks. On the way back to camp, Broken Knife said, "Take the horses, but do not tell anyone about this, except Black Brush. I have enough enemies without adding Bannocks to the list."

That night in bed, Wind asked, "What happened with your arrow?" She hesitated. "What is this sweetie?"

"The tip caught on the side of the quiver." He pecked her cheek. "A sweetie is someone very special."

"It better be. When we go to St. Louis, I am asking Jeannie."

Broken Knife grinned. "That is why you wanted to speak English?"

"Yes. You say things, and I do not know what they mean."

Smiling, Broken Knife pulled her close. His lips covered hers.

Wind and Broken Knife left Slow Fox's family by the lake. To the southwest, the country was not as steep as the East Side of Union Pass. Night camp was setup beside a river that rushed over large rocks. Finished eating, he and Wind sat on a large, flat rock next to the roaring river. The Grandmother's rays brought light to the meadow. Several deer fed not far away. Wind dropped her head to his shoulder. He realized that she had been quiet since leaving Union Pass.

"Honey, are you bothered about killing the Bannock?"

"No, he might have killed you."

"What is it then?" he asked. "Something is wrong."

"If Jeannie and Mrs. Walker find out, maybe they will not like me."

Broken Knife cupped her face in his hands. "How can they not help but like you?" He kissed her gently. "Yesterday, and with those traders, you have never looked more beautiful or feminine, to me. With that determined look on your face, I realize how strong you are. Then, when the love and warmth returns, I want to hold and protect you."

Wind pushed him back on the rock.

In a voice low and soft from their shared love, she asked, "What is feminine?"

His breath caught. He whispered, "Being a woman."

The travelers left the Seeds-kee-dee. It took two days to cross the Horse Creek meadows. Dropping off a rim into a valley bordered by the Gros Ventre range, the riders followed a good-sized stream down a canyon to the Snake River.

Wind and Broken Knife traveled along the East Side of the Snake into a large park. Straight ahead were four sage-brush-covered buttes. Riding around the one on the right, they saw the spectacular Teewinots hovering above the virginal valley.

The riders had not gone far when Broken Knife halted. A wide stream running over cobble rocks flowed beside them. He pointed east. "Wind, the head of that canyon must be where we first saw this valley."

Wind giggled. "If you had known where you were going, we could have ridden straight down here."

His eyes twinkled. "That is true, but then, I would have

missed finding out how feminine you can be on a flat rock."
Wind tried to hit him. His horse shied and she missed.
Laughing, he headed toward an isolated butte in the center of
the sagebrush flat.

The night camp was on the north end of the butte
between a vertical rock ledge and a stream. Opposite the camp
were the imposing peaks of granite. On this night, in this
valley, neither of them wanted to be in a wikiup.

Broken Knife lay on his back. He stared at: brilliant stars,
the Grandmother, the peaks. Enthralled by the breath-taking
beauty, he pulled Wind closer. Lying there together, they
watched wispy clouds float across glacier-carved canyons and
the granite faces of the Mountains of Stone.

The travelers followed the Buffalo River toward Tog-
wotee Pass. When the trail forked, Broken Knife and Wind
followed the south fork to its source.

Small patches of wind-bent trees dotted the vast open
country. Black Brush had called this area Buffalo Plateau. He
had mentioned to Broken Knife that a large herd of buffalo had
been snow bound there and perished. The riders crossed to
where the plateau fell off into a deep canyon. A switchback trail
led to the stream below. This tiny creek grew into the river that
ran past the entrance to their valley.

Following the Stinkingwater River, Broken Knife thought
of the tales from blacksmith shop loafers in Kaskaskia. Several
old timers said the western mountains formed a solid wall that
nothing could cross except birds. He admitted the granite-
peaked Wind Rivers looked that way, but Black Brush had
mentioned a broad, sagebrush-covered pass on the south end
of the range.

Broken Knife broke into a grin. He and Wind had traveled
through, over, and around these majestic mountain ranges, and
they were usually on an Indian trail wide enough to pull a
three- to four-foot travois over.

Wind rode beside him. She asked, "What are you

grinning about now?"

"Just wild stories about sheer-walled mountains that birds carried a lunch to fly over."

COLTER COMES

Wind and Broken Knife returned to find Eagle Plume, Waving Grass, and Dove gone. Broken Knife was glad when Grey Wolf said, "Redfeather and White Cloud will stay with them until they reach Cheyenne territory."

With a note of sadness in his voice, Broken Knife said, "Eagle Plume mentioned they might leave before we returned. Maybe it is for the best, good-byes would have been hard. Did he practice with the gun?"

"Yes, many times," Grey Wolf replied. "There were buffalo along the river. He killed two of them."

Owl Woman said, "Waving Grass and Dove wanted to stay, but Eagle Plume felt he must tell his people about the white man."

Broken Knife turned the packhorses loose. He and Grey Wolf followed them to the upper end of the valley where the rest of the horses were feeding. Broken Knife looked over the herd. "The foals look good. How many are there?"

"Forty-three with two mares still to foal."

"I hate to mention work, but we need a fence to separate the mares and stallion from the other horses."

When Broken Knife described what a fence looked like, Grey Wolf said, "There is a buffalo herd above the mud pots. It would be good to hunt before doing this fence."

"Could we wait a couple of days? Broken Knife asked. "My buffalo horse could stand a few days rest."

"If nobody bothers the herd, they will feed this way," Grey Wolf replied.

That evening, the family was sitting around the fire in Grey Wolf's lodge. Grey Wolf looked at Broken Knife. "Since you have said little about the journey, I will not bother asking you. Wind, how did it go?"

Broken Knife smiled and nodded, so she told where they had been and about the Bannocks. When she got to the part about the arrow and quiver, Owl Woman asked, "Is something wrong with your quiver?"

"There is a small, rough place, otherwise, I cannot see or feel anything." He looked at Owl Woman with a straight face. "Your daughter is always causing trouble. Take her back, and I will give you many presents."

Wind wrinkled her nose. "You have already promised to give my mother a present."

Before Owl Woman could say anything, Grey Wolf asked, "Bannock were following a Snake family?"

"Yes, Slow Fox, who is Black Brush's brother, said they were renegades," Broken Knife replied.

Grey Wolf said, "This is good. It will form a strong bond with Black Brush."

While the rest prepared for the buffalo hunt, Broken Knife built a long table with seats on each side for Owl Woman.

The hunters pitched the camp above the mud pots. By noon the next day, Broken Knife had killed three buffalo and was chasing the fourth one. His horse was running beside a young cow when it stepped in a badger hole. The horse went down. Broken Knife flew over its head.

He opened his eyes to see a hazy outline of Teal and Wind. "What happened?" His hands went to his head. "It feels as if it is going to explode."

Teal had tears in her eyes. "We were afraid. You have not moved in a long time."

Wind touched his shoulder. "Lie still. Your horse stepped in a hole."

He staggered to his feet. "I am just a little dizzy."

Wind asked, "Can you make it to the river if we put you on my horse?"

When he nodded, she and Teal boosted him on the mare's back. Wind held onto his leg. Teal led the mare. They were washing his face and side with cold water when Grey Wolf rode up. He held out a handful of warm buffalo fat. Grey Wolf said, "This will help the scraped places."

Broken Knife's head throbbed too bad to ride, so he walked back to camp. Teal stayed beside him with her hand in his. Wind walked along the river hunting two special plants. At camp, Wind made a tea with the herbs she had collected. After drinking the bitter mixture, Broken Knife lay down in the shade.

Warmth from the Grandfather's rays woke him. When Wind saw him stir, she took over another bowl of tea. Removing the buffalo robe that had covered him during the night, she said, "We thought you were going to sleep all night and all day. How do you feel?"

"My head feels better. Everywhere else hurts."

Wind kissed his cheek. Holding out the tea, she said, "This will make you feel better."

The strong tea turned the stinging sensation into a dull ache. Wind brought a kettle containing different herbs, buffalo brains, and large green leaves. She skimmed off the top leaves then placed them over the scraped areas. It was not long before the tea and soothing poultices had put him back asleep.

While the travois were loaded for the trip home, Broken Knife hobbled about camp. When Grey Wolf led a horse over, he shook his head. "I will walk." He looked around, then asked, "Where is my horse?"

"He broke his front leg," Grey Wolf replied in a hushed voice.

First Bird Tail and now the brown buffalo horse. Head down, Broken Knife followed the travois.

A week passed before Broken Knife felt good enough to start on the fence. While living with the Walkers, he had seen a fence made by tying two posts to form an X. The post were held together by three twelve-foot poles on one side, two on the other, and one across the top. With poles and posts close by, they could build one across the meadow.

Wind and Broken Knife cut down trees while Owl Woman and Teal trimmed and burned branches. When they finished a pole or post, Grey Wolf used the grey mare to pull it into the meadow. As Broken Knife tied the last pole on the fence, he said, "That went so well, let's build a corral and a catch pen for Wind and Teal's mares."

"A catch pen, what is that?" Grey Wolf asked.

"A small fenced pasture." Broken Knife paused, "That way, we will have a horse nearby to drive the horses into the corral."

Despite the moans and groans, Broken Knife knew no one really objected. They were all proud of the fence that divided the meadow. The upper pasture contained forty-five mares with foals and the stallion. The lower pasture held the buffalo horses, trading horses, and twelve unbroken colts.

Redfeather and White Cloud returned late that afternoon. Grey Wolf gave his son a black look. "Have you been waiting on the river until we were through?"

Redfeather laughed. "After we left Eagle Plume, we stopped at the Stinkingwater village. While we start on the horses, you and Broken Knife can shoot the two buffalo by the valley entrance."

The hunters quartered the meat then packed it to the storeroom. The cave stayed cold enough to keep meat for over a week without it going bad. Broken Knife was surprised at the amount of pemmican, jerky, wild onions, turnips, and berries the women had stored there.

Two days later, Wind and Broken Knife were riding across the meadow hand in hand when Broken Knife leaned over. He kissed her lightly. "What if we skip the trade fair? I would like to start on our cabin."

"I do not care about going either," Wind replied.

"Good, let's find Grey Wolf."

Grey Wolf saw them coming. He stopped by a beaver dam. As they rode up, Broken Knife said, "We have been talking about the trade fair. Would you go without us?"

"Redfeather and White Cloud are anxious to go, so there will be enough help," he replied. "What do we need?"

"If we give White Cloud a rifle, it leaves us with two extra ones. Get four more rifles and plenty of powder and lead. If Larocque is not there, tell the trader you want Pennsylvania rifles, or you will trade elsewhere. Other than that, get whatever you think we need."

Riding across the meadow, Grey Wolf said, "Redfeather and White Cloud believe only one of the colts will make a buffalo horse. We could trade off the others and the three mares that did not foal."

That night, Owl Woman said, "We have been talking about a garden. I could get seeds from Big Woman."

"A garden would be good," Broken Knife replied. "Wind and I noticed a couple of horses licking rocks. We will get salt for the horses and Little Man."

"Can I go," Teal asked.

"Of course," grinning, he added, "you can keep Wind out of trouble."

The three of them left early the next morning. After filling the panniers, they camped below the salt cave. Finished eating, Broken Knife asked, "Teal, would you like to live with Mrs. Walker, or Jeannie, and go to a white man's school?"

It was sometime before Teal said, "What if I do not like it there?"

"Wind and I will take you for a visit then you can decide. While we are there, I will make arrangements to have you brought back anytime you want."

Teal hesitated. "If you think it is best."

The rest of the evening, Broken Knife talked about St. Louis and all they could see and do there.

As soon as they were back, Broken Knife put out the salt. A day later, he and Grey Wolf checked the horses. There were elk tracks all around the chunks of salt. Grey Wolf shook his head. "Elk eat more than the horses."

"Wind and I can get more. Salt kept the elk here last winter; however much salt it takes is worth it."

Five days later, Grey Wolf and the rest of the family left for the Crow village. They would travel with Whistling Water clan members to the trade fair. Once they were gone, Wind and Broken Knife began on the cabin.

A week later, Broken Knife was peeling logs with a drawknife when Black Dog barked. He dropped the knife. Yelling at Wind, he run toward the gate. Through a gun port, he saw a white man coming around the bend.

"Colter! How did you find me?"

"I run into Grey Wolf an' he tol' me."

"How is Drouillard and the rest?"

"Ever' body's fine an' in St. Louie' by now," Colter replied.

Broken Knife started to ask more, but Colter held up his hand. "'Ere's ah time fer talkin' an' ah time fer eatin'. Now I'm partial ta tha lat'er." Colter stared. He blurted out, "Wagh! Who's that?"

Broken Knife turned to see Wind. Black hair flying, she bounded down the trail. She held her pistol in one hand, a powder flask in the other. Wind stopped beside him.

"This is my wife, Whispering Wind. Wind, this is John Colter."

Wind curtsied. "I am pleased to meet you, Mr. Colter."

Broken Knife smiled at the surprised look on his friend's face. Colter bowed. "The honor's mine, ma'am."

"Teaching the English was easy," Broken Knife said with a shake of his head. "Teaching her to curtsy was something else. When Colter quit laughing, Broken Knife grinned. "Let's go eat, so you can tell me the news."

Colter stopped just inside the valley. He stared at the horses. "Grazin' horses an' ah fence 'minds me ah' home." With admiration, he added, "Ya got ah fine place. Never think it's 'ere from below."

"Everything we need is here, or close by. This spring, our mares had forty-five foals."

"Ya raisin horses?"

"Yes. When you met Grey Wolf, they were headed for the Hidatsa's trade fair with fourteen horses and a pack of prime plews."

"My partners said thet next spring Lisa's bringin' close ta ah huntert men upriver. Ere'll be ah need fer horses ta ride an' pack."

"Is that Manuel Lisa?"

"Ya know 'im?" Colter asked.

"I met him once. Who are your partners?"

"Forrest Hancock an' James Dixon. They wur at tha Mandans an' wanted me ta stay an' trap. When I ask tha Cap'ns' iffen it wur alrit', they discharged me right then an' 'ere." He hesitated before saying, "Hancock carried word Chouteau wants ta see ya."

"Did he say why?"

Colter shook his head. "Hancock didn't know nothin' 'cept tha word 'ad been put out."

After Colter ate two helpings of stew, the old friends walked onto the meadow. When Colter settled down on a rock, Broken Knife smiled. "Now that you are full, you can start anytime."

"Goin' up river wasn't bad till we reached 'em falls on tha

Missouri. 'Ere 'as five differnt ones, spread out o'er nineteen miles, an' ranged from ten- ta fifty-feet high. Tha men cut twenty-two-inch wheels out ah cottonwoods an' used tha pirogue masts fer axles. These home-made wagons wur tha only way ta get tha goods aroun' tha falls."

"That does sound tough," commented Broken Knife.

"It wur, an' constant rain an' grizzlies didn't help none neither. Tha griz' wur bad. Near everbody 'ad ah scrape with 'em. Ah big sow with cubs chased Cap'n Lewis. He 'ad ta jump in tha river ta get away."

Broken Knife chuckled as he pictured a bear after Lewis. "How did Charbonneau pan out?" he asked out of curiosity. "Most Indians, especially the women, do not like him."

"He'd make ah big show ah cookin' intestines stuffed with meat an' baptized in Missouri River water which wur pretty good, otherwise, he 'as a sorry excuse fer ah man. Twice, wind squalls sceered 'im an' he nearly tipped oer tha pirogue with tha maps an' tha instruments in it. Tha last time, Cruzatte threaten' ta shoot 'im if he didn't quit screamin' ta God fer mercy an' grab tha tiller. It 'as sure ah good thin' Sakakawea 'as in tha boat when Charbonneau 'most scuttled it. She grabbed tha maps an' ah box ah instruments out ah tha river. Without them, we'd been in real trouble."

"He was not much help then?"

Colter's face showed his disgust. "Cap'n Lewis took him out once, an' thet 'as near tha Three Forks. An' 'ere, he 'as supposed ta be one ah our guides." He broke into a smile. "Cap'n Lewis regarded 'im as ah man ah no particular merit."

"What about Sakakawea?" Broken Knife asked.

"Lewis didn't 'ave nothin' ta do with 'er, but Clark kinda liked 'er. She membered three places on tha whole trip: tha Three Forks, tha Beaverhead on tha Jefferson, an' Bozeman Pass. Never did unerstan what tha Cap'ns spected from 'er. She 'as only ten or 'leven when tha Hidatsa took 'er from 'er people on tha Three Forks. In fact, when we got where she 'as took from, 'er lack ah feelins' caused Cap'n Lewis ta say, 'if she has enough to eat and a few trinkets to wear I believe she would be perfectly content anywhere.'"

Nodding his head, Broken Knife said, "I thought at the time the Captains were making a mistake. Except following a travois trail or gathering wood around a village, Indian girls know little about the country. I doubt if she knew much Hidatsa either. You do not learn to speak a language being a slave around a lodge. She had not been married to Charbonneau long enough to learn much, and the Hidatsa say he was to lazy to say anymore than absolutely necessary."

Colter started to reply when Wind walked up. She said, "Come and eat."

Colter stuffed himself on corn, wild onions, hump-ribs, fry bread, and boiled huckleberries. He smiled his appreciation. "Thank ya ma'am. It's been ah long time since I've 'ad anythin' this good."

Pleased, Wind said. "You are welcome. I built you a fire. Your pack is in Eagle Plume's lodge."

When Colter left, Broken Knife said, "Chouteau sent word upriver that he wants to see me. Colter did not know why."

"If we left now would we be back before winter?" Wind asked.

"It might be better to wait until spring," Broken Knife replied. "Pierre would have come if it was anything very important."

Wind snuggled closer. "We should get Teal and go. Otherwise, you will mope around all winter worrying about it."

On the way to look at the mares, Colter started in again. "Cap'n Lewis, Drou'ard, Shields, an' McNeal left us at tha Three Forks. It wur sometime 'fore, we saw 'em comin' with Snakes ta pack us oer tha mountains ta tha Lemhi Valley. They'd been gone better 'an two weeks. If they'd com back 'ithout findin' tha Snakes, we'd been forced ta turn back." He hesitated then added, "'Cept' fer horses, tha Snakes wur mighty poor. 'Ere 'as only two rusty gun an' ah few iron knives an' hatchets 'mongst tha bunch ah 'em. They lived on ah occasional deer an' antelope, fish, roots, berries, bugs, lizards, an' anythin' else they cun find. Despite bein' sceered ta death ah tha Blackfeet, they sneak onta tha Three Forks an' hunt buffalo ta git nuff food fer winter,"

"Did you find a river to the Pacific there?"

"Naw, tha band's Chief Cameahwait turned out ta be Sakakawea's brother. 'Fore we met up with 'em, Cameahwait 'ad told Drou'ard with sign language thet boats couldn't git down tha Salmon River. He said we'd 'ave ta cross back oer tha mountains. He promised ta git us horses an' send ah guide ta show tha way. I went with Cap'n Clark ta look at this Salmon River. Cameahwait 'as right. 'Ere 'as no way down it."

"Sounds like Sakakawea did not help much with the interpreting either."

"Cap'n Lewis didn't 'ave much faith in all thet translatin'. She'd take it from Snake ta Hidatsa, Charbonneau'd from Hidatsa ta French, an' Labiche from French ta English. Sides all that, Labiche claimed Charbonneau spoke mighty poor French. LaPage didn't think 'is Hidatsa wur up ta much neither.

"Ya had ta admire her though. She suffered every hardship tha men did an' carried ah baby most ah tha way. 'Sides thet, she 'ad Charbonneau ta look after. He 'as always hollerin' at her ta do or fetch somethin'. Another thin' she did 'as find plants an' roots we could eat." Colter paused then said, "After ah hard day, it seemed good ta 'ave ah woman an' baby around camp. Tha boys gave her an' York ah lot ah tha credit fer all tha help tha Indian tribes ah long tha way gave us."

Colter paused to scratch, then said, "We left Cameawait's camp an' went up tha North Fork ah tha Salmon ta git oer 'em mountains. Tha trail 'as steep an' narrow. It took us five days ta cross ta tha head ah tha Bitterroot Valley where 'ere wur a big camp ah Flatheads. We traded fer more horses 'fore goin on ta ah place tha Cap'ns named Traveler's Rest. We planned ta lay oer an' hunt, but 'ere 'as no game.

"We followed an' ol' Indian trail oer Lolo Pass. Believe me 'em mountains wur high an' rough. Tween no game, snow coverin' tha trail, an' freezin' nights, tha men wur sa cold an' hungry thet Cap'n Clark an' six others went ahead. When Rubin Fields an' ah guide cum back leadin' ah horse loaded with berries, roots, an' fish, it wur ah welcome sight. After spendin' three an' ah half months in 'em mountains, ta walk inta ah village wur a real treat. Ta find out ya could float tha Clearwater ta tha Snake, tha Snake ta tha Columbia, an' tha Columbia ta tha Pacific 'as like ah nightmare 'ad ended. It wur near fifty days 'fore we reached tha ocean after leavin' 'em Nez Perce. Believe me, it wur sure easier 'an 'em mountains."

"What did you do with your horses?"

"We cut tha foretops an' branded 'em with an iron stirrup 'en left 'em with tha Nez Perce," Colter replied. "Those wur tha friendliest an' best people we met on tha whole trip.

As they started back, Broken Knife asked, "How about Indians along the Columbia and around the Pacific?"

"They're short an' not well built as tha Nez Perce or tha Plains tribes. Most ah 'em had bowed legs an' knobby joints. Cap'n Clark figgered it 'as from sittin' in canoes, an' eatin' sa much fish. By ah place called tha Dalles, 'ere wur sum iron trade goods an' crude shelters made ah split logs."

"White men had been there?"

"We didn't see any, but ah Limey named Haley traded 'ere," Colter replied. "We left tha Nez Perce on tha tenth ah October, an' on December seventh, we started buildin' winter quarters – Fort Clatsop. "The boys wur sicker an' ornerier long tha ocean 'an anywhere else. It rained most everday, an' if it wurn't rainin', tha fog an' dew wur as bad. By 'en, our goods wur 'bout gone. We lived on stringy elk meat fer four months which didn't help none. We wur all glad ta get out ah 'ere an' 'ead back. Once we wur ah above tha Dalles, 'ere 'as not much ta eat, but nobody minded cuz 'ere 'as blue sky."

Broken Knife looked at his friend. "Nothing to eat?"

"Naw, tha tribes ah long tha Columbia lived mainly on dog meat when tha salmon wurn't runnin'. We didn't 'ave 'nough goods left ta trade fer many. Everbody 'as tickled when we reached tha Nez Perce an' started roundin' up our horses, but it didn't last long. Ah Nez Perce Chief tol' us thet snow blocked tha trail oer Lolo Pass til July. After waitin' round fer a month, livin' on horsemeat an' roots, tha Cap'ns decided ta try tha pass. It wur tough goin' in tha snow. We 'ad ta send back fer guides, but we finely made it ta Traveler's Rest."

Colter paused then added, "While we wur at Fort Clatsop, Cap'n Clark worked on his map. He figgered thet by followin' tha Missouri, we'd been six weeks longer, gone six huntert miles further, an' crossed 'em mountains twice. He fig'red thet from Traveler's Rest ta tha Great Falls 'as less than ah week away. Cap'n Lewis an' Drou'ard took part ah tha men an' went thet way an' tha rest ah us went fer a cache we'd left above tha Three Forks.

"It only took Cap'n Lewis four days ta reach tha Missouri. When they got ta tha Great Falls, tha cache 'as wet. While some ah tha men dried tha goods out, Lewis took Drou'ard an' tha Field brothers ta tha head ah tha Marias River ta 'stablish tha northern boundary ah tha Louisiana Territory. On tha way back they 'ad trouble with some Piegans. All I know fer sher is eight Piegans tried ta steal tha horses, an' two wur killed. When ya see Drou'ard, he can fill ya in on what hap'ned."

Colter smiled and continued, "After we 'as all back together at tha junction ah tha Yellerstone an' Missouri, Cap'n Lewis an' thet near-sighted Cruzatte wur huntin'. Cruzatte mistook Lewis fer' an elk an' shot 'im in tha butt. Luckily, tha wound 'as not serious. When tha Cap'n wasn't 'round, tha men sher chuckled 'bout it. Leavin' tha Mandans, tha Cap'ns figgered ta be in St. Louis 'round tha twenty-third ah September."

Broken Knife shook his head. "It is amazing you could spend two and a half years – sixteen months of it in uncharted country – and lose only one man."

"Ya, it is. An' tha only trouble we had, 'cept 'em Piegans, 'as when ah war party stole our horses along tha Yellerstone. Sakakawea figgered it 'as Crows." Colter hesitated before saying, "On ta other hand, we'd ah never made it without Indians helpin' with food an' guides. We might not 'ave made it thru thet first winter, if Hidatsa an' Mandans hadn't brought us corn an' squash fer iron goods thet Shields made. Ya know when we got ta tha Nez Perce, they already 'ad one ah his axes."

Broken Knife shook his head. "I could have my father-in-law find out if it was Crow that took the horses." Pausing, he said, "I guess it does not really matter now. You came down the Yellowstone?"

"Naw, Clark split us up at tha Three Forks. Nine ah us com down tha Missouri with Sergeant Ordway, an' tha rest ah 'em went with Clark thru ah pass thet Sakakawea said her people used ta git ta tha Yellerstone."

After a pause in the conversation, Broken Knife added, "I am glad it is hard to get to the Pacific, otherwise, settlements would spring up all along the Missouri. The towns will still come, it will just take longer."

"Some ah tha boys said thet vary thin'." Colter frowned. "Why's it white people 'ave ta change everthin'?"

"It is just the way things are," replied Broken Knife.

Wind stayed away while Broken Knife and Colter were talking. As soon as they finished, she suggested they take Colter after salt.

"Good idear, I cun git sum fer winter." Colter paused. "While we wur by tha ocean, we boiled ah lot ah water ta git tha salt out ah it. Tha boys wur salt hungry most ah tha time we wur gone."

The next afternoon, they camped below the salt pit. While Broken Knife and Colter sprawled out under a pine to talk, Wind went up the river to swim in a sun-warmed beaver pond.

Colter asked, "What ya been doin' since we parted on tha Missouri?" When Broken Knife got to the part about the three traders, Colter interrupted, "Ya mean Wind cut one thet bad?"

"Yes, and if I had not gotten there, she would have ripped at least one wide open."

Colter said, "That's 'ard ta believe."

"Do not be fooled by her looks. She is one of the best shots I have seen with a bow and is getting almost as good with a pistol."

Colter shook his head as Wind walked up and sit down. The campfire talk continued late into the night.

The morning after they returned with the salt, Colter said, "I best git goin. Those partners ah mine 'll think I'm lost."

"Do you want a horse or need anything else?" Broken Knife asked.

"Thank ya, but I couldn't winter it. We're gonna trap on Clark's fork ah tha Yellerstone. "Ere'll be too much snow fer horses."

Colter kissed Wind's hand. "Clint's mighty lucky havin' you."

"Please visit us again."

Colter had barely gotten out of sight when Wind whirled. She glared at Broken Knife then said, "Who is this Clint?"

Broken Knife laughed. "That is my white man's name."

Wind's face clouded, her voice quivered. "What else is there you have not told me? We are getting Teal and going to St. Louis. I want to talk to Jeannie." Sobbing, she ran up the trail.

Broken Knife stared. He was about to run after her when sounds of giggling drifted down the trail. He shook his head.

CHOUTEAU

Wind stopped on the knoll. She stared at: two ships under full sail, big wood buildings, wagons coming and going, streets crowded with people. It was several minutes before she nudged her horse toward St. Louis.

Broken Knife followed her and Teal off the hill. He stared at his wife's straight back and bouncing hair. His fears returned. Since picking up Teal at the Hidatsa village, he had had second thoughts about bringing them to St. Louis. Wind accepted life for what it was. Being mean and cruel were not in her. He did not want her hurt by white people's bigotry.

Wind looked over her shoulder. "We will be all right, quit worrying."

Broken Knife rode beside Wind. He pointed toward the river bluff. "The big house by the old fort is where Jeannie lives."

"Broken Knife! Over here."

Broken Knife saw Drouillard. Turning into a side street, they waited for him to cross the crowded road. After the old friends greeted, Drouillard smiled at Teal. "Look how you have grown and gotten prettier at the same time."

Teal curtsied. With a mischievous grin, she said, "How do do Miter Drourd?" She broke into a smile. "Thank you for the compliment." Chuckling, he grabbed her in a bear hug.

When Drouillard let her go, Broken Knife said, "My wife, Whispering Wind."

Wind pecked Drouillard on the cheek. She smiled at his red face. "We are already friends."

Still blushing, he replied, "Yes, ma'am." After a few minutes, Drouillard asked, "Could we talk alone?"

"If it concerns trouble, Wind and Teal can hear," Broken Knife replied.

"Two Englishmen are hangin' around the saloons. Seems they have more than a passin' curiosity about you. One of them killed a man in a duel two days ago. He is right good with that sword he carries. The other man packs a short-barreled gun in his right-hand coat pocket. You best keep an eye peeled."

"Why would they be interested in me?" Broken Knife asked. "Soon as Wind and Teal are settled, maybe we can satisfy this curiosity."

Drouillard said, "Meet me at the tavern across the street tomorrow. I'll mention it to Yves too."

Tobias answered the door. He stared at the longhaired, buckskin-clad figure. "Mister Clint! Is that you?"

"It is me," Broken Knife replied with a smile. "Tobias, this is my wife, Whispering Wind, and Teal."

Before Tobias could say anything, they heard someone running down the hall. Jeannie burst through the door. She threw her arms around Broken Knife and Wind. "Oh! You are here. Pierre sent word days ago you were coming. I could hardly wait."

Jeannie stepped back. She looked at Wind. Wrinkling her nose at Broken Knife, she said, "You could have at least married someone fat and ugly." She scowled. "Now, I am twice as jealous." With an arm around Teal and one around Wind, Jeannie steered them down the hall. The three of them were giggling like little kids.

Tobias smiled at the look on Broken Knife's face. "Mr. Chouteau will be here anytime. I lit a fire in the library. If you

249

want to wait in there, I will see to your horses."

"Thanks." Broken Knife touched Tobias's shoulder. "It is good seeing you again, my friend."

Broken Knife settled into a soft chair with a book. He had not been there long when Chouteau and Tobias came through the door. After a warm greeting, Chouteau said, "Tobias brought some brandy. With what I have to tell, you will need something stronger than coffee."

Chouteau poured them each a brandy. He took a sip. Setting the snifter down, he said, "Six months after you left, word came Mrs. Walker wanted to see you, so Jeannie and I went to Kaskaskia. She showed us the documents along with Dr. Fitzgerald translations." Hesitating, he said, "You have a Grandfather. He is the Marquis de Soissons. Your grandfather is one of the wealthiest men in France."

Broken Knife stared into the fire. A silence settled over the room. With a shake of his head, he looked at Chouteau. "My mother's gaunt face and never enough to eat are memories I carry of my white life. If he is so wealthy, why were we so poor?"

Chouteau's hand dropped to Broken Knife's shoulder. "I am coming to that part. I notified my barrister in France to contact the Marquis and inform him you had been in St. Louis. Your grandfather told my barrister French zealots had killed his son, your real father. Maure, his son's manservant, took you and your mother to Glasgow. The Marquis's men followed, but were unable to find any trace of you. Later, the Marquis learned from a ship's Captain that he had taken you to the Colonies. The Marquis sent men after you, but by the time they arrived in Boston, your parents had left for the Ohio country."

Chouteau went to the fireplace mantle. He returned with a thick envelope. "I sent the Marquis copies of the documents you left with Mrs. Walker, and a few months ago, this arrived. You are your grandfather's sole heir. A cousin is coming to take you to France." Placing the envelope beside Broken Knife, he left.

Broken Knife was re-reading the letters and what he could of the documents when Wind kneeled in front of him. Her fingers caressed his cheek. "Mr. Chouteau told me."

He gathered her in his arms. "My father was not my father. There is a Grandfather and cousin I never heard of." Squeezing her harder, he sighed, "To me, only you are real."

Wind moaned softly. Her hands cupped his face. Her lips touched his in a lingering kiss. She whispered, "Dinner is ready. We can talk about it tonight."

"You go ahead. I want to sit here awhile."

Finished with dinner, Wind took Jeannie aside. "I will help Tobias. Would you talk with Broken Knife? He needs someone who knows more than I do."

Jeannie smiled and hugged Wind. "It seems strange to hear his Indian name. This whole thing is so exciting, but I know what it is doing to him. It means choosing between the Indian and white worlds again."

Jeannie took Broken Knife's hand. She led him into the courtyard. Sitting on a bench, she said, "Uncle Auguste and I will help anyway we can."

Broken Knife smiled his appreciation, "The Grandfather has given me all I ever wanted: a family, a home. Should I give these up for something I know nothing about?"

Jeannie leaned over and kissed his cheek. "Maybe, Uncle Auguste can work something out." A warm smile crossed her face. "I am amazed at Wind's English and manners. She is such a beautiful girl." Pausing, she said, "Yet, I sense she is very strong willed. She is the perfect wife for you."

"Strong willed? Ah yes, that she can be," replied Broken Knife with a shake of his head and a smile. "When I told her about things Mrs. Walker taught me, I mentioned using knives and forks. She made me carve a wooden fork to see what one looked like." Pausing, he said, "Wind wants you and Mrs. Walker to think she is a lady."

"Well I certainly think she is, and I am sure Mrs. Walker would. Did my uncle tell you the Walkers are gone?"

"No, he did not mention it."

"Dr. Fitzgerald is ill. Before they left, Mrs. Walker sent you a beautiful colt."

Excited, Broken Knife said, "It is probably a son of the stallion I gave her. He will cross well on our mares."

"Do you raise horses?"

"We are starting to," he replied, then told her about Wind's parents and the valley. He talked for a long time before taking hold of her hand. "It is late. We better go inside."

Walking across the courtyard, he asked, "Would you take Wind and Teal shopping tomorrow? Buy them dresses and anything else they need." Broken Knife stopped and looked at Jeannie. "Two Englishmen have been asking questions about me. If anyone bothers you tomorrow, let Wind handle it."

Jeannie wanted to know more, but she did not ask. "Of course," she replied. "It will be fun taking them to the stores and dress shops."

Tobias said Wind had gone to the bedroom, so Broken Knife said good night. He opened the bedroom door. Before him was Wind's reflection in a full-length mirror. Her doeskin dress lay about her ankles.

Broken Knife moved behind her. He placed his hands on her shoulders. With his cheek next to hers, he whispered, "Now, Wind sees as I do."

"I have never seen all of me at the same time." She pointed at a reflection in the mirror. "Do we sleep in that?"

"Yes, it is called a canopy bed."

Wind's arms circled his neck. As her lips parted, she whispered, "I am pleased my husband likes to look at me."

Wind lay in bed. Her head rested on his shoulder. "You can go to this France." Her soft voice continued, "White men at the Mandan villages leave Indian wives. There is no disgrace for the woman in this."

Broken Knife reared up. "Do not say that again!" He kissed her forehead. "I would never leave you."

Light from the fireplace reflected in Wind's tearful eyes. She snuggled deeper in the feather tick. Stretching, she wiggled closer. "The white man has many good things. Maybe, we should see this France."

"We do not need to decide right away. Tomorrow, Jeannie will take you shopping. I can talk to Mr. Chouteau and Drouillard."

She raised on her elbows. "What is shopping?"

"It is going to stores to look at and buy things."

Excitement filled her voice. "Can I have a dress like Jeannie wears?"

"As many as you want." Pulling her head down, he kissed her. He said, "Nothing can make you more beautiful than our first night on the Stinkingwater, or standing in front of that mirror."

Wind's moist mouth covered his.

Chouteau told Broken Knife at breakfast he would be home early. As he walked out the door, he turned and grinned. "Now that you have so many obligations and responsibilities, we must discuss them."

"I am not sure about these obligations." Broken Knife answered with a grimace.

"Do not worry about us," Jeannie said as she, Wind, and Teal followed her uncle out. "We will have a good time."

Broken Knife found Drouillard with several trappers in the grog shop. As Broken Knife came through the door, Drouillard left the trappers. Going to a corner table, Broken Knife told him what Chouteau had said.

Drouillard asked, "Suppose this has anythin' to do with those men askin' questions?"

Broken Knife thought a minute. "Could be. If it does, they should be French not English. Let's wait and let them make the first move. What are your plans now?"

"Manuel Lisa is goin' upriver. He and his two partners, Pierre Menard and William Morrison, are planin' to build a tradin' post near the Three Forks. I am goin' as his partner's rep."

"I know Menard. He is from Kaskaskia." Broken Knife paused. "I talked with Colter a couple of months ago. He mentioned trouble with Piegans. What happened?"

"Capt'n Lewis took me and the Field boys to scout the headwaters of the Marias River. The last night out, we had barely setup camp when eight Piegans rode up. They acted friendly, so the Capt'n invited them to share our fire. Early the next mornin', four of them tried to steal the horses. Rubin Fields stabbed one in the heart. The Capt'n shot another one in the belly."

Broken Knife shook his head. "That is too bad. The Piegan along with the Bloods and Blackfoot make up the Blackfeet Nation. The Blackfeet and the Gros Ventre control the Missouri above the Yellowstone clear to the Three Forks country. The Blackfeet will not let anyone trap their territory. You be careful around them. Those tribes are fighters."

Drouillard nodded his understanding. "I figured they were tough. We had a hard time gettin' the Snake Indians to pack Clark and the men over the mountains. They were afraid of a Blackfeet trap."

Broken Knife and Drouillard discussed the Yellowstone, Big Horn, and Stinkingwater river country. Through with the geography, Broken Knife talked about the valley and horses. Finished, he said, "Regardless of this France thing, we could use a partner. Come and live with us?"

"I am obligated to Menard and Morrison for awhile," replied Drouillard. "Maybe later, if the offer still stands." Getting up, he added, "Your rifle made the trip with nary a scratch. It is in my room. I will fetch it."

"Keep it until I know what is going on?" Broken Knife glanced at the sun through a nearby window. "Chouteau

254

should be home by now. I better go."

Drouillard said, "I will let you know if I hear anything. If you need me, get word to the tavern owner. He is a good friend."

Tobias told Broken Knife Chouteau was in the garden. Broken Knife pushed a package under a bush before walking over to Chouteau.

Chouteau waved his hand over the town. "I enjoy watching the activity. There have been many changes since I first come to this place."

"For you there sure has been," replied Broken Knife. "I saw the pencil drawing on the fireplace mantle. The one of you laying out the first trading post here."

"That was for my step-father Pierre Linguest Laclede. It was in February of 1764," he said with a far-off look in his eyes. Chouteau turned to face Broken Knife. "I have had considerable correspondence with the Marquis. He has established a line of credit for you at a New York financial house. Besides an interest in that bank, he has a variety of investments in America. He owns several large companies and has vast land holdings in France. In fact, one of Maure's nephews manages your grandfather's vineyards." Pausing, he said, "Your grandfather is not well. Very soon, you will be an extremely wealthy young man. This is a wonderful opportunity for you."

Broken Knife shook his head. "Wonderful opportunity for what – to become a white man? An Indian village was not the same after living here, but all I know, or want, is in the mountains."

Broken Knife moved to the edge of the patio wall. He stared at the western horizon. The Mountains of Stone floated before his eyes. "Have you heard the stillness of a high mountain park, or seen the grandeur of glacier-carved peaks? Have you heard the rustle of aspen leaves, or seen the unmarred beauty of fluffy snow? Have you heard the sounds of crystal-clear water rushing over river rock, or seen elk calves frolic in fields of spring flowers?" Turning back toward Chouteau, Broken Knife said, "Why give up what is mine for something I know nothing about?"

Chouteau recalled his own youthful experiences. He stood sometime before replying, "I have not seen those things, but I know what you mean."

"Wind and I talked a little last night. She thinks we ought to go to France and then decide."

"You can always come back here and start a trading company." Chouteau broke into a smile "Or, do anything else you want. With money, all things are possible. There was a message on my desk that your cousin is on the Orleans Queen. The boat will dock by noon tomorrow, and I will invite him to stay here."

Broken Knife and Chouteau were still talking when they heard the shoppers come through the front door. Wind rushed out. "Come and see what we bought."

Broken Knife looked at Chouteau. "Sending them shopping may not have been a good idea. Are you sure I can afford it?"

Laughing, Chouteau said "I am sure. There is a good return on your four hundred and fifty dollar investment. Jeannie will take care of anything else you need until your credit is established here."

Surrounded by boxes, Teal and Jeannie waited in the hall. Jeannie said, "Most of these are Teal's." With a smile, she added, "Wind's things will not be ready until tomorrow afternoon."

"Wait until you see the beautiful gown." With a look that made Broken Knife go warm inside, Wind sighed, "Such a kind husband."

His fingers brushed her cheek. He said, "Tomorrow night, your new cousin will be here. You can wear it to dinner."

Jeannie looked at her uncle. "If he is coming, let's invite a few others." She grinned at Wind. "The Sorbies would give anything to be invited."

Chouteau said, "You told me you did not like her."

"It will be fun seeing the old biddy squirm."

Before Chouteau or Broken Knife could ask what she meant, Tobias announced dinner. After dinner, Broken Knife and Wind walked out in the garden. He led Wind over by the wall. "I saw the way Jeannie looked at you." He asked, "Did something happen with that woman?"

Wind's eyes twinkled. "Jeannie left Teal and me outside the dress shop while she went across the street to her uncle's office. When we walked inside the store, this woman and her daughter stared at us. The woman sneered and said something about filthy Indians in a dress shop. So, I said to Teal that white women must never take a bath, they use lots of toilet water instead." Wind broke into a smile. "The woman's face turned white, then beet red. She grabbed her daughter and stomped out."

Broken Knife laughed aloud. "I would like to have seen her face."

Wind's voice softened. "She was not any different than many others. In the stores and on the street people stared at us. I could see and feel the hatred their eyes held. One man refused to wait on us until Jeannie took him aside and said something. Then he was so nice it was worse."

Broken Knife pulled her into his arms. "Honey, many white people hate Indians. They have lost family or homes to raiding parties. Indians are blamed for everything," pausing, he said, "even if the white man starts it, Indians get the blame."

Going to a nearby bush, Broken Knife pulled out the package. Excited, Wind tore off the wrapping. It was a throwing knife. Raising her dress, she removed her skinning knife from a red lace garter. She smiled at the look on his face. "I bought this garter and a purse to hold my pistol." She touched his cheek, then said, "Since Drouillard told us about those men, I have carried my knife under my waistband."

Wind and Broken Knife stood for a long time overlooking the town. With the coming of darkness, coal oil lamps re-lit darkened houses. Wind asked, "How long has the white man been here?"

"Mr. Chouteau laid out a trading post here twenty-four snows after the Crow first traded for horses," Broken Knife replied. "Or if you mean in America, the Crow moved to the mountains about the same time the first Englishman crossed the Big Salt water."

Tears filled Wind's eyes. She said, "I fear for the People. You said the white man would come, but I had no way of knowing what you meant. Now I understand. First, the traders bring the iron goods, then the ones that dig and plant the ground come, then the ones that build the stores. The white man has many good things. My people will accept these things. Once that happens, the Indian way of life will vanish as does the smoke of our campfires."

Broken Knife placed his arm around her shoulder. "What you fear has already happened to the Delaware and many other tribes. The drunken Indians you see begging on the streets were once as proud as the Crow." Squeezing her arm, he said, "Most white men seek one thing, and that is money. Money is the best reason for going to France – with money – our family and our valley is safe from the white man."

THE PEOPLE

Jeannie led Broken Knife to a closet full of clothes. "These belonged to my brother. A tailor is coming to alter what you need until he can make new ones." Smiling, she said, "You in buckskin and Wind in an elegant gown would not look right."

Broken Knife spent the morning trying on shirts, pants, and waistcoats. He broke into a smile when Tobias stuck his head through the door and announced Mr. Chouteau and a guest waited in the library.

"Clint, your cousin Baptiste, the Count of Soissons; Count Soissons, Clint."

A plump middle-aged man, with a red puffy face, stepped forward. He grasped Broken Knife by the shoulders. He kissed both cheeks. "Welcome to our family."

When Chouteau excused himself, Broken Knife motioned Baptiste to sit. "I am glad you speak English. I was afraid we would have trouble talking."

Baptiste said, "I attended school in both France and England. After graduating from Cambridge, I ran several of your grandfather's companies in England."

"Do you still work with my grandfather?" Broken Knife asked.

"No, I left the businesses several years ago. I live in

259

Cannes. Now I spend most of my time painting along the sea coast." Baptiste paused. Smiling, he said, "Forgive me. You know nothing about France or England. Do you?"

Broken Knife shook his head. "Not very much. Please tell me more about yourself and the family."

Tobias knocked and said it was time to dress for dinner. Broken Knife was surprised. He and Baptiste had talked the afternoon away.

Baptiste said, "Before we go, I want to tell you how pleased I am. Bubonic plague and the revolution wiped out our whole family. Until the Marquis learned you were alive, I was his only relative. I dreaded taking over his affairs." He placed his hand on Broken Knife's shoulder. "Now, the businesses are yours."

"But I know nothing about such things."

"Do not concern yourself. Good men manage all of the companies. I will help in anyway I can," Baptiste grinned, "as long as it does not interfere with my painting."

Broken Knife went to the bedroom. Wind was not there. He was going to look for her when Teal came through the door. "Do you know where Wind is?"

"She is in Jeannie's room." With a grin, she added, "Wind does not want you to see her until she is dressed for the party."

"You should be getting ready too."

"I am going with Mary to her friend's house," Teal replied. She started out the door.

"Just a minute." When she came back in the room, he asked, "Would you like to go to France?"

Teal threw her arms around his waist. "Oh, yes." Her voice quivered. "I was afraid you would leave me here."

Broken Knife kissed her forehead. "How could I get along without you? Go ahead and go with Mary while I try to put these clothes on."

Tobias knocked and entered. He asked, "Would you like me to help with your tie?"

"I have no idea how to fix it," replied Broken Knife. "You better make sure everything else is right."

Tobias stood back. He smiled. "You look fine. Mr. Chouteau and guests are in the garden room."

Broken Knife saw two couples talking with Chouteau. Chouteau nodded with pleasure at sight of him. "Clint, I want you to meet Mr. and Mrs. James Sorbie. Mr. Sorbie heads our leading St. Louis financial house." He turned to the Sorbies. "Clint is a close friend of mine and Jeannie's."

Broken Knife bowed. He said, "I am pleased to meet you."

Mr. Sorbie grinned. He held out his hand, but Broken Knife could see the disdain in his eyes. Sorbie said, "I have heard about this young man."

"And this is Mr. and Mrs. Pierre Menard."

"We know Clint from Kaskaskia," Menard replied with a smile and firm handshake. "How are you?"

"I am fine, sir. I talked to Drouillard, and he mentioned going upriver with Lisa as your representative."

"Yes, we feel fortunate to get him."

Menard and Broken Knife were talking about the fur trade when Jeannie walked into the garden with Baptiste. "I would like to present our guest, the Count de Soissons."

Broken Knife smiled to himself. The Sorbies were fawning all over the Count. Jeannie talked a short while with Broken Knife and the Menards. She whispered in Broken Knife's ear. "Wait until you see our next guest."

Jeannie excused herself. In a few minutes, she returned. "I have someone else for everyone to meet. This is Clint's wife, Whispering Wind."

Mrs. Sorbie's gasp sounded around the room.

Wind stood in the doorway. She wore a white gown with a tight bodice and full skirt. Jeannie's green emerald hung from a gold chain about her neck. Standing there in the soft-green trimmed dress, Wind cast a spell over the room. Nothing had ever given him more pleasure, or pride.

Baptiste stepped forward. Bowing low to Wind, he kissed her hand. "No one mentioned a lovely wife. I am Baptiste." Offering Wind his arm, he escorted her into the room.

Just loud enough for Broken Knife to hear, Mrs. Sorbie whispered to her husband. "That is the dress I ordered. I did not like it."

Broken Knife turned toward the Sorbies. "Wind did mention the seamstress could not let the dress out enough to fit you." He looked Mrs. Sorbie up and down. He smiled at her red face. "It looks nice on her though," he said as he walked over to Baptiste and Wind.

Hearing Broken Knife's comment, Baptiste grinned. "After all we talked about this afternoon, you should have mentioned your charming wife."

Broken Knife squeezed Wind's hand. He kissed her cheek then whispered in her ear. "The Grandmother has given me a third image to carry."

Wind's eyes sparkled. She whispered back, "But I had no clothes on in the other two." Smiling, she said, "My husband looks very nice."

Broken Knife frowned. "This collar and these shoes are killing me."

"Oh, really. My shoes feel fine."

With a shake of his head, Broken Knife said, "Come and meet the other guests."

Wind was talking with Mrs. Menard when Tobias announced dinner.

Seated between the Count and Mr. Menard, Wind's easy laugh, quick wit, and occasional wrong word held sway over the dinner conversation.

Tobias was serving dessert when Broken Knife dropped his napkin. Bending down to pick it up, he saw that his elegant lady wore moccasins under her full-skirted gown.

After Tobias filled the wineglasses, Baptiste tapped his glass then stood up. "I propose a toast to my cousin and his wife. Clint and I talked this afternoon, but I did not tell him the best news. Before I left France, the Marquis transferred his estate and titles to his heir."

Baptiste raised his glass to Broken Knife. He bowed slightly at the waist. "Ladies and gentlemen, I give you the Marquis and Marquise de Soissons. May Clint and Wind have a long and prosperous life."

Baptiste's announcement surprised Broken Knife, but not nearly as much as Sorbie. The Banker's gasp was louder than his wife's gasp had been at seeing Wind. The announcement removed any doubts about accepting his inheritance. Broken Knife was the Marquis.

The congratulations over, Chouteau said, "Gentlemen, there are brandy and cigars in the study."

Broken Knife and Menard were talking about the Yellowstone and Three Forks country when Sorbie came over. He nodded to Broken Knife. "Could I speak to you for a minute?" he asked.

Sorbie maneuvered Broken Knife across the room. "I cannot tell you how happy I am for you and Wind. My bank is at your service. In fact, there is a couple of outstanding investment opportunities right now."

Chouteau and Baptiste came over and rescued Broken Knife. Baptiste said, "There is one other thing I should mention. I took the liberty of booking our return passage. We leave in three days." He grinned. "You can buy anything you need in New Orleans."

Broken Knife said, "Well if we are going, the sooner the better."

"Gentleman, let's return to the ladies," Chouteau said.

As they walked out of the study, Baptiste whispered in Broken Knife's ear. "I suppose Sorbie happened to have a good investment."

Broken Knife nodded.

Baptiste smiled. "You will get use to the Sorbies and their

good deals. France is full of them too."

When the men returned, the women were ready to leave. After the good-byes, Broken Knife and Wind went to their room.

"Baptiste booked passage for us in three days. When Drouillard goes upriver, he can tell Grey Wolf what has happened. Other than that, I guess there is nothing keeping us here. Do you need more time?"

"No," Wind replied. "I shall miss my parents, but I am excited about going."

"We can come back next year. By then, Drouillard might go there and help."

"That would be good. Do you like Baptiste?" Wind asked.

"Yes, I believe he is genuinely happy for us. The more we talked this afternoon, the more interested I become in my heritage. Baptiste told me my mother's uncle is head of the Stuart Clan in Scotland." Broken Knife hesitated. "As Baptiste talked about my parents and grandfather, a sense of belonging came over me. That feeling of not being part of the Indian or white world was gone. My spirit no longer cried out to know its path."

Wind touched his hand. "I am pleased you learned about your white family."

Broken Knife looked at Wind. "Why did you ask if I liked Baptiste?"

"No reason," she replied. "I just wondered."

He noted a hesitance in her voice. "You do not like him?" Broken Knife asked.

"Yes, but sometimes when you are not looking, his eyes do not say the same as his words." Wind shrugged her shoulders. "Maybe all men from France are that way."

Broken Knife said, "I noticed during dinner my pretty lady had moccasins on under her dress."

Wind giggled as she slid closer. "Shoes are not one of the white man's good things." She pulled his head onto her shoulder. "Jeannie gave me her emerald. I would like her to have one too."

Broken Knife and Wind were glad when the three days of hustle-and-bustle was over. Baptiste and Teal were in the carriage when Wind and Jeannie came down the walk. Broken Knife walked over. "Jeannie, we have been so busy I have not thanked you for all you have done." He placed an emerald in her hand. "We want you to have this."

Wind hugged Jeannie. "Now the green stones bind the three of us."

Jeannie broke into tears. Sobbing, she ran into the house.

The ship's Captain came down the gangplank and escorted them to two staterooms. Baptiste stopped in front of his door. As the Captain left, he asked, "Will you dine with me this evening?"

"Of course," replied Broken Knife. "What time?"

"The captain said he would have it served at seven."

Black thunderheads came up that afternoon. Choppy water forced Broken Knife, Wind, and Teal to stay in the cabin. When it came time to dress for dinner, Teal said, "I do not feel good. This rocking has made my stomach feel funny. Can I stay here?"

"Of course," Broken Knife replied. "Lie down, maybe it will make you feel better." Wind and Broken Knife were dressed and about to go when he said, "I will check on you in a little while."

"Do not worry, I am fine."

Finished eating, Baptiste had the dinner dishes removed. The three of them were talking when a knock sounded at the door.

Baptiste opened the door and a man wearing a sword entered. After the man whispered something to him, Baptiste whirled about. His red puffy face showed nothing but cruelty. He glared at Broken Knife. "My men say you have quite a reputation. If you do not want Teal killed, do exactly as I say."

265

Scorn filled his words. "Did you really think I would let a savage have what is rightfully mine?"

Broken Knife rubbed his neck – a lace collar. His eyes went to Wind. She cowed in the corner. He moved so the swordsman's back was toward her. Looking at Baptiste, he said, "Let Wind and Teal go, and you can have it all."

Baptiste held out a sheaf of papers. "There is one other thing I did not mention. The old bastard died before I left France. No one will ask any question when I say you renounced the inheritance." He sneered, "What else would one expect from a heathen Indian. Sign these, and you will be put ashore at the next landing."

Broken Knife slid the signed documents across the table.

Baptiste picked up the papers. His voice full of contempt, he said, "You are a bigger fool than I thought." He nodded at the swordsman then pointed at two steamer trunks. "Kill them while I get the girl. Those trunks will hold the bodies. Soon as it is dark and no one is around, throw them overboard. I will make sure no one on the boat says anything about them being gone."

The man's hand moved toward his sword. The sneer on his face faded. He took a half step forward and collapsed. Wind's knife protruded from his back.

Broken Knife lunged across the table. His hand locked over Baptiste's larynx.

Bug-eyed, the Count turned blue.

Wind grasped Broken Knife's wrist. "Let go! It is bad medicine to kill a relative."

Broken Knife threw Baptiste into the corner. "This is the last time I wear a lace shirt."

"It is not." Wind touched his cheek. "You look handsome in one. Hand me my knife, and I will protect you."

"Ah, yes," he said as he rolled the swordsman off the table. In a joking voice, he added, "He does not know how lucky he was. If he had torn your dress, you would have really

266

hurt him." Kissing her lightly, he said, "Wait here."

Wind stepped in front of the door. "If the man sees you, he might panic and shoot Teal. He will not be suspicious of me." She touched his hand. "My gun is under the bed pillow."

Broken Knife picked up the man's sword. "All right, but I will be outside the door."

Wind knocked then said, "The Count sent me to wait here."

Inside the room was a loud noise. She heard Teal gasp. The man said, "I got ah gun ta her head. If this is ah trick, I'll kill her. Com' in slow, 'nd 'ave yer hands where I cun see 'em."

Wind entered and closed the door. She stood with her back to it.

The man's vile stare made her cringe. "I 'eerd you wur ah real looker."

Wind forced a smile. Her hips swayed slightly.

The man lowered the gun. "Lock thet door." He pushed Teal into the corner. "Stay there, an' don't move." His lewd eyes stared at Wind's tight bodice. "Get on thet bed."

"There is no hurry," Wind said as she sat down at the table. "The Count said he and my husband would be busy signing papers for sometime. This will be my first time with a real white man." Smiling, she asked, "Could we have a drink first?"

The man licked his lips. "Traders said Indian women wur somethin'." He placed a bottle of rum and two glasses on the table. Dropping into a chair across from her, he said, "You pour."

Wind's hand was shaky. She spilled rum on the table. "I am sorry." With a smile of promises, she asked, "Would you please hand me that towel?" The man placed his hands on the table and lifted himself out of the chair.

Screams of agony drowned out the sound of the splintering door. Broken Knife had the sword point at the man's throat, before he saw that Wind's knife pinned the henchman's hand to the table.

"You bitch," screamed the Count's lackey.

Broken Knife lashed him across the face with the sword. "Watch what you say." He turned to Teal. "Are you all right?" When she nodded, he said, "Wind, get your pistol and watch him. I will get Baptiste and the Captain."

Broken Knife returned within a few minutes. Shoving his cousin through the door, he tossed a bundle of papers on the bed. The ship's Captain followed Broken Knife inside and closed the door.

Broken Knife grabbed Baptiste's arm. He dragged him to the table then growled, "Pull that knife out of his hand."

Baptiste's face turned a pasty white. He moaned, "I cannot do that."

"You pull it out, or else I will." Broken Knife snarled, "Then, you can pull it out of your painting hand."

Baptiste twisted the knife back and forth. Writhing in pain, the man passed out.

Once the knife was free, Broken Knife took it. He wiped the blade off on Baptiste's coat. "All that stands between you and the river bottom is being a relative." He stared at Baptiste. "You are the fool. Deep down, I never wanted this. You could have had most of it." Broken Knife's eyes hardened. His voice dropped. "I am giving the vineyards in France to Maure's family. If you cause them any grief, or try anything against us, you will spend the rest of your life in prison."

With a flick of his wrist, the point of the knife drew a red line across Baptiste's throat. Blood run down his neck onto his shirt. Broken Knife said, "If I cannot do that, I will come to France and kill you."

Wobbly legged, Baptiste leaned against the table. He stared at the blood spreading across the lace of his white silk shirt.

"Do you understand?"

Baptiste could only nod.

Broken Knife handed Baptiste a pen and paper. "Tell the Captain what you have done while you write it down and sign it."

After hearing Baptiste's confession, the Captain said, "I can turn him over to the authorities in New Orleans."

Broken Knife took the Captain aside. "We will not press charges. When he offers you a bribe, take it then turn him loose. Let him figure out what to do with the body and the wounded man."

The Captain nodded. "In about a half hour, there is a bend in the river where I could put you ashore."

"Good, I will leave his confession and those papers with Auguste Chouteau. If any problems come up over killing that man, Mr. Chouteau will provide the police with anything they need."

Broken Knife held out his hand to the Captain. After shaking hands, he glanced at Baptiste. "Take that scum and get out."

As Baptiste dragged his henchman out the door, Wind and Teal rushed into Broken Knife's outstretched arms. He held them tight. "Waiting outside was the hardest thing I have ever done. I was about to kick the door down when Lame Bear's hand rested on my shoulder. With my father's spirit beside me," he squeezed Wind, "our life's walk become clear."

Teal asked, "Are we still going to France?"

"Not now, we must go home."

Wind looked at him intently. She asked, "What did Lame Bear tell you?"

Broken Knife hesitated before saying, "Disease destroys the Hidatsa and Mandan. White soldiers come. The People's blood is spilled. Treaty words take Crow and Cheyenne lands. Buffalo are no more. Our People struggle on reservations." His voice dropped to a whisper. "This my father's spirit put before my eyes."

Tears flowed off Teal's cheeks. She asked, "When will this

happen?"

"I will see part of it, you will see it all."

BIBLIOGRAPHY

LEWIS AND CLARK EXPEDITION

Coues, Elliott (Ed.). *The History of the Lewis and Clark Expedition. Vol. I-III.* Dover Publications, Inc. New York. 1893 Coues Edition.

DeVoto, Bernard. *The Course of the Empire, pp. 435-553.* Bison Books, University of Nebraska Press, Lincoln, Nebraska. 1983.

Hawke, David Freeman. *Those Tremendous Mountains. The story of the Lewis and Clark Expedition.* W. W. Norton & Company, Inc. New York. 1985.

Jackson, Donald. *Thomas Jefferson & The Stony Mountains.* University of Illinois Press, Urbana, Illinois. 1981

Skarston, M. O. *George Drouillard Hunter and Interpreter for Lewis and Clark and Fur Trader 1807-1809.* Arthur H. Clark Co. Glendale, California. 1964.

Quaife, Milo M. (Ed.) *The Journal of Captain Meriwether Lewis and Sergeant John Ordway.* Cushing-Malloy, Inc., Ann Arbor, Michigan. 1965.

Thwaites, Rueben Gold (Ed.). *Rocky Mountain Exploration.* D. Appleton and Company. New York. 1904.

Thwaites, Rueben Gold (Ed.). *Original Journals Of The Lewis and Clark Expedition 1804-1806. Vol. I-VIII.* Arno Press, Inc. 1969.

271

NATIVE AMERICANS

Algier, Keith. *The Crow and the Eagle*. The Caxton Printers, Ltd., Caldwell, Idaho. 1993.

Bowers, Alfred W. *Hidatsa Social and Ceremonial Organization*. Bison Books, University of Nebraska Press, Lincoln Nebraska. 1992.

Catlin, George. *Letters and Notes on the Manners, Customs, and Conditions of North American Indians. Vol. I*. Dover Publishing, Inc., New York. 1973.

Ewers, John C. *Indian Life on the Upper Missouri*. University of Oklahoma Press, Norman Oklahoma. 1988

Ewers, John C. *The Blackfeet Raiders of the Northwest Plains*. University of Oklahoma Press, Norman Oklahoma. 1988.

Ewers, John C. *The Horse in Blackfoot Indian Culture*. Smithsonian Institution Press, Washington D. C. 1969.

Grinnell, George Bird. *Blackfoot Lodge Tales*, Bison Books, University of Nebraska Press, Lincoln, Nebraska. 1962.

Grinnell, George Bird. *The Cheyenne Indians. Vol. I-II*. Bison Books, University of Nebraska Press, Lincoln, Nebraska. 1972.

Grumet, Robert S. *The Lenapes*. Chelsa House Publishers, New York. 1989.

Hassrick, Royal B. *The Sioux*. University of Oklahoma Press, Norman Oklahoma. 1989.

Hoxie, Frederick E. *The Crow*. Chelsa House Publishers. New

York. 1989.

Hyde, George E. *The Pawnee Indians*. University of Oklahoma Press, Norman, Oklahoma. 1988.

Hyde, George E. *Indians of the High Plains*. University of Oklahoma Press, Norman Oklahoma. 1986.

Linderman, Frank B. *Plenty-coups Chief of the Crows*. University of Nebraska Press, Lincoln, Nebraska. 1962

Lowie, Robert H. *The Crow Indians*. Bison Books, University of Nebraska Press, Lincoln, Nebraska. 1983.

Lowie, Robert H. *Indians of the Plains*. Bison Books, University of Nebraska Press, Lincoln, Nebraska. 1982.

Mails, Thomas E. *The Mystic Warriors of the Plains*. Mallard Press, New York, N.Y. 1991.

McGinnis, Anthony. *Counting Coup and Cutting Horses: Intertribal Warfare on the Northern Plains 1738-1889*. Cordillera Press, Evergreen, Colorado. 1990

Roe, Frank G. *The Indian and the Horse*. University of Oklahoma Press, Norman, Oklahoma. 1955.

Schneider, Mary Jane. *The Hidatsa*. Chelsa House, New York. 1989.

Terrell, John Upton. *American Indian Almanac*. World Publishing Company, New York. 1971.

Waldman, Carl. *Encyclopedia of Native American Tribes*. Facts on File Publication, New York. 1988.

Wissler, Clark. *Indians of the United States*. Doubleday and Company, 1966.

GENERAL

Burpee, Lawrence,J. *Journals and Letters of Pierre Gaultier de Varendes de la Verendrye*. Toronto. 1927

Chittenden, Hyrum Martin. *American Fur Trade of the Far West. Volume I-II*. The Press of the Pioneers, Inc., New York, New York, 1935.

Coues, Elliot (Ed.). *New Light on the Early History of the Greater Northwest: The Manuscript Journals of Alexander Henry and David Thompson*. Francis P. Harper, New York. 1897.

DeVoto, Bernard. *The Course of the Empire*. Bison Books, University of Nebraska Press, Lincoln, Nebraska. 1983.

Harris, Burton. John Colter. *His years in the Rocky Mountains*. Bison Books. University of Nebraska Press, Lincoln Nebraska. 1993

Jennings, Francis. *The Invasion of North America: Indians, Colonialism, and the Cant of Conquest*. W. W. Norton and Company. Inc. New York, New York. 1976.

Lavender, David. *Westward Vision*. Smithsonian Institution Press, Washington D.C. 1985.

Mattes, Merril J. *Colter's Hell and Jackson's Hole*. Yellowstone Library and Museum Association. Mammoth, Wyoming. 1962.

McHugh, Tom. *The Time of the Buffalo*. University of Nebraska,

Lincoln, Nebraska. 1972.

Mirsky, Jeannette. *The Westward Crossings: Balboa, Mackenzie, Lewis and Clark.* University of Chicago Press, Chicago, Illinois. 1970.

Nastair, A. P. (Ed.). *Before Lewis and Clark. Vol I-II.* Bison Book, University of Nebraska Press, Lincoln, Nebraska, 1990.

National Park Service. *Exploring the American West 1803-1879. Handbook 116.* U. S. Department of the Interior. Washington, D. C. 1982

Newman, Peter C. *Company of Adventures.* Penguin Books, New York. 1987.

Newman, Peter C. *An Illustrated History of the Hudson's Bay Company.* Penguin Books Canada Ltd., Toronto, Canada. 1995.

Oglesby, Richard Edward. *Manuel Lisa and the Opening of the Missouri Fur Trade.* University of Oklahoma Press, Norman Oklahoma. 1963.

O'Meara Walter, *The Savage Country*, Houghton Miffin Company, Boston, Mass. 1960.

Parkman, Francis. *La Salle and the Discovery of the Great West.* Signet Classics, The New American Library of World Literature, Inc. 501 Madison Ave., New York 22, New York. 1963.

Russell, Carl P. *Firearms, Traps, and Tools of the Mountain Men.* University of New Mexico Press, Albuquerque, New Mexico. 1986.

Thwaites, Ruben G. (Ed.). *Early Western Travels 1748-1846, Vol. V, VI*. Arthur H. Clark Co. Cleveland, Ohio. 1904.

Wishart, David J. *The Fur Trade of the American West 1907-1840*. Bison Books. University of Nebraska Press, Lincoln, Nebraska. 1979.

Wood, W. Raymond and Thiessen, Thomas D. (Ed.). *Early Fur Trade of the Northern Plains: Narratives of John Macdonell, Francois-Antoine Larocque, David Thompson, Charles McKenzie*. University of Oklahoma Press, Norman, Oklahoma. 1987.

ABOUT THE AUTHOR

O. N. Eddins is a Doctor of Veterinary Medicine by profession. He was born and now resides near Jackson Hole, Wyoming and the Grand Teton – a landmark for Indian and Mountain Man. The majority of *Mountains of Stone* was written in a secluded camp along side an old Indian trail in a remote section of the Wyoming Mountain Range. By horse and pack string, Dr. Eddins has ridden many of the trails described in the book. His campfires have been built in the same places as those of mountain men and explorers one hundred and ninety years before him.

As a serious student and historical critic of the fur trade and the Lewis and Clark Expedition, he is well qualified to write a novel on early American Natives of the Plains and Mountains and how they were impacted by the first explorers, trappers, and traders to reach the Rocky Mountains.

Dr. Eddins is an approved judge of both the American Quarter Horse and the American Paint Horse associations as well as a certified ski instructor. He is researching and writing *Winds of Change,* the sequel to *Mountains of Stone.* The time frame of his next book is 1810 to 1843.

O.N. Eddins
neddins@silverstar.com
1-866-885-2400